An Unacceptable Conclusion

JB Millhollin

Grey Place Books —Nashville, TN
Paperback ISBN: 978-1-7358745-6-2
eBook ISBN: 979-8-3304-9467-5
Library of Congress Control Number: 2024921275
Title: *An Unacceptable Conclusion*
Author: JB Millhollin
Digital distribution | 2024
Paperback | 2024

This is a work of fiction. The characters, names, incidents, places, and dialogue are products of the author's imagination, and are not to be construed as real.

Published in the United States by New Book Authors Publishing

Previous novels by JB Millhollin

Brakus
    Brakus, Book 1
    Everything he Touched, Book 2
    With Nothing to Lose, Book 3
An Absence of Ethics
Forever Bound
Out of Reach
Redirect
Whisper of Hope
To Hide from a Northern Wind:
    Spencer Creek, Book 1
To Hide from a Northern Wind:
    Wilson County, Book 2
To Hide from a Northern Wind:
    Nashville Divided, Book 3
To Hide from a Northern Wind:
    River of Tears, Book 4
Plausible Deception
I Guess I'll Never Know

Coming soon:

The Reporter
My Turn
The Prosecutor
Life Altered   Book 1 of a two-book series
Life on Hold   Book 2 of a two-book series
One More Time

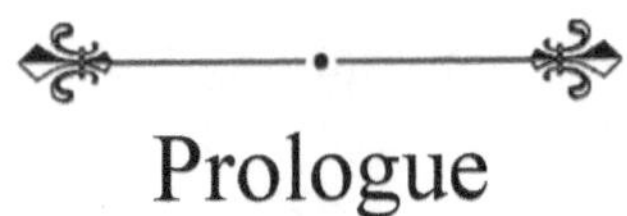

Prologue

May

Downtown Nashville

Robert Duncan sat across the table from his wife of forty-five years.

"Jean, I honestly believe you are as attractive now as you were all those years ago—I really do."

She smiled and said, "Thank you, sir. But those old wedding pictures I looked through this afternoon, show me *exactly* how I looked then. And I'm afraid they don't match up very well with how I look now. In fact, those old pictures look like someone I don't even know—nor ever did know."

He took another bite of his salad, smiled and said, "You still remember our first night? Both of us were scared to death just hoping our marriage would turn out the way we anticipated it would. We were both full of concern as to whether or not we had done the right thing. Our parents didn't approve. I guess we proved them all wrong, didn't we?"

"Yes, I guess we did at that. My, this food is incredible. I'm glad you brought me here."

He finished the last of his steak and waved to the waiter. As he approached, Bob said, "I need another glass of wine when you have a moment."

He watched as she finished the last of her meal. Once the waiter brought his drink, he picked up his glass and said, "Here's to you, sweetheart. I could not have found a better soul to be my partner. You are the best. Here is to another 45 years."

She picked up her glass, smiled and said, "I have no idea what I would have done without you, Bob. I love you with all my heart."

As they both finished their wine, the waiter brought a chocolate cake, with five small, flaming candles. As he placed it in the middle of the table, he said, "Congratulations to both of you. Compliments of the house."

Jean looked at Bob who was smiling from ear to ear. "Did you do this? Did you arrange this?"

"Maybe."

"Thank you. This just made it perfect. Now, cut it will you. I'm never too full to pass up a piece of chocolate cake."

He blew out the candles and as he picked up the knife and started to cut the cake, she said, "Any regrets?"

"Not really. Nothing I can think of anyway. My law practice has exceeded everything I could have ever imagined. Your advice concerning remaining a small law office without any additional lawyers involved, couldn't have been more on point. Luckily, you and I have been relatively healthy. We live in a beautiful home. Our relationship, while having many of the smaller issues most marriages have, overall has been incredible. I couldn't imagine being closer to anyone than I am to you. So, no, all in all, it has been a damn good run."

He placed a slice of cake on one of the two small plates the waiter had provided, as he said, "What about you? Anything you would have changed?"

She put her fork down and looked away for a moment clearly deep in thought. She then slowly turned toward him, smiled, picked up her fork, and said, "Not a thing, Bob, not a thing."

They sat quietly, each finishing their dessert, until he said, "Thinking about Donald?"

She never looked up as she said, "Oh, I guess. Maybe that was the one thing I regret. I know there was nothing we could have done, but I've often wondered if we would have been with them, if maybe…"

"We have discussed that before, Jean. If we had been in that car, there would have just been two more fatalities. We would have died too. There was nothing we could have done. I have no idea how Paul ever got out. He was so young then. I just don't know how he had enough sense about him to crawl out the way he did."

"Do you think about them, Bob? It's been twenty years now, but do you think of them often?"

"At least once every day. It never ends. And of course, it's been exacerbated by the fact that we never had any other children."

"What has it been now, five years since Paul disappeared?"

"Just about, yes."

"Where do you think he is now? Any idea?"

"None. As you know, I have tried every way I know how, to locate him. But it's not that hard to lose yourself if that is really what you want to do. And apparently that is what he wanted to do."

"The trauma associated with the accident, and then living with two old people like us, must have just made him snap. Is that what you think, Bob—he just went off the deep end?"

"I don't know. You know, we have discussed this so many times and every time we do, we come to the same conclusion. We have no idea where he is, what he is doing, or if we will ever see him again"

"I know, I just…"

He reached across the table and took her hand. "Come on, now. This is our night. There is nothing we can do about the past. It's you and me now and we are doing fine, in spite of the circumstances involving our child and grandchild."

He picked up his glass and said, "Here's to us. I hope we can make it another forty-five and remain as close and as much in love as we have the last forty-five."

She laughed as she raised her glass, and said, "I'm just not sure I am going to make it that long. But the one thing I do hope for is that when we do pass on, we do it at the same time. Because, at least for me, life without you, even for a moment would be one moment longer than I could handle."

"I feel the same way. I love you with all my heart." He smiled and said, "Here's to you, Jean—and to another 45 incredible years."

Chapter 1

Two years later
Law office of Robert Duncan
Downtown Nashville

Bob sat alone, staring out the window located immediately behind his desk. This morning, he arrived at his office much earlier than normal. He figured he would review a few messages and try to sort out the fires that had erupted since the last time he was here. But since his arrival, he had simply made a pot of coffee—that was it—he hadn't looked at one phone message, nor opened one file.

How long had he been away? He lost track of time. Had it been a week? No, surely it had to have been longer than that.

The rain continued to fall. He watched as cars drove past his office clearly exceeding the posted speed limit. Where were they all going in such a rush? What was the hurry? Maybe he should flag them down and tell them to enjoy each and every moment…because one never knows when…

He wiped away a single tear that quickly found its way to the middle of his cheek. How long *had* it been? What day did she….

It remained difficult to say the word.

Bob had come to the office early this morning for a specific reason. He had remained *home* long enough. Regardless of how much office work he might actually complete, it was time to do some planning—the rest of the week, the rest of the month—the rest of his life.

He could vaguely remember he had a trial coming up soon. He remembered it was on the schedule, he just couldn't remember what day. He had made no effort to continue the trial date, having concluded he knew enough about the case to try it with no more preparation than what he had already done. What the hell was the name of the case—what was…

"Bob. You are back. I didn't expect you in today."

Charlene, his secretary of twenty-plus years, had walked in his office without him hearing her.

A minute of silence later, she said, "What are you doing here? I did not expect you back for at least another week. That's what I told everyone—that it would be at least another week."

He continued to look out the window, failing to acknowledge her in any respect.

"Can I get you a cup of coffee?"

After Bob failed to respond, she said, "Oh, never mind. I see your cup there now. I didn't see it before, but now I…Should I leave you alone for a while?"

He never turned around, but finally acknowledged her when he said, "Yes. Give me a few more minutes, Charlene. I'll let you know when we need to discuss things."

"Certainly. You want me to close your door?"

"Yes."

As she walked out, closing the door behind her, tears started to flow down his face, as, one more time, he remembered Jean and the relationship they had enjoyed for all those years.

An hour later, there was a soft knock on his office door. He didn't have any desire to discuss business with her or anyone else. He never responded.

Again, came a knock on the door, this time a little louder, a little more assertive. He took a deep breath, wondering now why the hell he had come back this soon. "Come on in, Charlene."

"I am really sorry Bob, but since you *are* here, could we talk a minute?"

He slowly swiveled around and said, "I guess. Let me get another cup of coffee first."

He stood, walked into the hallway where a small table held the coffee pot and warmed up the coffee that remained in the bottom of his cup.

As she sat down, he said, "Can any of this wait? I really shouldn't have come back so soon. My mind is not on my work. I got up this morning, thought back over the past couple of weeks, and just didn't feel like I wanted to sit around the house for another day. But that might have been a mistake. To be honest, I'm not really sure where I should be right now."

"I am so sorry, Bob. I cannot imagine what you must be going through."

He grabbed his cup with both hands, looked down, and said, "It all happened so damn quick. She was there, she had cancer, she was gone. I couldn't believe it could happen that fast. Not today. Not with all the advancements we have seen. She was gone in the blink of an eye. I just...I just..."

"Being married that long to the same person and then watching them pass away—I can't imagine. As I said, I expected you to be gone at least another couple of weeks."

"I was thinking at about three this morning—don't I have some trial coming up? Isn't something scheduled for this week or next? I can't remember what..."

"Yes. You had that Morris dissolution set for Friday. But I called opposing council and told him what happened. He contacted the Judge and it's been continued for a month. I called Mrs. Morris and told her."

"Knowing her as I do, I'll bet she took that real well."

Charlene smiled, and said, "She wasn't happy about it being continued, but she understood. She said she would meet with you to prepare whenever you were ready."

Bob said nothing, continuing to look away in silence, until Charlene said, "What do you want to do today? Do you want to go through your messages, open mail, see anyone or just do nothing?"

"Is there anything that is really pressing? You took the phone messages. Is there anything in any of them that I should address or can everything wait?"

"Everything can wait. I have opened all the mail that was from other attorneys or that looked like it was something you should address immediately. But I either took care of it, or it can wait."

He never responded.

The office phone rang. She sat quietly waiting for him to respond. As the phone quit ringing and, the call went to voicemail, she said, "How do you want to proceed from here? Are you staying today or going home? And what about the rest of the week, or month? What should I tell those that call or walk in?"

He finally looked at her and said, "I am not staying here any longer today. I'm going home. As for the rest of the week, month, year, I have no idea what I am going to do. I may or may not continue to practice. If I had to decide today, I would tell you I'm finished. But I know it's best I don't come to any conclusions right now. It's just too soon.

He stood. "Just hang in there with me a while, Charlene. I'll figure it out. I just need a little more time."

She stood. "Bob, I will handle it any way you want. I'll be here until you no longer need me. You take the time you need and let me know when you finally decide. If there is something that comes up in which I must have some input from you, I'll call you. Now, go home. I will see you when I see you."

He sat at the kitchen table, opening envelope after envelope. Some were bills, and some were advertisements. But the rest were so many sympathy cards he couldn't count them all. He finally concluded he would need to open them some other time. His eyes were tired. He simply didn't want to read one more card telling him how sorry they were about Jean's death.

He stood, poured himself a short glass of bourbon and walked in his living room.

As he sat, his phone buzzed. He looked at caller ID and noticed it was Jack Raymond. He had ignored most every call that he had received the past two weeks, but this one he would take.

"Hi, Jack."

"Bob, how are you? I haven't had a chance to talk with you since the funeral. How are you getting along?"

Bob smiled. Some things never change. Jack said as many words in five seconds as most people said in a day. While both were in law school, many years ago, the professors would continue to try and slow down his manner of speech, knowing the stenographer in a court room would never be able to keep up.

"I'm doing fine, Jack. Thanks for asking."

"Why *wouldn't* I ask? You two were the best friends I ever had. I'll miss her as much as you will."

"To be honest, we are probably the *only* friends you ever had."

"What are you talking about? I got friends. I got a lot of friends. I just choose not to be with them—or even near them, actually. You are way off base there, buddy."

Bob laughed…for the first time since she had passed.

"Whatever. What do you want?"

"Let's go get a drink somewhere. I'll meet you in a half-hour somewhere. Where do you want to meet? We need to talk."

"Sorry, but I'm not going anywhere. I just poured myself one, and I'm staying right here."

"Oh, come on. I am just leaving the office. I don't want to drink alone, and you need to be with someone. Now, where should we meet?"

"First of all, drinking alone is nothing new for you. That's because, like I said, you haven't got any friends to drink with. But beyond that, I just don't feel like it. Sorry, but you are on your own tonight."

Jack hesitated for a moment, then said, "Do you have any idea what you are going to do from here on? Are you closing the office? Someone told me you might just close up. Is that true?"

"Hell, I don't know. I am just trying to survive right now. I don't even know what day it is, let alone what I'm doing with the rest of my life."

"That is why we need to talk. Let old Jack show you the way."

Bob laughed and said, "Oh sure. You know, I've followed your advice once or twice, and it never worked out very well. If you recall, if I had followed your advice, I would have never married Jean. You go drink on your own tonight, and we will get together when I've figured it all out—by myself—in my own way."

"What about next week? Will next week work for you?"

"Maybe. But don't call me. I will call you when I'm ready. I don't want you calling me every night to go out for a drink. Call all those *other* friends you have and go have a drink with one of them."

"Whatever. I'll call you mid-week, and we can discuss it then. Now, I need to go. I'll talk to you later."

Before Bob could even respond, the line went dead. Jack was a true character in every sense of the word, but he was also the best friend he ever had.

He sat in silence for an hour, until he fixed himself another drink and walked out on the porch. There were still two chairs sitting there, waiting for the same two people that had filled them for so many years—most every evening of every year since they had purchased the home.

He sat, thinking back over all those years, until it was dark. He then walked inside, shut the lights out, and as he had done for the last two weeks, crawled into bed by himself.

He thought how strange it was that when she died, many insignificant issues seemed to suddenly become so significant. Where was that gold necklace—that silly gold necklace? He searched for hours trying to find it—the one he had given her so many years ago when money was scarce and it took all he had to purchase it. He knew what it meant to her. He wanted to bury her with it on. How insignificant, considering the totality of it all.

Near midnight, he wiped the tears away and tried to fall asleep. He finally succeeded, only to awaken a couple of hours later and reach for her to determine if it had just been a bad dream or it had really happened. Once he concluded she was gone, he got out of bed and slowly walked to the kitchen, to start another day without the woman he loved more than anything else this world had to offer.

Chapter 2

He simply couldn't keep his eyes open any longer. As his elbow slipped off the table, he woke himself up.

Bob knew he must have flinched when his elbow slipped. As inconspicuously as possible, he looked around the courtroom, making sure no one saw it happen.

Everyone at the council tables, along with the Judge, were concentrating on the witness. No one noticed the elbow of an old man slip as it was holding up the head of that old man who was just plain worn out.

In the past, he had been advised that feeling consistently tired could be the direct result of depression. Now, he knew it was true—now he could discuss that issue based on firsthand experience. Bob continued to do the best he could to concentrate on the witness and not let his mind wander. But with each passing minute, it grew increasing difficult.

This was the first case he had tried since her death. He had concluded shortly after she died, that he would postpone those trials currently scheduled within the near future. He had religiously followed that plan until, at the constant urging of Mrs. Morris, he had her trial set for hearing as soon as a judge became available. He should have followed his initial conclusion involving indefinite postponement, both for the benefit of his client *and* himself.

The problem was that he just didn't care. Whether he won or lost was of no consequence. The only thing that mattered was getting out of the courtroom and back to the solitude of his own office, where he could continue to control the flow of traffic on his own terms until he really was ready to move on.

He glanced quickly at the opposing attorney. His opponent was clearly hanging on every word of every sentence the witness uttered. But for Bob, it made no difference who testified—each witness simply provided him with an additional opportunity to nod off.

His client's husband was now on the stand. Bob hadn't heard a full sentence of anything the witness had to say since his testimony began—nor did he care what he had missed. At this point, all that was important was that it end as quickly as possible.

Both parties wanted custody—that was why they were here. Bob would shortly be allowed an opportunity to cross-examine him, but he had concluded he would waive any cross—doing so would help end the hearing just that much sooner. He didn't care whether proceeding in that manner adversely affected his client's case or not.

"Mr. Duncan, did you hear me?"

Bob nervously cleared his throat, and said, "No, I didn't, Your Honor, I'm sorry."

"Cross-examine?"

"No, Your Honor, not at this time."

"Well, unless you, for some strange reason, call him back to testify, which I doubt you will do, this will be your *only* chance to examine him. I highly suggest, if you are going to do it you do it now."

"Thanks, Your Honor, but I don't wish to cross-examine him at this time…at all. No questions.

He turned toward his client and whispered, "Are you ready to testify? You'll be up next."

She looked as though her life had just been threatened. "I have to go *next*? Is there no one else that can testify so I can get mentally prepared? I didn't know it was coming so soon."

"You are next. That's it. There is no one else left. Now, are you ready?"

"Whatever. Yes. I guess I have no choice."

"You are correct—you have no choice. Now go."

As her husband stepped down, she stood and walked slowly to the witness chair.

The Judge swore her in, and after Bob had asked her a few essential basic questions, he was ready to question her concerning the issue of custody.

"Now, Ms. Morris, let's discuss your child… your child…" Bob paused.

"His name is Jack."

"Right, that's correct. How old?"

"Seven."

"Right, that's right."

Bob shuffled through some of his paperwork lying on the table in front of him, then looked up at her, and said, "And why do you want him with you? Why would he be better off with you than John?"

She stared at him for a moment, obviously expecting a correction, but hearing none, said, "Sir, my husband's name is David."

"Sure, that's exactly correct. Now, why you, not David?"

"Because that's where he would be best off. My husband travels all the time. The only reason he is asking for custody is because he wants to punish me for filing."

"And how do you know that?"

"Because he told me that. And I *told* you he told me that at the very beginning—and *have told* you that numerous times since then. Do you not remember I told you that?"

Bob sorted through his paperwork, then looked up and said, "Sure, sure, I just wanted you to tell the court what you told me."

He heard the back door of the courtroom open and turned to watch his friend Jack Raymond, walk in and sit down.

"Mr. Duncan? Mr. Duncan, are you done?"

Bob turned around, looked at the Judge and said, "No, I'm not. Your Honor, could I have a moment. Could we take a short recess?"

"Yes, certainly. Let's take fifteen minutes. Mr. Duncan, I would like to see you in chambers for a moment."

Everyone stood while the Judge left the bench. Bob escorted his client to a conference room across the hall. As he closed the door, leaving her in the room, Jack, who had followed him into the hallway, said, "Hey you old fart, are you okay? You sound a little shaky."

"I am fine. Now, what the hell do you want? I need to go see the Judge."

"How about a beer tonight? I'll meet you at that little bar down the street from your house after work?"

"Okay, okay fine. How about six?"

"Great I'll see you then. By the way, just from what I heard, you better get your ass back in the game buddy. It's pretty clear you are somewhere else today, because you are sure as hell not in that courtroom."

Without responding, Bob quickly walked to the open door of the Judge's chambers and remained there, as he said, "Did you want to see me?"

The Judge looked up from his paperwork scattered before him, smiled and said, "Yes, yes, I sure do, Bob. Thanks for coming in. Shut the door behind you and come on in."

Bob turned to shut the door, knowing being asked to do so was, most likely, not a good sign. He took a chair in front of his desk.

"You know, you and I have known each other a long time. You have tried many cases before me, and I might add, you have been quite successful."

"We have both been around quite a while Judge, that's a fact."

"What I am seeing before me today isn't the you that's been in my courtroom in the past. It is just that simple. Now, I know you have suffered a tremendous loss. As you recall, I was one of the first to call you and tell you how terribly sorry I was. But those days are over. Now, for the sake of your *client*, at least in the *courtroom*, those days of suffering because of your loss, must end here and now."

"I certainly can't know exactly how you feel. I have never experienced such a personal loss. But your clients shouldn't be made to suffer because of your loss. You have a good case, that's obvious. But you better start trying it, or you are going to get beat in a case you should have won. Now, there's still time for this one. But I strongly suggest you either get your head *in* or *out* of the game. If you are going to try cases, that's fine. But you must be fully engaged, and you know that."

Bob looked away as he whispered, "I know. I know you are right. My thoughts are elsewhere this morning."

He took a deep breath, turned toward the Judge and said, "Can I have a little time? Can you give me about 30 minutes to reintroduce myself to my client? I think that is all I'll need."

"Sure. Not a problem. See you in about a half hour."

Thirty minutes later, Bob walked back in the courtroom with his client. Four hours later, the Judge awarded custody of Jack to his mother. His mother then made it quite clear that she simply couldn't have been happier with the courtroom services of her friend and attorney, Bob Duncan.

Chapter 3

Jack was waiting for him when Bob arrived. He had already ordered a beer for both, but *Bob's* mug waiting for him across the table, was already half-empty.

As he sat down, Bob said, "What the hell is going on? Did you order me half a beer? I didn't even know you could do that. You drank yours, then you just decided to drink half of mine, didn't you? And once you were about half-way through mine, you figured it might be a fairly good idea to leave at least part of mine there, so you ordered another for yourself. *You know, I am not paying for this half a beer, don't you?* You are paying for it. Not only that, you can pay for *my next one too.*"

Jack watched Bob drink what was left in his mug. He finally said, "You cheap jerk, I never expected you to pay for it anyway—full or not. That's why I drank half of it. Now, before one of us dies of a stroke right here at the table, what happened in court today? Did you win? What did the Judge want?"

Bob set his mug down and carefully examined his friend.

"What the hell are you looking at?"

"Jack, do you give a damn how you look? Does your personal appearance mean anything to you anymore?"

"Okay, just what the devil can I do with my face? I am who I am and that's that. Sorry. I can only work with what God gave me."

"Have you ever given any thought to controlling your growth of body hair. You still have the ability to do that, you know. Your damn eyebrows look like a couple of caterpillars. The hair sticking out of your nose could be harvested with a lawn mower. You are disgusting Jack, you really are. You get a haircut about once every six months. Do you have any pride in yourself and how you look?"

Jack took another drink, smiled and said, "So, again, what happened in court today?"

"You know, you are impossible, you really are. I don't know why I continue to call you a friend."

Jack hesitated, then said, "So, again, what the hell happened in court today? Would it be too much to ask of you to answer that one question?"

Bob finished his half-beer and signaled the waiter to bring him another.

"The Judge was concerned about how poorly I was handling the case."

"Rightfully so."

"Oh, don't give me that bullshit. You watched all of ten minutes. You have no idea what went on either before you arrived or after you left."

"Hey, did I tell you I got myself a new girlfriend?"

"You know, you can't focus as well as a three-year-old! Have I ever mentioned that before?"

"Okay, okay what happened after I left?"

Bob just shook his head. He took another drink and said, "He told me to get my head in the game."

"What was your response?"

"I agreed with him. He didn't have to tell me to do that. My heart wasn't in it. I already knew it, and it just took a slap in the face for me to get it. He gave me a half-hour to get my thoughts together and become involved in the hearing."

"Were you able to do that?"

"Yes. I was just glad he had enough compassion to take the time and have that talk with me. I know other judges that would have just plowed right on through."

"How much longer did it last?"

"After you left?"

"Yes."

"About two more hours. Then it took another couple of hours for him to rule."

"Did you win?"

"Yes. It was a good ruling all the way around. I doubt her husband appeals."

"You know, you always were damn good in the court room when it came to civil cases. I never thought you were worth a crap in those limited criminal cases you tried, but you were always tough to beat in civil cases."

"I have never done very well in criminal cases because I just have a hard time believing most of my clients. They always say they are innocent, even when you know they aren't. I never tried one criminal case where I really trusted what my client told me. As you know, I never tried many of them, but the ones I did, I always felt lucky if my client was found not guilty. I'll never try another one—not at my age."

Jack hesitated before he said, "How are you doing? I don't mean in your practice, but, overall, how are you getting along?"

Bob took another drink, looked away and said softly, "I'm fine…I am getting along…fine…I just…."

Jack said, "Are you starting to establish a routine?"

Bob never responded.

"Don't get upset with me if I ask an inappropriate question. I'm not really sure at this point in time, what questions I *should* be asking. I have never been down the road you are traveling."

"No, no, you're fine. I understand. Obviously, I haven't either. In response, I am just doing what I can, at least at home, to get by. The office hasn't changed much. Jean was never involved with any of that. But the change in day-to-day activities at home are what have been difficult to accept and handle. Once I'm at the office, I can lose myself in my work, but walking through that front door at home, after a long difficult day at the office, has taken on a whole new meaning. It's just tough—day in and day out, it's tough."

"I am sure it is. I'm so sorry you are having to go through this."

Bob took a drink, set his mug down, and said, "It's time to move on. What about this new woman of yours? Tell me about her."

Jack smiled. "Lucy, is her name."

"Really. I didn't know anyone named their children Lucy anymore."

"They still did back when she was born. She's seventy years old."

"You got yourself a spring chicken there, don't you? How long have you been seeing each other?"

"Oh, about four months now, I guess."

"Are you serious about her or are just leading her on like you do most of them?"

"We are enjoying life right now. That's as far as it's gone and as far as it's going to go. I have not made any type of commitment concerning the future."

"Is she living with you?"

"About half the time. She still has her own place. She hasn't moved in with me. I don't think I will ask her to either."

"Why is that?"

"Because I've been to her place. It's a mess—it's worse than mine. Hell, neither of us would ever be able to find *anything*. We have discussed it, but I've always been able to divert the conversation in another direction. If she pushes it—if she pushes me toward moving in, she will be gone. I'll end it."

Bob emptied his mug and said, "I better go."

"Before you go, what are your thoughts about seeing someone else? Do you have any interest?"

"No."

"I realize it hasn't been that long, but do you think eventually you will ever be interested in seeing another woman? Because I got some pretty good ones that I know would love to date an attorney."

"Not now."

"So, an empty house is enough for you?"

He hesitated for a moment. "Yes. It about makes me physically sick to even consider a relationship with someone else. Maybe it just hasn't been long enough yet, but I feel like I would be betraying her…and her memory. I have no interest whatsoever."

"What if I found someone that I think you would *enjoy* being with. Would you consider…"

"Don't even think about it, Jack. I had an incredible marriage. *We* had a wonderful life together and I am just not interested in going through that effort with another woman. I am tired, plain and simple."

He stood. "I don't even know if I want to keep the office open. I'm not sure what I would do if I didn't, but it's a real effort just to crawl out of bed in the mornings."

"Is there anything I can do to help you get through this? Through the years, you and I have worked through a lot of messes together, Bob."

"Not this time. I need to figure it out by myself. I will. I just need a little time. Thanks for the beer."

As he walked away, Jack yelled, "Hey, you know you could at least pay for the one *you* ordered. You could help here a little you cheapskate."

As Bob continued to walk away, he smiled, and held up one finger, saluting him in the manner he felt most fitting. His smile continued until he inserted his key in the lock and once again opened the door to his quiet, empty home.

Chapter 4

"What happened?"

"I don't really know."

Charlene sat her coffee cup down and said, "You have no idea? Most of the time when you lose, which isn't very often, you have some idea as to what happened—what didn't go according to plan."

Bob had just returned to the office from the courthouse, where he waited patiently, with his clients, for the jury to return their verdict. They had deliberated for three days and had finally arrived at a conclusion. Unfortunately, it wasn't the conclusion they had hoped for.

"What did Mr. and Mrs. Masters say to you when the Judge read the verdict?"

"Nothing, nothing at all. They looked stunned. I told them I would meet both of them here in an hour. I can't believe this. We had a good case. We had good witnesses. She did a great job in describing the accident and all her injuries in explicit detail. I just don't understand this at all."

"So, they are to be here any minute then?"

"Yes. Unfortunately."

She stood, and said, "I'll send them back as soon as they get here."

While he waited, he went through his detailed notes, line by line. He tried to determine where the weakness in his case might have been, but he could come up with nothing. They were upset to say the least. But at this point it didn't really matter what frame of mind they were in—the case was over—they lost. End of story.

He heard them walk in the front door. His discomfort grew as he heard their slow, deliberate steps as they proceeded down the hall and approached his doorway.

He stood as they walked in. "Hi folks, have a chair."

They both appeared to have aged ten years. As a result of the accident, she would always walk with a limp. He helped her sit.

Once seated, he said, "Well Bob, that didn't turn out very well."

"Certainly not the way we had hoped."

"What happened? Do you know?"

"Not really. Everything we wanted to get into evidence we *got* into evidence. I am just as surprised as you are."

"I guess we should have accepted the insurance company's offer?"

"That is the hindsight we discussed before we made the decision to move forward. Those are tough decisions and once you make them, you live with them. Yes, *now*, that looks like what we should have done. But at the time, we all agreed their final offer wasn't enough."

"It is hard to believe they said we are entitled to nothing—nothing at all."

"They apparently determined you were at fault."

"All that time and effort—and we end up with nothing."

"I am sorry. I don't know what else to say. Remember, I get nothing either. I spent many, many hours getting ready and since I had a contingency fee arrangement with you, I don't end up getting a penny either."

She had been looking away for most of the conversation, but at that point she turned toward him and said, "But isn't that what you deserve—nothing? I mean, *really*, isn't that what you are entitled to? Obviously, since you were guiding us through this process—since *we* didn't have any idea what we were doing—the fact that we end up with nothing is your fault. Isn't that how *you* look at it? How could you look at it any other way?"

"Calm down, sweetheart, just calm down. Bob, what are our options at this point?"

"Well, basically, the only option available is to appeal. But normally appeals are based on mistakes in the record that were made while trying the case. I'll have the court reporter transcribe the record and I will read it all over, but to be honest, there weren't many mistakes the Judge made and certainly none of much significance."

"So, an appeal doesn't appear as though it would be successful, is that what you are saying?"

"Actually, the first thing I want to do is discuss the result with the

Judge. I know him—have for many years. He will tell me what he thinks happened. I also want to visit with a couple of the jurors and ask them what went wrong. Then, at that point, if it appears as though an appeal might be successful, we will visit."

She said, "I am assuming you are doing all this on a contingency basis too, correct?"

"Of course."

She turned away as she mumbled, "As if that's supposed to be a benefit."

"I don't know what else to say. You both always knew there was at least a chance we would lose. The insurance company would have raised their offer if they thought they were going to lose the case. They didn't. Obviously, they felt as confident as we did."

"We are just stunned. I guess I don't know how else to put it."

She turned toward Bob and said, "I think you should know that if this doesn't turn out better than it is right now, I am going to file a complaint with the bar association. I think you screwed this thing up. I don't know how—I don't know what you did wrong, but you have screwed this thing up, and they are going to hear about it."

Bob looked at her husband, waiting for him to respond, and when he said nothing, it was obvious they both agreed.

"I am sorry you feel that way. I really did the best I could for you. I tried to let you make all the important decisions along the way. I really can't think of a thing we could have done differently."

She stood. He helped her move toward the door. As they walked out, Bob said, "I'll let you know as soon as I have had a chance to talk to the Judge and some of the jurors."

He turned and said, "Thanks, Bob. We may seek another opinion as to an appeal through some other attorney, so don't be surprised if you hear from one."

Bob nodded, then listened as their footsteps faded down the hallway. He heard the outer office door open, then shut.

Charlene walked in a moment later and said, "What happened?"

"They were upset, as you can imagine. I spent a lot of time on that case. They are talking about filing a complaint against me with the bar association."

"You are kidding." She thought for a moment. "I don't remember that ever happening. Has it? Have you ever had a complaint filed against you?"

He turned to look out his office window.

"Yeah, once about 30 years ago. It amounted to nothing. Why don't you shut everything down. I think we will close a little early today."

He heard her stand and walk out of his office.

Maybe he needed to retire. All of these issues at the same time seemed to point toward one conclusion—maybe it was just time to fold up, to close the office and terminate his practice.

He was old, he was tired and he was sick of doing what he was doing. He would give it his all a few more weeks. If his attitude hadn't changed, perhaps he would close his office door one more time, permanently, then just move on. He would, of course, at some point in time, need to determine where he would *move on* to, because as of today, he had absolutely no idea.

Chapter 5

This was no ordinary Tuesday. Normally, Bob would, about this time of day, be opening his mail and getting ready for his next appointment. But he had decided to take the day off. He had decided he needed to pay some attention to the home front before it was completely beyond control.

The knock on his front door came fifteen minutes later than it should have.

He opened it to find an older lady, maybe 75 or so, who held out her hand as soon as he saw her.

"And you must be Mr. Jones."

Bob extended his hand, smiled and said, "I am. I assume you are Mrs. Hawks."

She shook his hand and started through the door, as she said, "I am. Sorry I'm late. I got caught in some of this damn Nashville traffic. Now, what have we got here? How many rooms in the house?"

"Well, counting the bathrooms, there are eight. I should count the bathrooms, shouldn't I?"

"You want me to clean'em, you better count'em. I assume I am to do the kitchen too—or are you doing it?"

"No, I want you to do it."

She turned and looked toward the kitchen doorway. "It's there, I assume?"

"Yes, yes it's through there."

She walked in the kitchen leaving him standing alone in the living room.

He heard her mumble something under her breath. A couple of minutes later she came out and said, "You told me your wife is gone, is that correct?"

"Yes, she is."

"How long?"

"It's been about five months now, I guess."

"How long has it been since you really cleaned the kitchen? By that, I mean since you did some deep cleaning beyond just washing dishes."

"I really don't know when she cleaned it that way for the last time. I have not done anything with the house but wash dishes since she died."

"It doesn't look to *me* like you have done very *much* of that dish washing—there are dirty dishes everywhere."

"Well, I really haven't done much today, I guess. But normally, I do it on a regular basis, like daily—or at least some of the time I do them daily. Sometimes I don't because…"

"I get it. What about the rest of the house? Have you done any deep cleaning since she died?"

"Well, no, I…"

"I will not clean if you are gone. I want you here so I can ask you questions and so you can make sure I don't take anything. Are you alright with that?"

"Well, it's hard for me to be here during the week. Do you work on weekends?"

"What the hell do *you* think? *You really think I clean houses on my weekends? Hell no.*"

She started to walk to the door.

He said, "Where are you going?"

"I can see right now this isn't going to work."

"Wait. I'll pay you well if you will do this for me."

"Pay isn't the issue."

She walked through the door as he said, "Could we just discuss…"

The door slammed shut before he could finish his sentence.

Later that morning, he called a couple of other housekeepers whose names people had given him, but they were all too busy to handle another home. He would need to start reviewing the want ads for people who were looking for that kind of work. He simply didn't have the motivation, time, nor basic knowledge to do what needed to be done with the products needed to do it.

Bob had delayed calling the utility company. He had received a notice his payment for last month was overdue.

"How can I help you, sir."

"I received a notice indicating my bill was overdue, but I sent a check a couple of weeks ago."

"Was it cashed? Was it run through your bank account?"

"I guess I don't know. I thought maybe you could tell me if it showed paid or not."

"Let me transfer you, sir."

He waited a full ten minutes listening to some pathetic song that repeated itself over and over, before someone finally said, "How can I help you?"

"You already have. You stopped that awful music. I just need to know why my bill is overdue. I sent a check weeks ago,"

"Name on the account."

"Robert Jones."

"Address?"

"1756 Jackson Lane."

"No such account."

"What do you mean? I am living here and we have been getting service here for 30 years."

"Sir, there is an account for that address, but it shows it is in someone else's name."

He hesitated. "Maybe it is in my wife's name, Jean."

"Let me look.".

Finally, after holding for five more minutes, he said, "Yes, that's correct. The account is in the name of Jean Duncan for that particular address. No one else's name is on the account and until a name is added, we can't talk to anyone but her."

"But she's now deceased."

"Not our problem."

"What should I do?"

"Not my department."

"Is that it? Is that all you're going to tell me? What am I supposed to do?"

"Not our problem. Have a good day."

The call was terminated.

"Hello! Hello. Shit."

He got up from his chair fifteen minutes later and walked into the kitchen, where he washed those same dishes that were so upsetting to Mrs. Hawks. The next time he interviewed anyone for that job, everything would be clean *before* the potential housekeeper walked in the door. Lesson learned.

As he started the dishwasher, the house phone rang. It was hardly ever used, and they had discussed disconnecting it. But every once in a while, a client, judge or attorney, would for some reason, have his home number and try to reach him through the home phone rather than his cell, so it remained an active number.

Caller ID reflected nothing.

"Hello, sir?"

"Yes."

"Sir, I very much need to talk to you, sir. We have tried repeatedly to reach you, sir, but to no success."

"Well, you found me. What's going on?"

"Sir, we are with the IRS, and sir, you owe a sum of money and if you can't get it paid within two days, sir, we will need to send out a warrant for your arrest, and place you in jail until paid."

Bob sat down. "I what?"

"Sir, you owe the sum of two thousand two hundred dollars and it must be paid as soon as possible to avoid going to jail."

"But I always pay my taxes and I have never received a notice. My accountant is really good and…"

"Well, he wasn't really good this time. You owe two thousand two hundred dollars and it needs to be paid as soon as possible."

Bob started to smile. "Okay, Jack put you up to this didn't he? That jerk. You had me going there for a moment."

"I know no Jack, sir. You owe the sum of two thousand two hundred dollars and it needs to be paid as soon as possible."

"For what tax year? Have you talked to my accountant?"

"Sir, if you don't get this paid by tomorrow at noon, we shall cause the sheriff to come to your home and arrest you. Now here's what you need to do…"

"Oh, now wait a minute. Is this one of those scammers? Are you one of those son-of-a-bitches that con people out of their money by telling them the IRS is after them."

"Oh no sir, I am *no son-of-a-bitches*. You owe the IRS the sum of…"

"I know, I know, the sum of two thousand two hundred dollars. Sorry, you asshole, but you're not getting a penny of my money, at least not today."

He terminated the call. A few minutes later the phone rang again and again, no one was identified with caller ID. He didn't answer.

So, this is what Jean went through on a daily basis. Now, he knew. Now he knew why there were days she was as tired as he was. He always figured she did nothing but watch tv and eat candy, even though there were days she told him how tired she was because so much had happened. He never gave it any thought. Now, he knew the *rest* of the story.

Charlene answered on the first ring.

"Hey, what's going on?"

"Not a lot, I guess. We have received a lot of calls, but nothing of much urgency."

"Are any of them wanting to come in today?"

"As a matter of fact, yes, there have been a few."

"What did you do with them?"

"I set them up for next week."

"Call them back. See if they can come in yet today. I'm getting out of here."

She laughed. "Is home too quiet for you?"

"Hell no. It's like a war zone here. I need to get out of here—get back to my own comfort zone. I know now how lucky I was that Jean didn't go stark raving mad on me. I'll see you in about a half hour."

"But I thought you were taking the whole day off to relax and…"

"I am. After what I've been through here so far this morning, that is exactly what I'm going to do. I am coming to the office—so I *can* relax. I'll tell you all about it when I get there."

Chapter 6

Bob sat alone as he finished a sandwich Charlene had brought in for him before she locked the front door and left. He had decided to stay in his office over the noon hour, rather than going home or to a local diner.

He had been alone now for six months. During that time, he kept thinking the loneliness would subside—that he would eventually reach the point where he would become comfortable with being alone. As of yet, that hadn't happened. The days *and* nights found him just as lonely now as he was the day she died.

He turned his chair so he could stare out the window for the remainder of the time he was by himself—before Charlene returned and the day began again.

Yesterday, they had finally settled the Master's case. His clients met with him and together, they decided they would threaten the insurance company with an appeal. The company ultimately concluded it wasn't worth the risk and settled. The Masters weren't happy, but it was an acceptable conclusion and the threat of filing a complaint with the bar association turned into a nonfactor.

His thoughts today were of his grandson. He would now be twenty-three. Bob thought about contacting the private investigator he had initially hired years ago. The firm did the best they could to locate Paul for over two years, but after turning up nothing during all that time, the investigator just told him his grandson did not want to be found.

He thought about starting the process again but ultimately concluded his grandson knew where his grandfather lived and how to reach him. He figured after so many years had elapsed, his grandson had no interest or use for him and he most likely would never see him again—a conclusion he would have never imagined could have been even a *remote* possibility before the accident.

"Hey, how was your noon hour?"

"Pretty uneventful, Charlene. Yours?"

"I ran home, had a sandwich, looked at the mail and put a roast in the oven. It will be ready to fall apart when I get home—so tender it will melt in your mouth. Why don't you come for supper? You won't be disappointed."

Bob said nothing.

Then she started to smile.

"Oh, that's right. You got a date! Tonight is the big night! Wow. Are you excited? You have to be at least a little excited…aren't you?"

He hesitated, before he said, "I… am… going. I told her I would meet her there, and I will honor my promise, but that's it. I shouldn't have listened to Jack—he has never been one to listen to about anything, ever. But I promised him I would go and I will. I am *not* excited. I am *not* apprehensive. I actually feel nothing. I will go, but I wish the evening was going to consist of me sitting at home, alone, drinking a beer and watching tv."

Charlene smiled and started to say something, but then thought better of it, turned around and left his office.

They had agreed to meet at Husk, an upscale restaurant not far from downtown Nashville, at 7:00 p.m. He noticed her as soon as she walked through the door. Susan Westerlund was an attractive woman, nicely dressed, big smile. As she continued looking around the room, he waived.

She noticed and waived back as she started to walk between tables to his table. He helped her with her chair. Conversation began immediately, and remained light with no particular direction, until half way through the main course, when Susan brought up Jean.

"Jack never told me much about your wife, Bob. What happened?"

Susan seemed interested in his life and in the direction his life was taking since his wife had passed away. But the specifics of Bob's marriage and of his wife had not been broached—until now.

"She died of cancer. It was quick and unmerciful."

"Funny how that disease works. Sometimes it's slow and unforgiving and sometimes it seems like it is over before it even began. Either way, it's a horrible disease."

"One day she was sitting beside me, the next day, I was planning her funeral. Her death ended a lot of good years for both of us. As you can imagine, it has been hard putting one foot in front of the other since she died."

Susan said, "We were married over 40 years before Tom was killed in a car accident. He has been gone a long time, but I still think of him almost every day."

"No children?"

"No. I never remarried either. Oh, I have gone out with a few guys since his death, but nothing serious. The conversation with most of them, many times turns to sex…or their children that don't want them to date at all…or to their lack of money…or to their health. To be honest, most of the time, their portion of the conversation consists basically of the words 'me' and 'I.'"

She studied him for a moment. "Now, don't get me wrong. Those words are necessary too—it's important to learn about whom you are with. But most of the time, at some point, I get tired of hearing about them and never asking about me or my life."

He said nothing.

"I'm sorry, I don't know why I told you that. I…just…get frustrated sometimes and wonder why I even bother. I am sorry. I'm just rambling."

Bob laughed, and said, "Hey, I feel good about the fact that you opened up to me about it. This is my first date since she died. To be honest, I am not sure I will go on another, but at least I'll know what to expect if I do. I have to admit, I didn't notice you falling into that trap. You really haven't dominated the conversation talking about only you and your life. I think we have both had plenty to say, and, I might add, at least for me, what you have said has been worth saying."

A few moments later, she said, "So, this is your first time out with someone since she died?"

"Yes."

"Is it uncomfortable for you?"

Bob said, "You have made it easy, but even so, yes, it is a little uncomfortable."

"I understand. It was for me too—and still is."

"To be honest, Jack is the reason I am here. I wasn't ready. I'm not sure I ever would have been. But you know him. He wouldn't leave me alone. He said I really needed to meet you. I will have to admit, at first, being with you was a little uncomfortable. But, as the evening has progressed, you have made it much easier than I thought it would be."

They finished dinner with a shared dessert and he walked out the door with her.

Bob said, "Do you have a vehicle here? If you don't, I can drive you home."

"No problem. I have my car."

"Well, okay. I…"

"I'm just parked across the street."

"Would you like me to walk with you?"

She smiled. "No. Thanks though. After all these years, I have grown very comfortable doing things by myself and walking across the street here, alone, is the least of my worries."

She hugged him and said, "Thanks, Bob. I've really enjoyed the evening. If you are interested in having supper again sometime in the future, give me a call."

"I will."

He watched her walk away, then walked to his own vehicle and drove home.

Later that night, he called Jack.

"Hi, Bob. You're up pretty late aren't you. You are always in bed by nine and up by six. How was the date?"

"It went well, Jack. She is a nice lady. We enjoyed the evening. *But no more*. Don't ever call me about another woman. I'm done. She was easy to be with and we both had a good time, but that's it— I'm finished."

"Oh, you're always so damn dramatic. Always the drama. But, it's your life. I'll leave you alone. What about her? Did you make any plans for the future?"

"No."

"Absolutely none?"

"No."

"Hmm. Too bad. I really figured you two would be a good match. Oh well."

"I need to go. Time for bed. Thanks for what you did, but don't do it again."

"Got it."

He terminated the call. Bob thought about his time with Susan and Jack's question concerning any future plans with her. While none had been made, he would give it some thought. A *permanent* future with her was, of course, out of the question, but he might just call her up sometime and see if she wanted to go out again. For now, it was time to get some sleep. He reached over to her side of the bed, patted it a couple of times and whispered the same words he had whispered before he went to sleep each night since she had passed away. "Miss you, sweet heart. I love you…always will."

Chapter 7

Bob sat alone in his office, waiting for Charlene to come in and tell him she was ready to leave for the week. It was Friday afternoon, *late* Friday afternoon. He was ready for a couple of days off. It had been an extremely busy week and, because of that, he had not had the time to plan anything for Saturday or Sunday.

He needed to buy groceries, and the house needed to be, at least superficially, cleaned up before the new housekeeper arrived on Monday morning. Those issues that needed to be resolved around the house, could be done tomorrow morning and then he would have nothing to do but sit the rest of the weekend.

That really wasn't how he had lived his life. When Jean was alive, he was *always* active. If *he* hadn't planned something, *she* had.

As he looked out his window, it was apparent the wind, which was blowing at a moderate clip when he walked in his office door earlier today, hadn't let up. The wind, combined with a cold spell, resulted in putting any and all of his outdoor activities that he might have planned, on the shelf until the temperature moderated and returned to normal for this time of year in Nashville.

But that near-term issue concerning what to do this weekend, was completely overshadowed by the issue that continued to consume his thoughts on an hourly basis—what should he do about his practice?

The office was extremely busy. For some reason, he had people coming to see him for advice that he hadn't seen for years. But he had never met the great majority of people that walked through his doorway. Maybe the increase in office actively was a direct result of his many years of experience in the practice of law…or maybe it was just because there were so many new people now moving into Nashville. But, for whatever reason, many weekends he found himself, for at least a portion of the weekend, handling office work, just to get out of the house for a while *and* because he was so busy.

But he didn't want to work weekends at the office anymore. He didn't want to take it home with him anymore either. The question was whether to slow down or just quit altogether. While his life outside the office was nonexistent, he still had no desire to fill those empty hours with office work. It appeared to him, at this moment, he was at a crossroads and it was time to move on, one way or the other, once and for all.

There was one other option concerning the totality of his life which he had considered, but not seriously—until just recently.

The only way he knew to stop the pain on a permanent basis, was by doing something which ran contrary to everything he had ever believed in. But, at this point in time, it no longer sounded like the worst option available.

If he *was* serious concerning a permanent solution, he would need to figure out a method. He hated guns—poison would most likely be painful. He never cared for heights…

His cell vibrated. He looked at caller ID. Should be answer? He really wasn't in the mood. What the hell…he really wasn't in the mood for anything else either.

"What?"

"Come on, Bob. Is that how you now answer the phone-- 'what?'"

"Not a good time, Jack. Get on with it. What do you want?"

"Why, what's the problem?"

"Nothing, I just…I was just…"

"Feeling sorry for yourself?"

"What the hell do you want?"

"You want to go get a drink somewhere?"

"Nope."

"Depressed, aren't you?"

"A little, yes. Now, anything else? I got a whole lot of things to do before I leave here tonight."

"Come on. Meet me somewhere for a drink, instead of sitting alone wallowing in self-pity."

"I need to go. I'll talk to you sometime over the weekend."

He terminated the call. As soon as he set his phone down, it buzzed again. This time he was conflicted. He didn't want to answer, but he did have somewhat of a desire to see her again.

"Hi, Susan."

"Hi, Bob. How is everything?"

"Fine, doing fine. You?"

"I haven't heard from you for a while and I was just wondering how you were getting along."

"Fine, I'm getting along just great."

She hesitated for a moment. He heard her take a deep breath, before she said, "Hey, what about meeting for a drink before you go home tonight? Do you have any plans? There's that little bar down the street, Randolph's, I think it's called. I could meet you there in a half hour or so."

He hesitated. "I don't know, Susan, I have a lot of things…"

"Oh, come on. It's only one drink. What about a half-hour from now?"

He thought for a moment and finally said, "Okay. I'll meet you there in about thirty minutes."

When he arrived, she was already seated at a small table and had a beer in front of her. As he approached, she said, "I told the waiter to watch for you. He said he would bring you a beer as soon as you walked in."

As Bob sat, the waiter brought him his drink. He smiled and said, "Were you already here when you called me?"

"No, no of course not, but I live near here. It didn't take me long to get here. There really weren't many here when I arrived. It's full now, but it wasn't difficult getting this table when I walked in."

During the next hour they discussed what had happened in each of their lives during the course of the day and, eventually, the past few weeks.

As they started to run out of small talk, she said, "You seem a little down. Are you okay? I obviously don't know you all that well…yet. But you do seem somewhat subdued tonight. Am I wrong?"

"It was a long day. I need to figure out what I'm going to do about my practice. I am getting a little tired of it. It's just getting old. I think I need to make a few decisions concerning the office, one way or the other, then move on."

She studied him a moment, before she said, "I can certainly understand. Your practice has probably been a huge part of your life up until now. I'm sure all your priorities have changed since Jean's passing."

He remained quiet, as did she.

Finally, she broke the silence as she said, "You never did tell me about your grandson. He sounds like the only family you have left. Why did he run away or what happened with him?"

Bob cupped his hands around his beer mug and stared at his half-empty glass as he considered whether to discuss a subject so personal with someone he had only just met. He finally concluded perhaps talking about it might be therapeutic. Maybe verbalizing the loss with someone other than Jack or Charlene would somehow provide him with a new prospective.

He looked up at her, and said, "He was here one day and gone the next."

"I believe you told me he was only sixteen?"

"Yes. He had lived with us for a number of years after his parents were killed."

"Was there something that triggered that kind of reaction?"

Bob leaned back, and said, "We were much older than his parents so there was a significant generation gap which many times was hard to overcome. We established a number of rules for him to follow, as we had done for his father when he was young. They worked for our son; they *didn't* work for him."

"It had to have been a horrible shock when he left."

"He was an angry young man. The death of both his parents seemed to fuel an anger in him we had trouble understanding or controlling. But we never, ever thought he would take off like that. We tried to find him for years."

"And you never did find him?"

"Never did. I hired a private detective and his firm tried to find him for two years, but with no success."

"He was the only family you had left?"

"Yes."

He looked away, having said all he was going to say about the subject.

She remained quiet for a few moments, until she, apparently concluding he was done discussing his lost grandson said, "Let's change the subject. What happened at work today? How did the day work out for you?"

An hour later, after they had both gone their own way, he sat at home, watching TV and finishing up leftovers from the night before.

Bob thought about his time with her. He concluded he had enjoyed being with her, if for no other reason than she had provided a great change of pace. He had no desire to be with her on a regular basis, but he would not be averse to seeing her again. If she didn't call him within the near future, this time maybe he would call her.

33

Chapter 8

"So, what did you do during your weekend?"

"Friday, I stayed here, at the office, until about six when Jack called and I had to deal with him. I guess I finally got home around eight-thirty. I did nothing the rest of the weekend."

Charlene said, "You talked to Jack that long? He must have had a whole lot to say, because your conversations with anyone never, ever last that long."

"Well, I did spend some of that time with Susan."

"Who is Susan? I don't remember a current client named Susan."

Appointments would not begin for another hour. Bob and Charlene had been reviewing his schedule for the next couple of weeks. There discussion in that respect had come to an end. But Charlene stood, leaning against the doorframe making small talk, before she walked down the hallway to her desk where her day on the job would then officially begin.

"Well, she isn't really a client. She…"

"Oh, okay, okay, now I remember. You have gone out with her a couple of times…or maybe…more. I remember you talking about her. So, how many times *have* you been with this 'Susan'?"

"Not that many. There was last night and I guess maybe another time. That's about it."

She smiled. "Do you…like her?"

"She is a nice person, yes."

"You know what I mean. Do you *like her*?"

"No, not like that. I enjoy being with her and I'm glad we met, but beyond that, no one will ever replace…no one will ever…"

"No, I understand. But that doesn't mean you couldn't love someone else *too*, does it? I am not talking about replacing Jean. I'm talking about some other woman you could be with, enjoy life with, and maybe have a common goal or two. I mean, you are absolutely right. I have known you a long time and no one could or ever will, replace Jean. But that's not really what I am saying."

"I understand. In answer to your question, I have really enjoyed our time together, but that is it. I may, or may not see her again, and if I don't, I enjoyed the time we spent together—nothing more, nothing less. It wouldn't bother me if I never saw her again."

"Really?"

"Yes, really. Now, go to work."

"You know, I get the feeling you are not being entirely truthful with me. Are you? Is that really the way you feel? I know you pretty well, Bob and somehow…"

"Okay, okay this conversation is over. Now, go to work before I have to fire you,"

She smiled, and said, "Fine, I'll go to work, but not because you threated me. You got no bite. You talk big, but sorry, you got no bite."

He had to smile. She had worked for him way too long. He couldn't and wouldn't fire her no matter what she did. She was as important to this office as he was.

The remainder of the morning crawled along. He saw four different people and they all wanted the same thing—to end their marriage. Bob had heard the same story four different times—only the names changed. He was just getting ready to leave for lunch at a local bar near his office when he heard the steps of Charlene as she walked down the hallway. He didn't normally notice. She normally walked quietly and took her time to reach his office door—not so this time.

She turned the corner into his office and quickly walked up to the front of his desk. "Bob."

He never looked up as he said, "What."

"Look at me."

He looked up and said, "What do you want? Why haven't you left for lunch?"

"We got a call and when I looked at caller ID it said it was from jail. That was all it said—jail."

"I'm not ever taking another criminal case, Charlene. Not now, not never. You know that. Don't answer it if they call back."

"I already did."

"Big mistake. Tell them I will call them back or something. Just get rid of them."

"I can't."

"Why?"

"It's your grandson. It's Paul on the line. He is on hold."

He never moved.

"Pick up. It's Paul and I don't know how long he will be able to stay on the phone. I know they restrict the use of the phone when you call from…pick up the damn phone."

He picked up, and said, "Paul, is this you. Is this really you? How are you?"

"Not very damn good—*Bob*. I've been holding here on the phone for way to long and I have no idea how much longer it will be before they terminate the call."

"Are you really in jail?"

"Yup, I really am. Yup, sure am, *Bob*"

"What are you charged with?"

"Murder."

His heart skipped a beat. "Where are you? Are you here in Nashville?"

"No, I'm in Knoxville."

"Who did you murder?"

"I murdered no one, Bob, absolutely no one."

He sat back as he reconsidered the conversation so far.

"Okay, bad choice of words—who did you allegedly murder?"

"One of the people I worked for. A woman I worked for."

"Do you have an attorney?"

"They appointed one for me. I don't have any money or assets of any kind. I don't have enough money to afford an attorney, so they appointed this asshole prick to represent me. He knows nothing. He's belligerent, cocky and I can guarantee you I know more about representing myself then he does about representing *anyone*."

"You don't want to go there, Paul—believe me, you don't want to represent yourself."

"And that brings us to my reason for the call. I need help. I have no one else to turn to. I am afraid if I don't have someone represent me who knows about criminal law *and* that I can trust, I'm going to end up in prison the rest of my life."

"Well…I need to tell you I don't really do any work in the criminal law area. I do a lot of civil work, but very little criminal defense work. In fact, it's been a while since I tried *any type of case* in criminal court."

"Here's the deal—*Bob*. I do *not* have enough money to retain an attorney. I am *not* going to let this dumb ass court-appointed jerk represent me. That means you either help me, or I represent myself. You think that over—Bob, and let me know what I should do. You got the number for this place. You think it over and then call and tell me how you want to proceed. Well, gotta go. Enjoy your evening. I'm sure I will."

He hung up the and looked at Charlene.

"That was interesting."

"What did he say? What is going on?"

"He is in jail. He's charged with murder. He wants me to help him."

"Where is he?"

"Knoxville."

"Do you know anyone there that could represent him?"

"I know a couple of guys, yes, but he wants *me* to represent him. Maybe I could hire one of those guys, and I could pay him to represent Paul. I don't know, I..."

"You finally find him and he has been charged with murder? What are you..."

"I don't know, Charlene. I need to think. I'll see you in the morning. Go ahead and go home.

The office was quiet. He had done nothing the past hour but think about Paul...about his problem... about what he needed to do to help. First of all, he needed to discuss it with someone. He needed to verbalize the problem and hopefully come to some conclusion.

"Jack, are you busy?"

"Hey. Are you still at the office? What are you doing there so late?"

"I need some advice."

"Well, you called the right person. Now, what do you need?"

"I heard from Paul today."

He hesitated. "Your Paul? Your grandson, Paul?"

"Yes."

"You are kidding me. Well, hallelujah! Good for you. What's his story?"

"He is in jail, in Knoxville. He is charged with murder. He wants me to represent him."

Jack said nothing.

"I don't know what to do. You know I don't practice in that field. I just don't know how to handle this. I finally hear from him and this is what I'm faced with."

"What about just paying someone else that specializes in criminal law, to represent him?"

"I thought about that. I don't know if he will go for that or not. I have a feeling, in talking to him even the short while I did, he may have a few trust issues."

"How much is his bail?"

"We never discussed that. The call was short and to the point. He just provided the basics. He was afraid the call might be terminated before he was able to provide me with all the details."

Jack was quiet for a moment before he said, "You have two choices. You either pay to have someone else represent him or you need to do it yourself."

"I *can't* do it myself. I don't practice in that field. *I can't help him.*"

"If he doesn't want anyone but you, then buddy you better learn criminal law quick, because you have no other option. If he wants you and he needs you to do this for him, that's the end of the discussion. You have to help him."

The call ended a few moments later. Bob never left his office until near 10:00 p.m. He studied the criminal code and reviewed the applicable statures that pertained to murder in the State of Tennessee.

He knew Jack was right. If Paul didn't want someone other than him to represent him, he would be left with no choice. He had finally found his grandson! He would do whatever needed to be done to save him. If that meant practicing within an area of law he wasn't comfortable with, then so be it.

Chapter 9

He hadn't slept but a few minutes all night. After tossing and turning for a couple of hours, he finally fell asleep, but woke up shortly thereafter. It was now 5:00 a.m. Bob finally just got out of bed and ready for work. After an abbreviated breakfast, he drove down empty streets and subsequently found himself turning on the lights in his office at six-thirty.

First, he checked the Knoxville online newspapers for the past couple of weeks and finally found the article he needed to read. Paul had been working for the victim. They were also apparently romantically involved. She had been murdered—he was the prime suspect. Bond was set at three hundred thousand dollars, of which the paper noted he was unable to pay. The bond was set so high because he was considered a flight risk.

Bob then reviewed the charges against him. Paul was charged with premeditated first-degree murder.

Charlene walked through the front office door at seven-thirty and down the hallway about fifteen minutes later. She wanted to know what he had found out. He briefly explained what Paul was charged with and then told her to go ahead and open the office for the day. As she turned to walk out, he told her to close the door as she left his office. He wanted it quiet while he tried to contact Paul.

He put in the call, but was unable to talk with him at that time. A couple of long, uneasy hours later, Paul called him back.

"How you getting along?"

"Oh, never better, Bob, and you?"

"We need to talk about how you want to handle this attorney business. Have you had any second thoughts about using the court appointed attorney they assigned to you?"

"No."

"I assume by that you mean he is not an option for you?"

"Correct."

"What about retaining a local attorney to help you?"

"What do you mean?"

"What if I could find an attorney locally there in Knoxville to help you? I would pay him. I would find someone that I felt could represent you and that was qualified to do so."

"Aren't you qualified?"

"To be honest, probably not. I just haven't done much work in the criminal field. I would feel better about the situation if you retained someone that really knew what they were doing."

Paul laughed. "You know, I don't know why, but that is really not a surprise. You just don't want to deal with me. Is that it? You just don't want to take the time to deal with me?"

"No that is not the case at all. I'm just afraid…"

"Look. Just forget it. I will represent myself. I think I'm as smart as that idiot public defender. By the way, to be perfectly honest, I do have a few trust issues. Especially as concerns strangers. Just forget it, Bob. I'll handle this myself."

"Wait a minute. Just give me a minute here. I need to think about this. Can you call be back in a few minutes?"

Paul said nothing.

"Are you still there?"

"Yes, Bob, I'm still here. I'll call you back in ten minutes."

Paul terminated the call.

He stood, walked over to his office door and shut it. He then walked back to his chair and swiveled to face the window.

It was time for him to make a decision, one way or the other. Either way, whatever he decided to do, his decision was going to significantly affect the rest of his life.

Should he just shut down. Should he turn his back on his grandson, close the office, perhaps travel, read a book or two and live the sedentary life he had observed so many acquaintances do at his age?

For the following hour he continued to sort through other available options associated with slowing down. Finally, he simply stopped assessing his position, slammed his hands down on the arms of his chair, and said, "No way. Not yet."

He just wasn't ready. Her death had caused him to conclude, because of the sorrow, the grief, the lack of drive, that it was time to shut down.

But now…now that Paul had finally contacted him, he felt a resurgence he hadn't felt since she died. There was no way he would vary from the energetic way of life he had enjoyed with her so many years, even though she was no longer with him. He was absolutely not going to follow an uncommitted, uninvolved pathway during the years he had left on this earth. That was simply an unacceptable conclusion.

His cell rang. He turned around, picked up the phone, and before Paul could say anything, he said, "I will handle it for you."

Paul, said nothing.

"Do you understand? I'll do the best I can for you."

"Thank you."

"I will be down to see you, maybe tomorrow. Will that work? And if it will, what time is the best time to come?"

"Tomorrow is fine. I'll certainly be here. The best time is probably around ten."

"Okay, you take care of yourself, and I'll see you then."

Paul said nothing before he terminated the call.

Near noon, Charlene walked through his office door, and said, "Jack is on line one. You want to talk to him?"

"Yes."

"By the way, I cleared your calendar for tomorrow, all day."

"Better clear it for the following day too. I may be back, but I may not be either. Better move everyone to another day."

Bob picked up the phone and said, "Jack, what are you doing tomorrow?"

"Good morning to you too. Working my ass off as I do every minute of every day. Why?"

"I guess I am going to take Paul's case. He doesn't seem to want it any other way. I have offered to have someone else handle it and I would pay the bill, but he doesn't want that. He said he would represent himself first. I don't know what else to do other than just try the case and do the best I can for him. I am going down tomorrow and visit with him—to see what he has to say about what happened."

"That's a good idea. You can take time to look over the location where it happened too. Let me know what you find out."

Bob said nothing.

"Okay then, is that it? Let me know what you found out when you come home. Maybe we can meet somewhere and discuss it over a beer."

"Well, Jack, I was wondering…"

"Oh *shit*, I knew this was coming as soon as you said you were taking the case. *Don't* ask me to go with you. Please, please, please *don't* ask me to go with you tomorrow. I've got a million things going on and…"

"No problem. I'll go alone. No problem with that at all. I will probably screw the whole thing up, but I'll go alone. If I do, just remember you were the one that said I had no choice but to…"

"Just shut the hell up. I'll go. I will have to move everyone off my schedule, but I'll…go…with you, I guess."

"Great. I'll pick you up about eight at your house."

"Yeah, whatever."

"Oh, and one more thing."

"What's that?"

"We may be gone two days, not one, so plan accordingly."

"I can't be gone…"

Bob terminated the call, before Jack finished his sentence.

He quickly punched in one more number.

"Hi, Bob. What's going on? You never call me during the day."

"Susan, I won't be in contact very much the next few days. I found my grandson."

"You what? Are you kidding me? Where is he?"

"He is in Knoxville, in jail. He has been charged with murder. He wants me to help him."

She took a deep breath. "Are you going to represent him?"

"He won't have it any other way. I am going down first thing in the morning. Jack's going with me. I have a million things to do here today and tonight before I leave in the morning."

"I thought you told me you weren't at your best in the criminal field. But you are still going to represent him?"

"I tried to talk him out of it, but he's insistent. Otherwise, he's going to represent himself. I don't have a choice. I won't be in touch for a while and I…just felt you should…know, I guess."

"I understand. If there's anything I can do while you are gone, let me know. If I need to do something with the house, or you need something done here in Nashville, just call."

"Okay, thanks."

"Oh and Bob."

"Yeah."

"Good luck. I'll be thinking of you."

"Thanks. I will need all the luck you can provide. I'll keep you informed."

Chapter 10

As they approached Knoxville, Jack said, "Where are we staying tonight?"

"They have a nice Hilton here. I just figured we would stay there," Bob replied.

"You know, they are expensive. I assume I am paying for half of the cost of the room?"

"If you are staying in the room, sure you are. If you want to stay in the car, then no, you are not paying anything. It's up to you."

"Well, obviously I am staying in the room. But if I'm paying half the bill, I want some say in where we stay."

"Sounds fair to me. By the way, I talked to Paul earlier. I told him we would be in to see him tomorrow. I want to take today to figure out where this happened, talk to the cops and just determine exactly what went on before we see him. We can then ask him questions based on our own investigation, rather than trying to figure it all out while we are visiting with him."

"Do you have the name of the cop that investigated?"

"Yes, he's a guy by the name of Glen Majors. I thought once we checked in, we could go see him first thing."

As they reached the outskirts of Knoxville, traffic picked up significantly.

Jack said, "Hey, that looks like a decent place to stay. Turn right at the next intersection."

"Where? I'll turn but I don't see the place you're talking about. Where is it?"

He turned off the interstate onto an access road. As he stopped at the stop sign, he said, "Which place? What are you talking about?"

"The Sidewinder Motel. Right over there. We can drive right up to the room."

"Are you nuts? I'm not staying there."

"I have no doubt the rates are low. You know, I've stayed at many drive-up places before. They are fine. If it's not okay, we can move tomorrow. That's where I want to stay Bob. And if I'm paying half the bill, then you owe at least that much to me to try it for one night."

Bob, not wanting to argue, drove into the parking lot, walked in the office and checked in for one night. They parked in front of the door to their room and unloaded the few items each had brought with them for the one-night stay.

Jack smiled. "See, this isn't so bad. We each have a relatively clean bed, the bathroom isn't bad, we have easy access to our vehicle—all is good."

"We will see. Let's go visit with the cop."

A half-hour later they were downtown, asking where they might locate officer Glen Majors. The officer informed them which precinct Majors worked in, then directed him toward that office.

When they arrived, they were told the officer happened to be working on paperwork but further indicated he was available. After introductions, Officer Majors took them to a small room normally used to interrogate.

After being seated, the officer said, "You know, I don't normally do this. I don't normally sit down and discuss this type of situation with people. But I decided since you were Paul's grandfather and not from around here, this would be an exception."

Bob said, "Thank you. I know so little about what's going on, I was hoping you could fill me in on exactly what happened the day the murder occurred."

Officer Majors leaned back in his chair, clasped his hands together behind his head and said, "Well, to be honest there's not much to tell. Paul had an ongoing personal relationship with a woman he worked for. Her name was Lynn Baker. Her house had security cameras in front and in back, although she wasn't using the one in back—the light illuminating the area was out and had been for quite some time."

"This would have been about a month ago?"

"Yes. He was seen going into her house during the afternoon and coming out about two and a half hours later. When he came out, he came out in a hurry. No one saw her. A number of the neighbors heard yelling involving the two of them about 30 minutes before he left."

"Her daughter then tried to reach her the next morning. Lynn never answered her phone. She went to the Baker home and found her dead—murdered. When they conducted the autopsy, Paul's DNA was found inside her."

"So, the assumption is that they had an ongoing relationship, they then became involved in an argument, he raped her and then killed her?"

"That's what the evidence indicates happened, yes."

"Are there any other possible suspects?"

"No."

"The outside camera shows no one else entering or leaving the house after he left and before she was found?"

"No."

"Was anything taken?"

"We aren't sure. It looks like there might have been, but of course Paul never admitted taking anything and her daughter just couldn't be certain whether there were items missing or not."

They visited about apprehending Paul and the fact that he, at that time, vehemently denied committing the murder. Bob then asked for and was given the address of the location where the crime occurred.

The two of them located the home and took the time to look over the general area before stopping at a McDonalds and eating an abbreviated lunch.

Officer Majors had mentioned they might want to talk about the case with a reporter for the local newspaper—Carrie Thompson. She had apparently taken an interest in the story and had followed it from the beginning. That would be their next stop.

Upon arriving, Bob asked to talk to the reporter that covered the murder of Lynn Baker and confirmed it was, in fact, Carrie Thompson. They asked if they could meet with her for a few minutes. The front desk contacted her and shortly thereafter they were both taken to a small conference room, where Carrie was waiting for them.

She stood as they entered the room.

Bob shook her hand, and she offered them a seat.

"I understand you are Paul's grandfather, is that correct?"

"Yes. I haven't seen Paul for a number of years, and when he called, he asked me to help him. I told him I would. I felt I needed to jump into the situation as soon as he called. Do you know any more than what you have already reported? I assume what you've reported, is consistent with what Officer Majors just told us."

"I don't know any more beyond what he might have told you. I am the only one from the paper that has covered it from day one, but I didn't investigate—I only followed along. Lynn was an important lady in this community. He seemed to be the exact opposite of that. I just found it interesting she became involved with him. I followed it from the beginning and anticipate following it until the end."

"Well, you will probably be seeing a lot more of us while the case is pending. I'm not only his grandfather, but I am also going to represent him. Both Jack and I are lawyers. We are here to try and do whatever we can to help him. Paul ran away from home after his parents were killed, and we haven't seen or heard from him for a number of years…until he called."

She smiled and her blue eyes sparkled as she said, "Wow. That's an interesting twist. Grandfather/grandson estranged for years, and now you are here to save the day. Interesting."

"I guess."

They continued discussing the facts of the case as she knew them for another fifteen minutes and until Bob turned toward Jack and said, "We better move along."

As Bob stood to leave, she stood and said, "Let me ask you something. As I said, I've followed this story closely from day one. Would you mind if I tag along? Could I tell this story as it unfolds—somewhat from your point of view?"

"You mean what goes on when we're not in court? Maybe just kind of report on it as a human-interest story starting with the preparation and continuing through the trial itself from the inside rather than just watching with the spectators from the outside?"

Bob looked at Jack, then turned toward Carrie and said, "I don't know why not. It won't bother me, but I'll need to ask Paul. I'll let you know tomorrow."

Later in the day and after having a quick supper, they retired to their small room at the Sidewinder Motel.

Bob had a hard time falling asleep. He figured it probably had something to do with Jack's snoring. He had no doubt Jack could be heard in the parking lot.

About 2:00 a.m., Bob sat straight up in bed as the sound of breaking glass filled the room. He heard something hit the wall above his head and after turning on the lights, they were able to determine a bullet had entered the room through the window and lodged itself in the wall.

They immediately packed up and moved to the Hilton where Bob stuffed toilet paper in his ears and slept soundly the rest of the night.

Chapter 11

The following morning, since the bathroom had dual sinks, both men found themselves shaving next to each other at the same time.

"Jack, I don't know if you know this or not, but you snore as loud as a goddamn freight train. Anybody ever tell you that?"

"Yeah, I've been told that before. Obviously, there is nothing I can do about it. Did I bother you last night?"

"What do you think?"

Jack stopped in the middle of a stroke, turned to Bob and said, "It's nice you told me about it, but why bother? You know there is nothing I can do about it so why even bring it up?"

"I just wanted you to know. I felt you should know how horrible it is to sleep in the same room with you—you know—for future reference. I have no idea how you ever get a woman to stay with you in the same room longer than one night."

Jack returned to shaving, as he said, "Obviously, what I provide them during the evening, is worth accepting the snoring."

"Oh, give me a fricken break. You are a joke. My conclusion is that the women you pick up have nothing else to fall back on other than a broken-down piece of shit like you. They have nowhere else to turn. Now, that's just one man's conclusion but…"

"Whatever." Jack turned toward Bob and said, "Are you ready or is it going to take you another hour to clean yourself up."

"Just about done."

The drive to the jail took little time. As soon as they arrived, Bob asked to see Paul. Both were escorted to a room where they were able to sit and visit with Paul through the glass separating them. He walked in five minutes later.

If Bob hadn't known better, he would have sworn it was his *son.*

He looked enough like his father to be a twin.

Bob smiled, and said, "Hi, Paul. Been a while."

"Yes, it has. Who is this with you?"

"Jack Raymond. Do you remember him? He is an attorney in Nashville that I've known a long, long time. He has been a friend forever. Jack has agreed to work with me on your case. You most likely met him when you lived with us."

"Whatever. Are you going to be able to help me or not? If you can't, I will represent myself. There's no sense in all three of us appearing to be fools. If you two can't help me, I will do it myself."

"I think we can help. But before we go any further, I guess we need to discuss what happened. Yesterday, we drove by the house, we met with the officer that investigated the murder and talked to the reporter that handled the story. So, we have at least acquired a little information about what happened."

"What's next?"

"Why don't you tell us, in your own words, how you ended up in Knoxville and what happened that day. Then maybe we can talk about where we are going from there."

He stared at both of them for a moment, then looked away.

Once he turned to face them again, he said, "I have a small lawn and garden service. I started it from nothing. It had grown extensively, to the point where I had even considered hiring another guy or two."

"Lynn Baker was a client. She wasn't married. We became involved. I really cared for her."

Again, he looked away.

"When this all happened, I had worked for her off and on most of the day. She fixed me supper. We made love. But as the evening progressed, we both had had our share of wine. We started to argue. The yelling eventually got pretty loud, which I attribute to the booze—we had never, ever argued like that in the past."

"She told me it was time to go. I agreed. I walked out the door, slamming it as I left. I went to a bar I've frequented many times and was there for a couple of hours before the cops came and picked me up. I was charged with murdering her right after that."

Bob said, "I am sorry for asking you this Paul, but I have to. Did you kill her?"

"No, *Bob*, I didn't kill her."

Jack said, "Do you have any idea who might have? Did she have enemies? Was she having a relationship with anyone else who might have taken issue with her because of you? Do you have any idea where we should look to determine who might have done this?"

"No. I, in fact, have very little knowledge about the rest of her life. We did little together beyond the boundaries of her property."

Bob said, "Okay, Paul, we will start asking around to see what we can find out. We will probably fast track the proceedings to trial. There is no reason to delay it. Jack and I are going home tonight, but we'll be back next week for your arraignment. Do you have any questions for us?"

"No. Just get me out of here. Just get me off, that's all. I didn't do this. I really don't want to spend the rest of my life in jail for something I didn't do."

Bob turned to Jack and said, "I need to visit with him…alone… before we go. Do you mind?"

Jack said, "No, go ahead." He stood. "Nice meeting you, Paul."

Paul looked away and said, "Yeah, right."

Once Jack left the room, Bob smiled and said, "It's so good to see you again. I tried to find you after you left. I hired private investigators and did everything I knew how to do to find you. Can you tell me why you left? What did we do? What happened?"

"You really want to know?"

"Yes."

"To many rules, Bob. Do this, do that, don't do that. I heard that from the time I got up, to the time I went to bed. I just got damn tired of it. By the way, where's Jean? Apparently, she didn't care enough to come with you. No surprise to me."

Bob looked away for a moment, then turned toward him, and said, "She died. She's been gone not quite a year."

"Got it. Is that all we have to talk about today concerning the case? If it is, I know my time is about up anyway. When will I see you again?"

"I will be here for your arraignment next week, after you are indicted by the grand jury. I'll see you then."

"So be it. By the way, why don't you put up the three hundred thousand and bail me out of here…show me just how much you really care."

"I don't have that kind of money, Paul. I have a little put away, but I can't raise that kind…"

Paul stood. The guard walked him out of the room.

An hour later they were on their way back to Nashville.

They said little to each other, until Jack said, "Your grandson is one angry dude. I hope we can help him, but that attitude is definitely going to need to change if he's going to testify."

"I know, I know. I'll work with him on that. So, what do you think?"

"I think we got a tough case. The evidence clearly points to him—all of it. It may come down to his own testimony. I don't think there is any doubt but that he will need to testify on his own behalf. We will see what you and I can turn up. But witnesses for him that actually know about the facts of the case will be hard to find, based on what he told us today. And if this persona is who he is on a day-to-day basis, *any* witness for him will be hard to find. That's my thoughts. What about you?"

Bob thought for a moment, then said, "I agree. I think he is going to be a tough man to represent. I'm afraid we have really got our work cut out for us, Jack. He wanted me to bail him out. I told him I didn't have that kind of money. I wasn't quite truthful with him. I have it, but at this point, I'm just not sure whether he would run. I believe it's best to leave him where he is until we get to know him a little better. If he were let out after I put up his bail, it wouldn't surprise me if he skipped town and we never did get this resolved."

"I agree completely."

Chapter 12

Bob quickly sorted through all his messages he had received during the last couple of days. While out of his office, all the messages received, and the appointments made, involved divorce. The caller provided basic information concerning their situation, then made an appointment to see him.

Fees were always a major issue. All the new clients needed was a *"simple"* divorce. No one *ever* had a *"complicated"* divorce. He learned long ago they would all lie during their initial conference, concluding that might keep the fees down. It was only after he had thoroughly examined the essence of each client's issues, that he learned his estimate of fees, based on the client's assertion as to how simple it would all be, was considerably short of what it would take to complete the matter.

Of course, after the proceedings were initiated, any request for payment of additional fees always met with resistance. He had learned long ago to overestimate the cost right up front. If his estimate was then too high, and he had an overage of fees which he paid back to the client, it left the client thanking him rather than cursing him for continuously asking for more.

"You are back. I wasn't sure you would be in today. I didn't schedule any appointments for you, not knowing for certain you would be here."

He leaned back in his chair, and said, "It was a long couple of days, Charlene. Being with Jack, made it even longer. I am glad he is helping me, but to be honest, he's difficult to deal with for an hour and *impossible* to deal with for two straight days."

Charlene smiled and said, "Did you two share a room?"

"Oh, yeah."

"I cannot imagine staying with him."

"Actually, *I'm* probably not much better." He smiled. "We are just a couple of old men set in our ways, trying to make it through the night."

"What about Paul? Are you going to be able to help him?"

He leaned forward and said, "I'm not sure. The evidence is really solid. I cannot believe he would murder anyone for any reason, but I also haven't had contact with him for years, so what do I know?"

"When are you going back to Knoxville? What should I do about your schedule?"

"I need to talk to Jack. He will be here this afternoon around two. I've got plenty to catch up on, so it's a good thing the calendar is clear. Let's keep it that way for today. I am thinking we will probably go back down on Friday and stay until Sunday, but I will let you know."

Bob prepared for a couple of trials, reviewed paperwork and called witnesses until a few minutes after three. He heard Jack walk in the front office door. He notified Charlene to send him back.

As he walked through Bob's doorway, he said, "So, when are we going back to Knoxville?"

"Hello to you, too. I thought maybe Friday. Do you have anything going on Friday through perhaps Sunday?"

"Yeah, I got plenty going on, but most of it I can get out of doing. Is that when you want to go?"

"Yes. So, clear your schedule. Do you have some time today to talk about the case?"

"A few minutes, sure."

Bob said, "This looks, unfortunately, like it is open and shut unless we can come up with something while we are in Knoxville that hasn't already been discovered."

"I agree. Let's talk about potential witnesses and what their testimony might be, at least based on what we know now."

"From what we initially learned; we have the neighbor who heard them fighting. We have the medical examiner who will testify as to her cause of death and also testify the semen he examined was from Paul. We most likely have a bartender that will testify as to Paul's state of mind and we have the cop that investigated."

Jack said, "Do you think the bartender will testify?"

"I'll bet he does. From what I have noticed about Paul's demeanor, I can't imagine he didn't say something to the bartender about the argument. We need to find out what his name is and the name of the bar where he works. We can get that information from Paul. They are going to indict him next week. After they do, we'll know the names of all the witnesses and we can go from there."

"You know, unless somehow we can uncover witnesses of our own that can provide some *substantial* evidence concerning who committed the murder, I have a feeling we are not going to have much to offer."

Charlene interrupted the conversation as she leaned around the doorframe and said, "Paul is on line one."

Bob picked up and said, "Paul, how are you? Jack is here. We were just talking about you."

"I'll bet *that* is an interesting conversation. It's probably a good thing I'm not there. When are you coming back?"

"We thought we would try to drive down on Friday and stay until Sunday. Will that work for you?"

"I'm just not sure. Let me check my calendar." After a slight pause, he said, "Sure, that will just work fine. See you sometime Friday, or maybe Saturday, and then perhaps on Sunday. You drive safely."

Bob heard him terminate the call. He set his phone down, turned to Jack, and said, "I hate to say it, but my grandson is an ass."

Jack smiled and said, "From my standpoint, I completely agree, at least based on what we have seen so far—which brings us to our next and final question for the day."

"What's that?"

"*What the hell are we going to do when we have to present our case?* Clearly without a response of some kind from us, they will convict him. We need to find someone that will testify on his behalf."

"I know that. I am just wondering if maybe one of his friends might agree to testify as a character witness for him. We need to discuss that issue when we get together with him."

"I mean, the problem is he was at her house around the time she was murdered, they were clearly involved in an argument, and they clearly had just been intimate around the time of the murder. She was strangled, which probably means someone used their hands. As a result, no one is saying there was a weapon used, so there is no issue concerning where it went. The State has all they need—motive, method, opportunity. That obviously begs the question—what's left for us to respond with?"

"I agree. I understand. In addition to all of what you just said, I am really concerned about him getting up on the stand to testify on his own behalf."

"Well, since you raised that issue, what *are* we going to do about him testifying? He, at least at this stage, would be a horrible witness. He is so angry, so full of rage, I have a feeling he would be his own worst enemy. What are we going to do if we decide not to put him on the stand, but he demands to testify?"

"I think, Bob, based on what I've observed, we need to protect ourselves. If he testifies, I think, unless we can get him to calm down and testify in a civil manner, we need to make a record, and preserve the fact we advised him not to testify—that we told him, but he wouldn't listen, and he wants to testify contrary to our advice."

"I agree. But let's see what happens between now and the time of trial. I might be able to work with him and get him to calm down a little, although from what I've seen, he's certainly going to be a challenge."

"That is an understatement. I am really afraid from what I've seen, if he gets up on the stand with that much anger, he's going to be his own worst enemy. Unfortunately, if he does that, he could very well convict himself with his own testimony."

Chapter 13

As soon as Jack left his office, he sent Charlene home for the day. After he had considered his abbreviated conversation with Paul and the comments made by Jack, he sat alone, wondering which way to turn. Should he stay here, at the office and clean up some of the issues that had surfaced while he was in Knoxville? Should he put together some type of overall plan for Paul's defense, even though the facts and witnesses were still somewhat sketchy? Should he…?

Bob finally concluded he was in no frame of mind to come to any conclusions concerning Paul. He was hungry—and to be perfectly honest, he missed Susan. Perhaps he would take care of those two issues with one phone call.

After briefly discussing what they had done during the day, he asked her to join him for supper, to which she agreed. He suggested Sambuca, an upscale restaurant in the trendy Gulch area of Nashville. She agreed and suggested they meet each other there, but he said he would pick her up, rather than having two cars to park, which met with enthusiastic approval from her.

Once seated and once a glass of pinot noir had been provided to both, she said, "Okay, now tell me, how was your meeting with Paul? I'll bet he was so, so happy to see you."

He hesitated, before he said, "To be honest, it didn't work out very well."

"Really? Was he glad to see you?"

"I wouldn't say that. It…just…didn't work out as I had hoped it would."

"Were you able to spend time with him discussing personal matters?"

"Not really. He didn't want to talk about anything but the case. I told him Jean had died…" He looked away for a moment, cleared his throat, and said, "And that didn't appear to affect him one way or the other."

He looked up at Susan and said, "He is an angry young man. I hope I get some time alone with him the next time we are in Knoxville, but, unfortunately, I'm not sure there is much I can do to alter his attitude. He seems full of contempt and completely wrapped up in his own world. Of course, being charged with a crime he insists he didn't commit is, to some extent, driving that attitude and I understand that. But, I am really concerned that even if he is exonerated, his relationship with me is irretrievably broken."

"Are you going to continue to work with him, to continue to represent him, or would it be better if you just completely removed yourself from the picture?"

"No. I have a feeling this is my last chance with him—with the only family I have left. I am going to hang in there with him as long as he will let me. Along the way, I'll do what I can to move him back into everyday life as the rest of us know it, because right now he is totally immersed in a world of his own. There is no one but him. I matter only because I might be able to help him out. I am just hoping we can somehow develop a relationship and at least be friends."

"Is the case against him a good one?"

"Right now, it's overwhelming. It even looks to *us* as though he *is* the one that did this. We have a lot of work to do. I not only need to figure out how to use the facts to his benefit, but I must study criminal law and get used to practicing in that area."

"Sounds like your work is cut out for you. I know I shouldn't probably ask this, but I would like to be there for the trial, if it gets that far. Is that too much to ask?"

He smiled. "I appreciate your interest, Susan. But let's just wait and see how this all unfolds. I don't have a problem with you being there, but let's see what happens between now and then."

"You mean, between us…or what might happen with the case?"

"Both, I guess. Let's move on. Paul's situation has consumed me since I learned of it. Let's eat a little supper and talk about what's happened in *your* life during the past week or so."

"Just one more thought. When do you go back?"

"Friday. We'll probably stay until Sunday."

The waiter arrived and they ordered supper. While waiting, Susan said, "Is it all working out with Jack being involved?"

"Oh, I guess. It is the first time I've stayed with a man in a hotel room in a hell of a long time. It's taking a little getting used to. But as far as the case is concerned, yes, *that's* working out fine. He has had much more experience and been much more successful in this field than I. If I can just get by the snoring and all his little idiosyncrasies, I think we will both survive until the time of trial. He should be a great benefit when we actually try the case."

The waiter brough their order a short time later. Both quietly continued eating, until she said, "I've missed you."

He hesitated a moment, then smiled and said, "I have missed you too. That's why I called you."

"So…what *are* your thoughts about this relationship—you and I?"

"Well, to be honest, I must say I do enjoy spending time with you. When we first met, I was still pretty absorbed and immersed in self-pity as a result of losing Jean. But time does help and I must admit I was looking forward to seeing you again."

"I've gone out with a few men since my husband died, but *very* few. I just wasn't interested. But when Jack talked about you…about who you were…because you sounded like a good guy, I thought maybe I would just take this one more chance. I am really glad I did. Are you wanting to continue this—you and I? Believe me, I don't want to interrupt everything you have going on right now, but is our relationship something *you're* interested in continuing?"

He put his fork down and finished the last of his wine. "Yes, it is. I'm making no promises, Susan. I can't. I'm too old. I have to many things going on right now to promise you anything. We will just have to see what happens and how everything else in my life plays out. I do not want to mislead you in any respect. So, all I am going to say about us, is that I enjoy being with you, I missed you while I was gone, and at this point, I'm glad you are a part of my life. Now, what about dessert?"

After they finished eating, they ordered an after-dinner drink and listened to some of the live music presented on a nightly basis at Sambuca. As it approached ten o'clock, he told her they needed to leave.

He drove her home, walked her to her front door and kissed her goodnight. She hugged him and told him she would wait to hear from him.

As he drove home, he thought of her, of their night, of their kiss…but not for long. Moments later, all his thoughts once again turned toward Paul and his situation. He had no doubt his grandson's dilemma would continue to remain the focus of his attention to the exclusion of most everything else, until all his issues came to a conclusion, one way or the other.

59

Chapter 14

Bob had made an appointment with Arnold Camp, the District Attorney General for Knox County. However, the only time he was able to see him was Friday at 9:00 a.m. Jack didn't want to travel that early in the morning, so they decided to drive to Knoxville on Thursday night, check in to the hotel and be prepared to meet with Mr. Camp the following morning.

After another restless night, and as they prepared to meet with the District Attorney, Bob said, "Did you know you snored last night?"

"Figured. Did you hear me?"

"What the hell do *you* think? I need to buy some earplugs. We need to go to a Walgreens or somewhere that sells earplugs before tonight."

"Whatever. Do what you need to do, I don't give a shit. You're driving. Let's find one before we meet with the Prosecutor."

"Oh, don't worry I will. By the way, do you use some kind of mouthwash?"

Jack stopped what he was doing and said, "Why? What difference does that make to you?"

"Because your breath smells like you just drank sewer. It actually smells like you literally ate shit last night. It's awful. You need to do something about it before we see him. No sense offending him the instant we meet. I'm sure you will do a good enough job doing that at some point during the conversation anyway. But there's no sense in *starting out* on the wrong foot."

"You know, I'm getting sick and tired of all this crap you are giving me about me and my body. I haven't said a damn thing before today, but you know you got issues too. Just so you know, this isn't a one-way street here, buddy."

Bob had his pants pulled about half-way up and stopped as he said, "What the hell do I do?"

"You know what you do. I don't have to tell you."

Bob said, "You got nothin'. You know it and so do I. Let's go."

"Fine. I'll tell you about your issues when we have time. No need to discuss them now. There will be a right time and place, and then…"

"Oh, just shut the hell up. Good god, just shut up."

An hour later, after a short wait in the reception area, they walked into Arnold Camp's office. It was at least four times the size of Bob's office and appeared to be full of antiques and other items that came with a lofty price tag. Bob was adequately impressed, as he assumed he was supposed to be.

After they shook hands and exchanged names, Arnold said, "Have a seat. Both of you have a seat."

As he sat, he said, "It is my understanding you gentlemen are here to discuss the Paul Duncan case, is that correct?"

Bob said, "Yes, that's right. Did you present his case to the grand jury this week?"

"Yes, we did. Yesterday in fact."

"What happened?"

They indicted him for murder. Now, where are you boys from? Did I hear you were from Nashville—is that correct?"

"Yes, it is. When is his arraignment?"

"The middle of next week. Now, as I understand it, one of you is his grandfather, is that correct?"

"Yes. That would be me. What time is he to be arraigned?"

"Sometime between ten and twelve. So, how is your friend here involved in the case?"

"We are both going to try Paul's case."

Arnold smiled as he said, "You all are trying to gang up on me, huh? Well, you don't have to worry about me as concerns *this* case. I got my best man on this one—George Jensen. He'll give you a run for your money, boys. I assume you both specialize in criminal law, right?"

Bob looked at Jack, then turned toward Arnold as he said, "Not really. But we'll do the best we can. Could we just take a moment and informally discuss the case against my grandson? That's why we are here. Who are the witnesses against him, and what do you anticipate they will say? I just want to discuss the case in generalities. Then perhaps we can discuss whether we might work out a plea bargain."

"Sure, sure, as you wish. Well, first of all, we have the neighbor's testimony who testified before the grand jury, indicating that he heard them arguing near the time of day she was murdered.”

Bob started to write, but stopped for a moment to ask, “Did the neighbor testify before the grand jury?”

“Yes, he did. We also have the testimony of a bartender who waited on him after the murder and who told the grand jury that Paul told him he had just left her house. All he could talk about was his argument with her. From the time he sat down, until he left, he continued to call her every name in the book and was clearly beside himself with anger.”

Bob looked at Jack, and said, “We assumed he would be a witness.”

“Of course, we have the medical examiner’s testimony that his DNA matched DNA from the semen. His testimony also indicated it was clear their sexual involvement was very recent.”

“Is that it?”

“He will also indicate she died of strangulation.”

“Can you tell me, in that respect, did Paul have any marks on him…as if he had been in an altercation with her?”

“He had one recent scratch on his arm. That was it.”

“Were there any other witnesses?”

“No one that appeared before the grand jury. But we have talked to a couple of his friends who indicated Paul was a bitter person and that he was very, very quick to anger. They will say he jumped into an argument as if he enjoyed the conflict. It wasn’t hard to rile him up—that was just part of his character.”

“Anything else?”

Arnold smiled. “No, not right now. But to be honest, we probably don’t need much more than that.”

“Have you investigated the possibility that it might have been someone else that killed her?”

“Not really. No need to. Every shred of evidence points toward him.”

“But he says he didn’t do it. Doesn’t that count for something? Wouldn’t that, in and of itself, indicate at least a little more investigating would be in order?”

“Maybe, in some cases. But not this one. In my opinion, this is an open and shut case. All the evidence we have points toward one person and one person only. If there was anything that pointed us in a different direction, we would take a little time and effort to look that way. But there is absolutely nothing that indicates anyone else was involved."

Bob put his pen back in his pocket and his legal pad back in his briefcase.

"Okay, let's discuss a plea bargain. What are your thoughts?"

Arnold leaned forward, and the smile quickly left his face as he said, "I'll take the death penalty off the table if he pleads to premeditated murder. How's that?"

"That's not much of a bargain. Especially when he is so emphatic about not committing the crime."

Arnold sat back and said, "That's about the best I can do."

Jack spoke up for the first time when he said, "You don't really believe he went there to kill her do you? How are you going to prove some type of premeditation?"

"You can read about that in the indictment. We know through one of his friends that Paul and Lynn Baker were not getting along. We know that from what all of his friends told us. Our position is that they might have had sex, but we also know he was upset and angry with her. We will just let the jury figure it all out from there."

"What about manslaughter—maybe her death occurred during a spontaneous argument which got out of hand and he caused her death."

"Not going there. Of course, if you boys come up with something that indicates that was the case, certainly let me know. But I have nothing that indicates that is what happened and *plenty* to indicate he went there that day with an attitude consistent with hurting her."

The conference ended shortly thereafter.

On their way to see Paul, Bob said, "What do you think? I wonder if we should even tell Paul about the offer at this stage of the game."

Jack said, "I think we should. Regardless of how he might react, he still has a right to know. He is no different than any other client we might have in any other criminal case—he has a right to know and to make up his own mind about accepting or rejecting it."

"You tell him. I'll wait in the car."

Jack smiled, as he said, "We will *both* tell him *and* we will both feel very fortunate there's a piece of shatterproof glass that separates us from him when we do."

Chapter 15

Bob reluctantly pushed himself out of bed. It had been another long night to say the least. In spite of the earplugs, Jack's snoring kept him up half the night—the other half he spent worrying about his meeting with Paul.

They arrived at the jail a little after 9:00 a.m. and waited for them to bring Paul to the conference room.

Once he arrived, Bob said, "Morning, Paul. We had the opportunity to meet with the Prosecuting Attorney and discuss their witnesses. I think probably it would be a good idea to go through their testimony, then get your take on what they have to say. We also had a chance to discuss a plea. But I think we need to discuss witnesses first."

"Go ahead. It doesn't matter to me which comes first."

"Alright, let's start with the neighbor. He is going to testify he heard the two of you arguing that afternoon. Is he correct?"

"Yes."

"Can you just give us an overview of your relationship with her and what happened that day involving the two of you, this time with a little more detail," Jack said.

Paul looked down for a moment. He took a deep breath, looked at Bob and said, "I first started seeing her about a year ago. It started out only as a working relationship. She put an ad in the paper saying she needed someone to handle all of her lawn work and her flowers around the house. We were involved in a relationship for about six months prior to the time she died."

"In the beginning, is that all that was going on? Is that all you were doing for her was lawn work?"

"Yes. That is my business. That's what I do and, like I told you before, it was growing like gangbusters—until this."

"So, what happened concerning your relationship? What changed?"

"One hot day when I was working for her, she asked me to come in and have a cold glass of water. Over the next few weeks, a relationship developed, and we became very, very close."

"What about the day it all happened?"

Again, he looked away.

"Paul?"

"Paul, what happened that day?"

He turned toward Bob, and whispered, "You need to know old man, I loved this woman. I'm *still* trying to get over the fact that she is dead. She meant a lot to me. Give me a moment."

"I'm sorry. Yes, certainly. I'm sorry. Take all the time you need."

He took a deep breath, then said, "She wanted me to move in with her. She wanted to get married. She had mentioned that to me a couple of times But, after we had sex early that evening, she became demanding. She wouldn't take no for an answer. She wanted me to marry her. I wasn't ready for that."

He took a deep breath and looked away.

When he turned to look at Bob, he said, "That issue led to an argument. It got pretty loud. She is…or was, a demanding woman. I started to leave. I walked to the door and opened it to go. She grabbed for me as I turned away and scratched my arm. I turned to look at her for a moment, then walked away. That was the last time I saw her alive. I got in my car and drove to the bar. That's it. That's what happened. That is the truth."

"So, the neighbor would have heard her yelling at you while all this was going on. Did you ever yell at her?"

"No."

"Are there security cameras inside the house?"

"No. However, we had discussed that issue. As many antiques as she had, I told her a number of times to have someone put up cameras inside her home. She has a guy she uses for household repairs, but I don't think she ever said a thing to him about that. She does have them outside, above the front and back doors, but I don't know if either of them was on. They wouldn't have mattered much anyway—they don't show what was going on *inside* the house."

"True, but the outdoor cameras would have caught someone else going in and out. We will check with law enforcement on that. Apparently, the bartender is going to testify. What might he have to say?"

"Hell, how would I know?"

"Did you go straight from the house to the bar?"

"Yes."

"What did you tell him?"

"I don't remember everything I said. I know I was upset with her and with myself. I said some things that I now regret. You know— just about how mad I was at her and about the whole situation."

"The Prosecutor also said something about a couple of your friends testifying that you said, prior to that night, Lynn continually suggested that you marry, but you weren't having any of that. Did you discuss this particular issue with other people prior to that night?"

"Yes, but nothing about wanting her dead."

"What were the discussions about?"

"As I recall, something about the fact that we just wanted different things in life. I didn't want to get married and she did. I think maybe I said her comments were getting really old, and I was getting tired of discussing marriage, I don't know. I guaranty you I never said anything about wanting her dead."

"Okay. Those people, along with the medical examiner and the cop that was at the scene, are the ones that are listed as witnesses for now. They could add others, but those are the ones we know about."

"So, what do you think? What's next?"

"Well, for one thing, we need to figure out whether to have you testify. For another, we need to figure out who we may want to have testify on your behalf."

"I want to testify. I want to tell them I didn't do this."

Bob said, "You think you can hold your temper while the Prosecutor cross-examines you? He will call you basically every name in the book, as he tries to make his points with the jury. You think you can handle that?"

Paul leaned back and smirked. "Obviously, you don't."

"Let's just say, from what I've seen, suppressing your temper is not one of your better attributes. That is why we need to determine whether or not it's a good idea. You have a choice. You don't have to testify and they can't use that against you. Now, what about other friends? Do you have other friends that could testify you are not violent—that you can control your temper?"

"Let me think about that. I'll let you know. Let's move on. What's next?"

"You will be arraigned, where we will plead not guilty. Then I want to take depositions of all the witnesses they have listed. You will be there with me. We need to know what they are going to testify to before we get to court."

"When is that going to happen?"

"I will get them set up as soon as I can. I want to keep this moving along. We want it before a judge and jury as soon as possible."

"Good. Now, you said you wanted to discuss a plea bargain. Did you discuss that with the District Attorney General's office?"

"Yes, we did. He said if you would plead to murder, he would take the death penalty off the table."

Paul leaned back and said, "Is that it?"

"Yes. He wouldn't discuss any other charge but murder."

Paul hesitated for a moment, then said softly, "You know, I wouldn't plead to something like that if I *was* guilty. Why the hell did you even bother bringing it up?"

"We have to. It is part of our responsibility to you, our client. We don't have a choice."

Paul stood and leaned forward, against the small table abutting the glass. "You can tell him to go straight to hell. I find it really hard to believe, first of all, that was the best you could do, and second, when you *couldn't* do any better, that today you even brought up the subject at all. That's an insult. Well done, gentlemen, well done. Drive safely on your way home, you idiots."

As the officer took him away, neither of them said a word.

Finally, Jack turned to Bob and said, "Well, all in all I think that went well, don't you?" He stood. "You know, I've had about all this shit I want. Let's go home."

As Bob stood, he said, "Yeah, I agree. Let's go pack up and drive back to Nashville."

Chapter 16

They both waited patiently, on a hard wooden bench in the hallway, while an officer brought Paul for his arraignment. Bob had decided he didn't need Jack to handle the arraignment so he left him in Nashville. Since Carrie had indicated she wanted to be a part of each and every element of Paul's proceedings, Bob had contacted her and told her to meet him at the courthouse prior to the hearing.

"So, how long have you been with the newspaper?"

"About a year now. I worked for a small-town paper in North Carolina before I came here."

"Do you report on everything or do you specialize?"

"Whatever they want me to do."

"Let me ask you this—do you have any information about Paul's case that hasn't been reported? I mean, I have read most of what you wrote for the paper, but is there anything else you have turned up and not reported in any article that you think might be something we should know about?"

"No. I reported everything I had. To be honest, I was just going to do one more follow-up article on what happened after he was convicted. But of course, after meeting you, this story has suddenly taken on a new meaning for me."

"Do you intend to do anything other than just report? Do you intend to investigate any of this yourself, or will you just report what you see and hear when you are around us?"

"Only what I hear while with the two of you. That's all I have been authorized to do. I just don't have the time nor authority to do anything other than that. I am simply to report what happens and what your investigation turns up, if anything."

"I understand. That's fine. I just wanted to make certain what your position was concerning the case. Thanks for being honest with me."

He noticed Paul coming down the hallway in handcuffs, with an officer on each side of him. As he passed by and walked through the door of the courtroom, he never acknowledged Bob in any respect.

They followed him through the door and into the courtroom. As the officers took him forward to be arraigned, Bob followed along behind, then sat down by him waiting for the Judge to start the process.

"Are you charged in your true and correct name, son?"

As he stood, Paul said, "Yup."

"Mr. Bob Duncan, are you his attorney?"

"I am, yes sir."

After proceeding through all the obligatory questions and answers necessary at every arraignment, the Judge looked at Bob and said, "Mr. Duncan, what is your client's plea to the charge?"

Before Bob could say anything, Paul said, "Your Honor, I'm absolutely not guilty. This is the biggest pile of crap I ever saw. I loved that woman. I…"

"Hold on there. This is a conversation I am having with your attorney, not you. Now keep still."

"But Judge, he wasn't there. He doesn't know what the hell happened. He's only…"

The Judge slammed his gavel down on the sounding block three times, before Paul quit talking.

"Son, if you say one more word that is not in response to a question I ask you and you are going back to your cell. Your attorney and I will handle this without you. Do you understand?"

"Whatever. I'm just telling you I…"

"Officer, take him back."

Both officers looked at the Judge, but neither moved.

He quickly slammed his gavel down once more and said, "Did you two hear me? Get him out of here."

Both of the officers jumped to their feet and took Paul from the courtroom.

"Now, Mr. Jones, how does your client plead?"

"Not guilty, Your Honor."

"It is my understanding you and the Prosecuting Attorney have agreed on a date for trial—let's see March 16 is the date I was given. Is that correct?"

Bob answered in the affirmative.

"So be it. This hearing is concluded. Next."

Paul walked up to the window and as he sat, he said, "What are you still doing here, Bob? I figured you would be halfway to Nashville by now."

"Nope. I just wanted to see you one more time—just make sure there is nothing you need that I can get for you. Is there anything I can do to help right now?"

"Get my ass out of jail would really help. Maybe like yet today. Can you do that—can you handle that for me—Bob?"

He sat there quietly for a moment, carefully considering whether this was the time and place.

Deciding it was, he said, "You know, it might be best if you called me something other than Bob. Either Mr. Jones, or grandpa, or pops, or most anything would be better than the way you spit out the word, *'Bob.'* It has really gotten old and to be honest, it has lost its effect. You think you can handle that... *Paul*?"

Paul leaned forward and said, "Just do your goddamn job old man, just do your job. Then, when I'm out, I'll figure out what I'm going to call you."

Bob leaned forward just inches from the glass and said, "What the hell happened to you? You were a good kid. I loved being with you. You are a complete jerk now. You could give a shit about anyone but yourself. You are mean, you're inconsiderate. What the hell happened to you? You are hardly even human anymore. You are more like an animal than a human being."

"I am like I've had to be. I've been this way ever since I started stealing food to stay alive—ever since I begged for a place to stay during the winters in Kentucky, where I was before I came here. Everything I've done, I've had to do on my own, without an ounce of help from anyone. You know what that's like? You ever lived that way old man? Try it. Try it sometime and then I'll critique you—the way you talk, the way you act."

"You know, you have no one to blame but yourself. You had a home, school, food, shelter—you gave it all up for the lifestyle you now complain about."

"I guarantee it was better than living in your home under your rules. Anything would have been better than that."

"Then quit your goddamn complaining. You got what you wanted. You made a choice and you got just what you wanted. Everyone I've talked to that has known you for any length of time say the same thing—you have been this way—easy to anger, short tempered—

ever since they met you. I don't understand why. You were living exactly the way you wanted to. That being the case, why the hell don't you just drop that chip on your shoulder, quit bitching about everything and enjoy the life you wanted from the time you left our home?"

Paul leaned back and said nothing.

"Look. You've got me working my ass off for you. I love you, Paul. At least I love who you were. I'm not sure who you are now, but I would like to get to know you—again. Jack is trying to help you. Carrie is interested in what you're doing, what happened to you and what's going to happen to you. It's time you started working *with* us instead of *against* us. *We are on your side. Don't you understand. We are with you. We are trying to get you out of here.*"

Paul looked away.

"You know, this attitude, this know it all, 'I'm smarter than the rest of you, I'll say what I want when I want to' approach, isn't going to work. It might have worked prior to all this going on, but it's time you changed your attitude, Paul. You have a decision to make and it needs to be made now. Either work with us, and lose that attitude you have, or get someone else to represent you. *Or* you can represent yourself! I'm giving up a hell of a lot to help you, and so is Jack. I *want* to be here with you. I *want* you out of here. I *want* a relationship with you. But this know-it-all approach to life, doesn't cut it with me, and I've had about all of it I'm going to take."

"Whatever." Paul stood to leave.

"I'm telling you, if you don't change your approach toward us, toward this hearing, toward life in general, we are out of here. We're done."

Without saying a word, Paul walked through the door and out of the room.

Bob sat quietly for a moment, then stood, shook his head and walked away.

Chapter 17

“Are you heading straight home, or are you going to do some Christmas shopping while you’re here. There could be some interesting shops in Knoxville which you might not find in Nashville.”

Jack said, “I want to stop at the mall after we check out of here and see what I can find.”

Bob continued to shave as he said, “So, not to belabor the point, but now, after you have had a while to think about each individual’s deposition yesterday, what are your conclusions?”

“You know, I didn’t think there were many surprises. I didn’t sleep very well…I kept waking up and thinking about them. I really feel like they were pretty much what we expected and nothing I am very pleased with. They all testified confidently and were believable to me. I really don’t know what we are going to do to refute their testimony—any of them. We just have so little to go on. Paul’s testimony is now, as it was when we first became involved, about the only thing we have.”

“Unfortunately, I feel the same way. When I talk to him today, that is one of the issues we will discuss. By the way, thanks for driving down in your own car. I knew I would need to spend some time with him, alone, this time. I want to discuss his history and go through the witnesses’ testimony one by one. I hope the last time we spoke had an impact on him. I’ll find out today.”

“Good luck—you will need it. Oh, by the way, what are you doing for Christmas? Do you want to come over home?”

Bob hesitated. “No, I don’t think so but thanks. It’s the first Christmas without Jean. I think I will probably leave it at that and spend the day alone.”

“What about Susan? She is probably planning on spending at least part of Christmas with you.”

“I don’t know whether she is or not, but this year, I just really want to spend it by myself. I don’t want to hurt her, but this is the first one without…without Jean. I want to spend it thinking of her and all the good Christmases we spent with each other."

"I hope Susan understands."

"So do I, but whether she does or doesn't, that's the way it is going to be this year."

An hour later and after Jack had left for Nashville, Bob sat waiting for them to bring Paul.

As he walked in, he said, "Hi…Pops." He sat down, and said, "You okay with that? You alright with 'Pops'? I decided last night I just don't want to piss you off calling you something you don't like anymore."

Bob smiled and said, "Anything is better than *Bob*', at least the way *you* were saying it. Yes, Pops is fine."

Bob noticed the smile, along with a slight change in attitude. He thought he had noticed a small change while they were sitting through depositions, but he wasn't sure if it was wishful thinking or that he had finally got through to him. Now he knew it was the latter.

"Let's talk about the depos. Is there anything we need to discuss concerning those? I mean, were there any of those witnesses whose testimony was incorrect or inaccurate?"

"No, not really. They were all pretty much on the money. Of course, none of them really know what happened in the house. Nobody saw me walk out the door nor knew she was still alive when I got in my pickup and left. All of it is circumstantial, but it was also pretty accurate. I might dispute those two witnesses who said I'm quick to anger and that I lose my temper frequently, but again, they know nothing about the facts. If that is their opinion concerning my personality, I guess there is probably not much we can do to refute that."

"Is there any one you want to call as a witness on your behalf? We need to visit with them if there is."

"That guy that did her repairs around the house and I got to be pretty good friends. He wasn't there very often, but he never saw me lose my temper, and we always got along. Other than that, we could call a couple of my other friends that might testify they felt I was normally under control."

"Okay. When I come back here, I'll contact them, and we can issue subpoenas to make sure they show up. Now, let's talk about you. Do you still want to testify?"

"Absolutely. I think I *have* to. We do not have many other witnesses and I would think the jury would want to hear from me. Am I right on that? Won't they want to hear me say I didn't do it?"

"Yes. No doubt about that. But, Paul, you have no idea how hard it can be to sit there and have someone grill you for possibly hours on end. I am just afraid—I'm just afraid—."

"I understand how you feel and rightfully so. But I really believe I can hold it together and not want to strangle—oops, bad choice of words—not lose my temper. Maybe we can go over everything a number of times before the trial."

"Oh, we will. No question about that."

"So, what's next?"

"We need to get you ready to testify and subpoena some witnesses. In the meantime, we will continue to search for answers. This newspaper woman you met—Carrie—I think she will work with me. We will just hope someway, somehow, before trial, we can figure out who did this. In the meantime, you keep your mind working concerning what might have happened and whether there might have been someone that wanted her dead."

Paul looked away and remained silent.

"I suppose I better hit the road. I need to get back to the office and go through what all has happened the last couple of days before my secretary starts closing everything down."

Paul hesitated for a moment, then said, "When did grandma die?"

His comment caught Bob completely off guard.

"Well, actually not long ago. Early this year."

"What happened?"

"Cancer. It took her quickly. It just seemed like one day we were planning a vacation and the next day, she was gone."

"She was a special woman."

"She was at that."

"Has life been difficult without her?"

"I cannot describe how difficult."

"*My* life has been like a roller-coaster. First, my dad and mom are killed. Then I run off. Now the love of my life is gone. That's why I was so excited to hear your voice. You and I are the last of the family."

Paul looked down and remained silent.

"Can you tell me a little about what happened after you left us?

Where did you go? What did you do? How did you survive? Can you talk about it?"

He stood. "Maybe later. Maybe we can discuss that later. When are you coming back?"

"Most likely the first of next week. Do you want to talk a little more yet today?"

"I'll just see you then."

As he sorted through his list of phone messages, Charlene walked in and said, "Is there anything you need me to explain or do for you before I leave."

He looked up, leaned back in his chair and said, "Yeah, just give me a quick summery, will you? I don't want to go through all these messages one-by-one."

"Sure. Really, the only important messages were those that set up appointments. I put those on your calendar. It wasn't all that active while you were gone."

"I am afraid that slowdown might just continue as people discover I'm out of the office all of the time anymore."

"Is there something you want me to say—to do—to explain what's going on and then explain to them you will be back practicing full time in a few months?"

"No. Just keep doing what you are doing. Hopefully, they will find Paul not guilty and this will all come to an end."

"And if they don't?"

"Then there will be a sentencing later, then an appeal, then—well, if all of that doesn't work, we will probably have to accept the results, but not until then. Oh, and by the way, this could literally take years. If he isn't exonerated, I may be forced to close up and either move to Knoxville or just work out of my home here."

"Let's think positive."

"Oh, I am, but I'm not sure that is working. We have some real issues."

"How are you getting along with Paul now?"

"Better." He folded his arms, smiled and said, "You know, I think we had a breakthrough this week. He was actually more human and less animal today for the first time. It's a work in progress, for sure. Our relationship is much better now than it has been, but it is all still just a work in progress."

Chapter 18

Bob had discovered a new method of surviving the Christmas holiday season, but it had come at a tremendous cost—he now needed to replace all those recently emptied bottles lying around the house, with a fresh supply of liquor. Every bottle in the house which contained an alcoholic beverage had been emptied during the days leading up to and including Christmas day. He saw no one. He called no one. He never answered the phone. He wanted to be alone, to remember her—to remember what they had enjoyed together, to remember their life with each other—and that is exactly what he did.

When December twenty-sixth arrived, he wasn't sure he was actually better off for handling the holidays as he had, but he had definitely honored her memory. She certainly deserved to be remembered, especially at a time of year she had always made so special for both of them.

As he drove to Knoxville, he tried to remember how many times Susan, Jack or Charlene had called him. He finally left a message on each phone indicating he was tied up for a couple of days and would return their call sometime between Christmas and the first day of the new year. His message stopped each caller from calling again.

He was waiting outside the jail for Carrie to arrive. She had agreed to meet him at 1:00 p.m. They would both discuss the upcoming trial with Paul in attendance. Paul hadn't met her yet and today that would change.

Once she arrived, they walked into the building together. Paul was brought out shortly after they were seated.

"Paul this is Carrie Thompson. She is the reporter I was telling you about."

Paul nodded, but said nothing. He looked at Bob and said, "So, has anything else turned up. Have we got anything else to go on, or are we just going with what we got? We only have a few weeks left."

"We have nothing else. I've uncovered nothing new, and clearly law enforcement is through investigating. We are going to have to use just what we have, I'm afraid. The next time I come, I'll go through your testimony, explain how we select a jury and what all the different aspects of the trial mean. I will also bring you a jury list so you can go through it and determine if there is anyone on the panel you don't want on that jury."

"Are you going to subpoena the guy I work with? Have you had a chance to talk to him yet?"

"Yes. Briefly. He is willing to testify. He doesn't really know you all that well, but he is willing to testify he never had a problem with you. He will also testify that at least from what he saw, Lynn and you never even said a cross word to each other. I will visit with him more in depth sometime prior to the trial."

He turned to Carrie and said, "So, what's your story? How did you end up being involved in *my* problem?"

She smiled and said, "Well, I covered the story for the paper from the beginning. I continue to provide updates concerning what is going on and your grandfather and I discussed perhaps a human-interest story, with me being closely involved until we have a verdict."

"I get it. You are looking to tell a story that might be career-defining for you, is that it?"

Bob said, "I don't think that was what she had in mind. We never discussed her career, but only a story that might tell our side of the issues rather than, you know, just…"

"Sounds like to me you got your own interests in mind—and your own agenda. It doesn't make sense to me that you would spend your time on a story like this unless it could somehow benefit you—further your career. Are you at the bottom of the barrel with that job of yours? Are you just looking for that one career-defining story? Maybe that's not such a good idea. Maybe I don't want my story told. No one ever asked *me* about this."

Carrie turned toward Bob and said, "You know, I'm thinking this probably wasn't a good idea." She stood, and said, "Good luck. Good luck to the both of you."

As she walked out the door, Bob said, "Nice job. What the hell were you thinking? We can use her. She is the only one out of jail *living in Knoxville* that might possibly be able to help us."

"Listen. She is in this for one reason and one reason only. And that's to…"

"How the hell do you know that? You don't even know her. You never even gave her a chance to explain or discuss it. You prejudged why she was here and summarily sent her on her way. You know, you got to stop burning your bridges before you're sure you are not going to need the bridge. You have continually done that since we started down this road together. She could help us—I mean she could *really* help us. You opened your big mouth and now she's gone."

Bob stood. "I'm going after her and try to undo what you just did. I'll get down on my hands and knees if I have to. Hopefully, she will stay with us. If she agrees to at least discuss continuing to work with us, *you too* will get down on your hands and knees if you have to and tell her you're sorry for the way you acted. You got a hell of a lot to learn, Paul, and I'm not sure I got enough years left to teach you. But you better by God get it all figured out or your life, no matter where you end up, is going to involve one disaster after another. I'll see you the next time I come back."

As Bob walked away, he heard Paul say, "Hold on. Wait a minute, will you?"

On the way back to Nashville, Bob called Carrie and discussed the problem. She laughed about it, said she understood and further indicated that she would continue to work with them. He only hoped taking care of Paul's *legal issues*, would somehow become as easy to resolve as the mess he had created with Carrie. But he concluded that might be wishful thinking.

Once back at the office, he noticed a couple of calls from Susan. Bob needed to talk to her and explain.

He shut his office door and punched in her number.

"Hi, stranger. Where have you been? I've been trying to reach you for a couple of weeks now."

"Yeah, well, I'm sorry. Christmas was tough this year. I really don't want to talk about it other than to tell you that even though I was alone, a large quantity of alcohol was involved. I think I drank up everything I had in the house."

She laughed, then said, "I assume you were most likely thinking about Jean and your holidays with her."

"Yes. I figured I owed her that. After all the incredible Christmases we spent together, I owed her one in which the only thing I thought about were all those incredible years and how she made Christmas so special. Maybe that might seem silly to others, but it wasn't to me."

"I understand. I did somewhat the same thing after my husband died. I just didn't leave the house—for months. You will hear no criticism from me for what you did. In fact, I respect you for doing it."

"So how was Christmas in your home?"

"Quiet. I went to a friend's house on Christmas eve, and that was about it. How is everything proceeding in Knoxville?"

"Let's just say that every day presents a surprise and a new challenge. It is moving along as expected, I guess. We just can't figure out who did this. The trial date is getting close. I am really concerned. There is nothing I can do but move along and hope the jury finds him not guilty. But at this point I'm afraid that might be just wishful thinking."

"Why don't we get together and have a couple of glasses of wine—your house, my house, downtown, I don't care where."

"You know, I just got back from Knoxville and I need to get this desk cleaned up. I think I'll take a raincheck for now. Are you going anywhere in the next few days?"

"No."

"Let me give you a call and we will get together in a day or two if that's all right with you."

"Sounds good. Oh, and Bob."

"Yes."

"I've missed you."

He hesitated, but finally said, "Same here," before he terminated the call.

Chapter 19

“ **G**ood morning, Mr. Jones, have a seat.”
Bob walked in the Prosecutor's office, looking around the room as he did.

Certainly, the expensive amenities he noticed in the District Attorney's office were forbidden or not affordable when it came to the office of his Deputy—his office was drab and unimpressive with furnishings which were clearly outdated and well-used.

“Good afternoon, Mr. Jenson. Thank you for seeing me. I was in town and thought I would stop by for a moment to discuss Paul's case with you.”

As they shook hands, George Jenson said, “Not a problem. Have a chair. I wondered if I would be hearing from you. We only have a few weeks before his trial and you and I haven't had a conversation yet about trying to resolve the case. In fact, this is the first time we've talked at all. It is my understanding you discussed a resolution with Arnold, but that conference didn't end in settling anything.”

“Yes, that is correct on both counts. We did talk and did discuss a resolution. He indicated if we pled to murder one, he would take the death penalty off the table. That just isn't going to work. That conversation was quite a while ago and I figured it was time to discuss a possible resolution once again before the trial starts. Do you have any other thoughts?”

“It is my understanding he is your grandson, is that right?”

“He is, yes.”

“I have been reading the stories in the paper following the progress of the case through the eyes of both you and Paul. Actually, it has been pretty interesting.”

“The young lady is an intelligent woman and a good writer. She has done a good job of explaining what's going on, but not divulging any of our strategy.”

George smiled. “Do you have a strategy? This case seems pretty open and shut to me.”

"Well, I will agree we don't have much to go on, but we are still working on it. I will let you know what we have when it's time for us to present evidence."

"Fair enough. Tell me, Bob, what are *your* thoughts about resolving this?"

"I would be happy if you would just dismiss it."

George smiled and said, "Well, short of that, what are you thinking?"

"I am thinking he didn't kill her. I think I could get him to plead to an assault if you could accept that."

"Can't. I just can't. We are way too far apart to resolve this. I could probably take murder one off the table. Honestly, I have a feeling he didn't go there to kill her that day. I assume something angered him and he eventually strangled her. If you could get him to plead to a manslaughter charge, I might, and the operative word is *might,* get my boss to go along with it."

Bob stood. "Okay. Let me visit with him and see what he says. I'll get back to you."

Later that day, Bob sat down with Paul to discuss the different elements of the trial.

"Go slow for me, Pops. I haven't been down this road before, so take it slow."

"The first thing that will happen is the selection of a jury. Now Paul, this is a really important element of the trial. Those jurors will decide your fate. We don't want anyone on the panel that already has a problem with you. I gave you the list of prospective jurors. You absolutely must make certain you don't have a problem with any one of them. If you do, you need to let me know, and I'll make sure they are not a part of the final twelve."

"I've gone through the list a couple of times, but I'll go through it again. I think we are fine. I don't recognize any of the names."

"Okay, good. When we finish the selection process, we will have twelve regulars and most likely a couple of alternates. I just don't want you getting upset because I am taking so long to pick them. It is going to take however long it takes, and we aren't going to hurry the process. It is really important that we get the right kind of people on the panel."

"I understand. What happens then?"

"The attorneys make an opening statement and then they start introducing testimony. The State presents their witnesses first, then it's up to us to respond. I really don't anticipate a lengthy trial. There just aren't that many witnesses for them to call. And, of course, we have only two or three of our own. So, in terms of time, I don't know that this will take all of a week to try. Then, once the testimony has been introduced, we have instructions to the jury from the Judge, and closing statements. Once the attorneys give their closing statements, the jury will deliberate."

"How long do they have to deliberate?"

"As long as they want."

"What happens if we lose?"

"We can appeal, although an appeal is really only relevant if there were mistakes made by the Judge during the proceedings. So, first of all, we will think optimistically about the verdict and then figure out what we're going to do if we end up with a guilty verdict."

"What about me?"

"I don't understand."

"Am I testifying?"

"I don't know, Paul. Do you want to? Do you think you can handle the Prosecuting Attorney's cross-examination? I know it will be very intense, and if you lose your temper once, we are done."

"I understand. But, Pops, I really do think it's necessary. I really believe I should tell my story my way."

"I'm just saying—you better not..."

Paul leaned forward, glared at Bob and said, "I know, I know, you've told me that a thousand times. But like I have told you, I feel I need to tell them I didn't do it. I am *going* to testify, and I am *going* to remain calm. Now, old man, just plan on it, because that's the way it's going to be, understand?"

Bob leaned forward, his nose almost touching the glass, as he said, "And that, right there, what you just did—that's what I'm talking about. Just one outburst like that and you might as well give all your clothes you wore outside this jailhouse to the Salvation Army, because you'll never wear them again."

Paul thought for a second, then leaned back. He smiled and said, "Hey, that was pretty good. You were pretty quick there, Pops."

"Whatever." He stood. "I need to go. The next time we meet, we will go through how you are going to handle yourself on the stand a few more times. I will also go through the questions I am going to ask you. One more thing. Do you want to plead to manslaughter?"

"Hell no."

"Would you like to discuss it at all?"

"Nope."

"Didn't figure you would. See you next week."

On the way home, Bob called Jack.

"Hey. I talked to George Jenson. He wants a plea to manslaughter. I discussed it with Paul. He isn't interested. I called George back and told him. So, we are pretty much set for trial."

"Okay. You want to get together sometime next week and determine what part of the trial each of us is going to handle?"

"Yes. I have a pretty good idea already, but I want you to be comfortable with whatever aspect of it you want to take. Why don't we get together on Monday—do you have any free time?"

"I'll make time. By the way, do you miss me? I bet it seemed a little strange without your roommate."

"Strange my ass. I finally got some sleep. I'll see you next week."

"Hey, what are you doing this weekend?"

"Working. I'll talk to you later."

He terminated the call. At the next stop sign, he punched in her number.

She answered immediately. "Hi, Bob. Are you home?"

"No, but I'm on the way."

"How was Paul?"

"Good. I think we are basically ready to go. I'm still quite concerned about the lack of evidence we have, but you can't make this stuff up. It is what it is I guess."

"You don't have a lot of time left, do you?"

"It's getting close but I think we have the time we need. I talked to Charlene and I have a number of issues to handle at the office. By the time I drive home, go to the office and clean up any issues there, it is probably going to be after seven. I'm already tired and I still have all that to handle. Let's cancel for tonight and have supper tomorrow night. You okay with that?"

She hesitated. "Okay, sure, that's fine, I guess. I was looking forward...yes, yes, I'm fine with that. Give me a call tomorrow morning and let me know when and where we are going."

"Certainly. Thanks for understanding."

"No problem. Drive safely."

He terminated the call.

His thoughts turned to Paul and their discussions of the past week. His grandson had changed. There was a definite change for the better in his outlook on life, his demeanor and his approach to the issues that he needed to address.

He hoped and prayed he could find a way to convince a jury to set him free. But the way it appeared to him at this point, he was extremely concerned that just as quickly as he found Paul, he was going to lose him. If that did happen, this time there would be no hope left—*this time* he would be forever separated from the grandson he had so desperately searched for all these years.

Chapter 20

He couldn't sit still—so he paced. Bob was waiting for them to bring Paul. It had been a long fifteen minutes since they left for him, and the longer he waited alone with all his concerns, the more anxious he became.

Only one week remained before they would select a jury. He had second guessed himself all week. Why didn't he just do what he felt was right for Paul when all this first started? Why hadn't he just hired a specialist in criminal law to represent him? But was he given that choice at the time? Paul didn't *want* someone else. He wanted his grandfather to represent him. But, should he have listened to him or should he have retained someone else?

Paul would have surely found out before the process went too far, that he wasn't capable of representing himself and most likely would have accepted whoever Bob retained for him. But, is that *really* what he would have done? When they were first reunited, Paul had such a chip on his shoulder he might have, out of sheer spite, tried to represent himself, regardless how difficult the task.

So, was there any other way this situation could have been handled other than the way it *was* handled? Did it really matter now anyway? Here they were—less than a week away. What had he done? *What had he done?*

He should have told Paul he had retired. He almost was! If he had taken a different path and accepted the fact that he was old and tired, maybe everything would somehow appear much more favorable at this point in time.

But the point is he *didn't* take that path. He *didn't* accept a life of passive resignation, he *didn't* retire, and as a result, here he was. *No. no, no, this was not the time to second guess yourself.* But what happens if he…

"Hi, Pops. How are you?"

"Good to see you, Paul." He quit nervously wringing his hands and sat down. "Are you all ready to go? We only have a week. I'm planning on staying down here from then on, until it's over."

"Are we going to go through everything again—you and I?"

"Yes. We will do that later today. By then, Jack will be here and he can go through whatever I forget to tell you."

"Did you contact John Reed, yet?"

If Jean were here, she could calm him down. So many times, before a big trial, when it was apparent he was extremely worried about a case, a word or two from her was normally all it took. Just a word or…

"Pops, did you hear me. Did you talk to John?"

"Yes…yes, I did. I am to visit with him Sunday afternoon. Because of his work, he is hard to tie down. He couldn't get together until then."

"Let's go through my testimony just briefly. Now…"

That civil case he had that one time—he was so worried about trying it. Jean knew when he walked through the door that night, the night before the trial started, that he was so nervous he couldn't stay seated for supper. She knew. They took a walk. She told him to relax—that no matter what happened, the sun was still going to rise in the morning, the roof would still remain over…

"Pops, are you alright? You seem a little off today. Do you want to wait and do this some other time?"

"No, no I'm fine. Let's get down to business. I've been meaning to ask you… did you get into trouble any other time between leaving home and now, other than this?"

He leaned back and said, "No, why do you ask?"

"No reason. I just wanted to know. I just wanted to make sure there was nothing in your past they could at some point during the trial, try and get into the record."

"No, there's nothing."

Bob studied him a moment, then finally said, "You know we've never discussed what happened after you left home—where you lived, how you lived. I guess I always thought you would bring it up when you were ready to discuss it. But maybe we better go through it now, at least briefly."

"Okay. What do you want to know?"

"How did you survive? You had virtually no money. You didn't have a car, you apparently left Nashville and I have no doubt you knew no one anywhere that could help you to any extent. How did you do it?"

He hesitated, clearly reflecting on those years carefully, before he spoke. "Well, at first, as I mentioned before, I hitchhiked to Kentucky. I slept in famer's barns and asked for food handouts until I came to a farm that was looking for help. I asked the guy for a job and he gave it to me."

"How long were you there?"

"A couple of years. I put a little money together and one morning I just told him I was quitting and going to Knoxville."

"You know, you broke your grandmother's heart. She was really never the same after you left. We both did everything we could to find you."

"I thought about what the two of you must have gone through. But I couldn't justify staying with you, or going back just because it was what you wanted me to do. I had a life too and living with the two of you just wasn't working."

"So, you went to Knoxville and what then?"

"I found a job with a farmer near there and continued to put together a little money. While there, the farmer taught me a lot about farming, crops, and just generally appreciating the land. I ultimately decided I wanted to try taking care of people's lawns and grounds. I had enough money to get me by, at least for a while, and I started picking up clients. By the way, while I was doing that, I found the time to get my GED."

"That is unbelievable. So, is that occupation what you want to continue to do once this is all over."

"You're pretty optimistic there, Pops. You are assuming I'm going to get out of this mess and have a choice. *If* I am found not guilty, yes, I want to continue doing what I was doing. I really do enjoy it. But I also want to save up enough to go to college on the side. I am not really sure I can handle both, but I want to at least give it a shot."

"Has there ever been a woman in your life?"

"Oh, there has been one or two, but nothing of any consequence. As you know, I have this small issue with trust, and that has created a problem in my relationships along the way, more than once."

As they continued to discuss his past, Paul said, "Did you invite Carrie to be a part of this today?"

"Yes, but apparently, she had something else going on. She said, she would be here but…"

"She is coming now. She's just walking in."

Bob stood as she walked up behind him.

"Hi, Carrie. Glad you could make it. We were just going through Paul's life history from the time he left home until now. With everything that has been going on concerning the criminal charge, we just haven't had the time to talk about his past. To be honest, I'm not sure we really do now, but I felt it would be a good idea to know where he has been and what he's done."

She sat down and as she pulled a legal pad and pen out of her oversized purse, she said, "Paul, would you mind going through it all briefly again. I'm sorry I'm late, but could you just generally go through your life from the time you left home until now."

She turned toward Bob and said, "Do we have time? Is that alright with you?"

"Certainly. Yes, we have the time. I still need to review the questions that I want to ask him again, but we have a little time for him to describe his past with you."

The summery of Paul's life, didn't take long. Carrie sat by quietly, while Bob then went through all the questions he would ask Paul when Paul was finally called as a witness on his own behalf.

Once that was finished, Bob said, "Paul, I need to go. I have a few other things I need to do here in Knoxville this afternoon before I head back to Nashville. I will see you Saturday or Sunday. Jack will be with me and we will probably not see you until after I meet with Mr. Reed. Once that's completed, we will come here."

He stood and looked at Carrie, fully expecting her to walk out with him.

She looked up at Bob and said, "There are a few things I want to discuss with Paul—you know, just some questions about his life and who this guy really is. Do you mind if I stick around for a few more minutes?"

"No, no certainly not. Is that okay with you, Paul?"

"Sure. They will kick me out of here before long, but I got a little time left."

As Bob walked across the floor towards the doorway, he turned ever so slightly and watched as the two of them seemed deep in conversation…and then he heard Paul laugh…for the first time in years.

Chapter 21

Bob arrived at the office early, opening the front door shortly after 6:00 a.m. He made a pot of coffee and checked messages until he heard Charlene arrive. Bob knew it would only be a matter of minutes before she walked back to his office to fill him in on the days he was in Knoxville. So, he leaned back, put his feet up on his desk and waited.

"Morning. How is everything in Knoxville?"

"About the same. Not much has changed. There is absolutely no way Paul's case can be resolved short of a trial. So, we are just putting the final touches on everything and we will start the trial Monday morning. How was everything here while I was gone?"

She sat down and said, "You know, you have a lot of loose ends with some of your cases. For instance, what do you want me to do with both of those divorces you have set for trial in a couple of weeks—you know, Jackson and Reardon?"

"I thought about those driving home. Draw up a motion to continue both. Sign my name and get them in the mail. Call the attorneys on the other side of both cases and tell them what is going on. I know them. There shouldn't be a problem."

"Okay. I set up appointments for you late next week not knowing for sure when you would be home. You want me to move them too?"

"Yes. Don't set up any appointments for the next two weeks. If this trial only lasts for a week, we can schedule them back in."

"So, what do you think…about…the trial?"

He looked away and said, "To be perfectly honest, I'm scared to death. We just don't have much to work with. The State's case seems airtight. I really believe we are in trouble. Of all the cases for me to say that about, who could have imagined it would involve my own grandson. I have been second guessing myself all week. I should have paid someone to handle it, Charlene, I really should have. I feel like I'm caught in a living hell and can't get out."

"Oh, quit being so dramatic. Bob, you are as good an attorney as I have ever known. Through the years, I worked for a couple of attorneys before I came here, and I've been in contact with many more that I have met as a result of working in this office. You are the best attorney Paul could possibly have to represent his interests. I've never seen you like this. You are always confident and self-assured. You know as well as I, you can only work with the facts your client provides you, whether it's your grandson or someone else. You can only work with what you have, Bob."

"I know and I have told myself that a thousand times. But this one is so much different. This one involves by own flesh and blood."

She stood. "Right now, at this point, it is business, plain and simple. You have a job to do—a job you are good at. Now go give them hell. I hate to end my little pep talk, even though I'm sure you are glad it's over, but I need to get to work. Is Jack coming over? I see he is on the calendar."

"He should be here by ten. Oh, and Charlene…."

"What?"

"Thanks. I needed that."

Thirty minutes later, Bob had gone through many of his phone messages and now needed to review files concerning his pending cases. He would then leave notes for Charlene on each file and have her take care of those issues while he was away next week.

Charlene peaked around his doorframe and said, "Paul is on line one."

Bob picked up immediately. "Are you alright? Is everything okay?"

"Yes, everything is fine here. How are you doing?"

"Good, I'm good. Jack is to be here about one and we will go through everything again. We figured we would leave here about nine Friday morning. We are meeting with John Reed, then we'll see you later Sunday."

"I know. We have been through all that about five times."

"Why did you call?"

He hesitated for a few moments, then said, "Oh…I'm just…a little nervous, I guess. What do you think is going to happen, Pops?"

"At the trial?"

"Yes. What is your honest opinion?"

Bob leaned back in his chair, as he considered how to respond. Finally, he said, "We are fine, Paul. It's a tough case with the limited testimony we have, but we will be fine."

"That is all wanted to hear, I guess. I just wasn't sure what you were thinking when I talked to you earlier this morning. You seemed preoccupied. You seemed uncertain. I'll let you go. As you can imagine, I'm worried out of my mind."

"I understand. I'll see you soon."

"Sounds fine…and Pops."

"Yes."

"Thanks for all you have done for me."

Bob hesitated. He quickly blinked away his tears as he said, "You are certainly welcome, Paul. Oh, by the way, how was your visit with Carrie?"

"Good. She's a nice woman. We know a few people in common and we had a good talk. I'm glad you decided to make her a part of all this. I'm thinking it might have really been a good move."

Bob smiled. "Hope so."

At two, Jack walked in his office door and said, "Are we all ready to do this?"

"I guess. Have a seat."

Jack sat down, pulled his file out and said, "Are you still planning on handling our witnesses?"

"Yes. Unfortunately, that won't amount to much other than Paul. I have those two guys you and I discussed, lined up as character witnesses, but they will be brief. I doubt the State even cross-examines them. I have to talk to John Reed and then we meet with Paul Sunday afternoon. That's it. That's all we got."

Jack said, "I will take care of the medical examiner, the cop, the neighbor, the bartender, and Paul's so-called friends who will apparently testify he is short-tempered. I'm not exactly sure what points I can make with any of them, but I'll do what I can. Their testimony is pretty clear-cut. You know as well as I, this is all just coming down to Paul and what he says concerning what happened."

Bob took a deep breath thought for a moment, then said, "What do you think?"

"What do *I* think? Hmm, how can I put this and not piss you off? Let's see. I think I made a mistake agreeing to help you with this case. That's about as subtle as I can be. We have a big problem. That's not your fault, that's not my fault. We just have a tough case to win. I think all we can do is make sure all the testimony we *do* have is admitted into the record and hope for a miracle."

"You know, somewhere out there, someone other than the killer, knows who did this. I believed that from day one and only hoped that between then and now, something would turn up. Maybe it still will, but like you, I think we are in all kinds of trouble."

They spent the next two hours going through testimony and trial strategy. However, Bob knew they could strategize all they wanted, but without the facts to back them up, they were in a an extremely tenuous position.

Jack had been gone about an hour, when Bob's cell rang. It was Susan. She wanted to meet for a drink. He indicated he couldn't make it tonight but would love to see her Thursday night, the night before he was to leave for Knoxville, to which she agreed,

Chapter 22

She was waiting for him when he arrived. Susan had found a table for the two of them at a small bar not far from his office. It was full of people when he finally arrived, which was just after five-thirty. It was necessary for him to squeeze between people to reach her.

As he sat, he said, "Whoa, this is crazy. How did you ever get this table?"

She smiled. "I waited nearby until the two people that were sitting here had finished and started to stand. Then I made a mad dash for it and sat down before anyone else could. It was like musical chairs without the music."

Bob waived at one of the waiters,. He noticed the waive and walked to their table.

"Is beer okay with you?"

She replied, "Yes…that's fine."

"Two beers."

"Yes sir. What brand?"

"Whatever you bring us."

As he walked away, she said, "What are you doing ordering beer? You are a wine drinker."

"Not tonight. Tonight, I just feel like beer—lots and lots of beer."

"It must have been a tough day."

"Tough day, tough week, tough next week. It is going to be tough from now on. That's why I said 'lots and lots of beer'. Finally coming to a conclusion on anything calls for something special, however, tonight *something special* just might be forgetting about what *has* happened *and* what is *about* to happen."

The waiter delivered their drinks and Bob drank half of it as quickly as it could exit the cold mug.

He continued to look around the room full of people, until she pulled him back into the conversation. "So, how do things look? Are you ready?"

"We are as ready as we will ever be with what we have to work with."

"Okay, now, that told me absolutely nothing. Let's start again and this time, answer me so even I, a poor layman, can understand."

He took another long drink, noticed his mug was nearly empty, and waived at the waiter to bring him another.

"Summing it all up, there's nothing else we can do. We leave Friday morning for Knoxville. I have one more witness to talk to. Then Monday morning it all begins."

He finished his last few swallows effectively emptying his mug and handed it to his waiter as it was replaced with a full one.

"What are your expectations? Are you still as negative about the possible outcome as you have been?"

"Yes."

"What about Jack? Does he concur?"

"Yes. Change the subject. What did you do today?"

"Okay, sure. Let's see, I went to my book club meeting. We reviewed a book we had all previously read and then discussed it today. Pretty good book too."

"Oh really. Anything I would like?"

"It was called Out of Reach. You might like it. It's pretty dark but sometimes so are you. It's about a prosecutor and his kidnapped daughter. The novel should generate lots of discussion, that's for sure."

"Sounds interesting, but to be perfectly honest, I wouldn't give a plug nickel to read a story about the practice of law, no matter *what* it was about or *who* it was about."

She said nothing, nor did he.

As he continued to look around the room, he whispered, "I made a mistake."

"I'm sorry, Bob, you'll need to speak up. There is so much noise…"

He raised his voice, "I made a mistake. I never should have taken this case, regardless of what Paul wanted."

He waived at the waiter for another.

"I've never seen you drink like this. Are you sure you want another one."

"I made a mistake. What was I thinking of? What have I done? I'm going to lose a case that sends my grandchild, my *only* grandchild, to prison. What was I thinking?"

"You know, you could win this case. Don't write it off yet."

The waiter brought another beer, just as he said, "There is no way we are going to win. It's just not possible, Susan. The facts aren't there, the witnesses aren't there, we just don't have enough."

He had trouble opening his eyes. He rolled over on his back. The smell—what the hell was that smell. It smelled like roses—something sweet.

He slowly opened his eyes. A dry mouth and splitting headache helped him begin the process of recalling some of his activity from the night before.

He concluded the smell was of fresh fruit emanating from the sheets. His sheets never smelled like this.

He smacked his lips. The taste in his mouth was like nothing he had experienced—somewhat like he figured well-worn socks might taste like.

As he continued to regain awareness, he looked around. This wasn't his bedroom. Where the hell was he? There was too much light. The furniture wasn't his. Had he ventured into a third dimension? Maybe he was dead. *Was this dead?* If it was, it really wasn't so bad.

He sat up. One thing was for certain—he remembered yesterday he had a shirt on—but not any longer. The sheet and blanket covered him from the waist down. He quickly lifted both to see what he might have on below his waist.

He had retained his boxers, but everything else had been removed. He quickly looked around, finding his cloths hanging over a chair which was situated in front of a small desk.

Bob could now make out the faint aroma of food—bacon and coffee. The smell was coming from beyond a closed door which apparently led to somewhere. If this was hell, he was glad it wasn't nearly as bad as he had imagined.

He shoved the blanket and sheet off of him and got out of bed. His headache was beyond belief. Slowly, he began to remember bits and pieces of the prior night.

He put on all his cloths, then opened the door and walked into the kitchen where Susan was standing over the stove.

"Good morning."

She turned around, smiled and said, "Is it? I mean, is that really how you feel about this morning? If it is, more power to ya, big guy."

He sat down at the table, as she said, "How about a cup of coffee?"

"Please."

As she placed the cup in front of him and slowly poured it half-full of black coffee, she said, "Would you like to know what happened last night, or have you concluded it might be better not knowing?"

He took a short swallow of hot coffee and said, "I guess I better know."

"You got blasted drunk. That's the long and short of it."

"What happened after that?"

She walked over to the stove and started to turn the bacon, strip by strip.

"Well, I got you out of the bar and to my car. There was no way in hell you could drive home. I strapped you in, then brought you here instead. I'll bet you have a doozey of a hangover."

"Like you cannot believe. How did I get in…what happened then?"

"I helped you in here, took…most of your clothes off and put you to bed. You were out like a light as soon as I covered you up. I hope you slept well. It's a pretty comfortable bed and…"

"You undressed me?"

"Sure. You weren't going to sleep in your clothes at *my* house."

"If you don't mind my asking…"

She turned, smiled and said, "No, I never looked. I figured if that was something I was going to see, it would be under more favorable circumstances. That wasn't going to happen while you were drunk and without any ability whatsoever to make a rational decision concerning what you were doing. Your secret is safe—at least so far."

"I am *so* sorry I put you in that position. That has never, ever happened…"

"Forget it. You would have done the same for me. Now let's have a bite to eat and I'll take you to your car."

He stood, walked up behind her, turned her around and kissed her. "Thank you. I cannot thank you enough."

"Not a problem. Like I said, you would have done the same for me. Now, let's eat so you can be on your way. I think you told me you needed to pick Jack up later this morning, so let's get moving. When we are done eating, I'll take you to your car, and you can drive home from there."

"Did I say anything that was offensive or that…"

"Absolutely not. Now go sit down."

He walked to the table. As he sat down, he said, "I owe you. I really do. I'm so sorry…"

As she served the bacon, she said, "No problem. You are under a hell of a lot of pressure, Bob. I understand. Next time though, the sleepover is at your house. And…the next time, you can fix breakfast for me."

He smiled and said, "It's a deal."

Chapter 23

Bob picked up Jack early the next morning. He told Bob he had done nothing but prepare the entire evening, then asked Bob what he had done.

Jack indicated he had done nothing but prepare. After quickly describing his evening to Bob, he then asked him what he had done.

"It was a short evening for me. I went out and had a drink with Susan then went to bed."

"You look awful. Did you have trouble sleeping?"

"Sure. Yup, sure did."

"Hmm. Did you drink too much last night?"

"I might have. I certainly could have. Why do you ask?"

"Because that is not like you. Nor is that like you to drink beer. Were you at Susan's house?"

"When?"

"*Anytime*. Were you at Susan's *at any point in time?*"

"Why?"

"Jesus, Bob, what the hell is wrong with you? The questions are simple, the answers are simple. Why are you avoiding answering my questions?"

"I'm not. Now, is there anything else we should go through for…"

"Wait a minute. Were you with her…all night?"

"No. Absolutely not. I was *not* with her all night,"

"Let me rephrase, counselor. Did you sleep at her house last night?"

"What the hell is this? Why all the questions?"

Jack thought for a moment before he responded.

"You know, Bob, it is not a sin and it's not against the law for you to start a relationship with another woman. I'm not sure you understand that. We all move on, you know—all of us move on. We all move on in our *own way,* but we must, and we do move on. The fact that you might enjoy a relationship with another woman now that Jean is gone doesn't make you a bad person. You aren't cheating on her. You are just moving on the best you can. You have absolutely no reason to feel any guilt."

"I don't want to discuss this. Move on."

"She's gone, Bob. Plain and simple. You have a right to enjoy the life you have left. You will never forget, you will never ignore, but you have a right to be happy and to be involved with someone else, if it makes your life livable"

"Thanks. I'll be sure and keep that in mind. *Now, dammit move on!*"

"Don't you think that would be what she wanted—for you to enjoy the rest of your life? Do you really think she would want you to mope around and live the rest of your life in the past. That's not what Jean would have wanted, Bob, and you damn well know it."

Neither of them said anything for the following few minutes until Bob brought up some aspect of the case and the conversation returned to the trial that would begin in less than twenty-four hours.

His appointment with John Reed was to take place in the lobby of the Hilton. As he waited. he considered Jack's comments made on the way to Knoxville.

Jack was most likely right. He had considered his involvement with Susan many times—just how far should he go—what Jean would have done if he was the one that had died. Those questions haunted him and before his relationship with Susan moved to another level, if it ever did, he would need to somehow handle the guilt he felt every time he was with her—every time he laughed with her, or he kissed her. Jack had definitely hit the nail on the head. The guilt issue was a problem. He would need to somehow justify his relationship with Susan, before he would be able to move forward with her.

John Reed arrived precisely on time.

Bob saw him walk in the door, alone, with no baggage and quickly assumed it was him. He stood and as John approached, he smiled, stuck out his hand and said, "Are you John Reed?"

As he reached out to shake his hand, he said, "Yes sir, I am,"

He presented a good picture. He was clean shaven, hair cut short, nicely dressed. Since this was the only witness that could really comment about the relationship between the victim and Paul, it was necessary he be as believable as could be and appearance was always a factor in that respect.

"Have a chair." As they both sat down, Bob said, "John, I thought maybe you could just tell me what you observed about both Lynn and Paul. Maybe tell me a little bit about how they acted when they were with each other, and just in general what you observed about the two of them. Now, first off, why don't you tell me what you did for Lynn."

"Certainly. I did whatever she needed me to do. I worked mostly around the outside of the house, but sometimes she had me do a few small jobs inside too. Whatever she needed me to fix, I did it."

"How long did you work for her?"

"Almost five years. I wasn't there on a regular basis. I just helped her out when she called me."

"How did you get along with her?"

"Great. She was really a good person. I miss her,"

"Tell me about Paul. How long have you known him?"

"Just the last couple of years. I met him when he started to work for her."

"How did you get along with him?"

John smiled. "He's a good guy. I never had a problem of any kind with him. We never really worked together—he was always working on the flowers and the lawn. But we took our breaks together and always talked for a bit when we were there at the same time."

"What about his relationship with Lynn? How did they get along?"

"Great. Never a bad word between the two of them. That is why I was so surprised when I heard she was murdered and he was charged. That made no sense to me then, and it doesn't now."

"Do you have a family?"

"Yes. I am married and have a couple of children."

"Have you lived around here long?"

"All my life."

"Can you further describe the relationship between Paul and Lynn as you observed it."

"As I mentioned, it was good. I didn't know it had apparently reached the point where they were involved with each other. But now, looking back, I can see that was probably the case. I could remember a number of times she would get a little handsy with him. She would touch him on the shoulder, or grab his arm while they laughed about something. Thinking back, I can remember little things between the two of them that I just never put together while I was working. *Now*, it's no surprise they were involved."

"Did he ever lose his temper around her?"

"Not around her. I saw him kick at a dead plant a time or two, or kick up some dirt in disgust. But I never saw him show any anger of any nature toward her. Now, he's your grandson, right?"

"Yes."

"I can't imagine what you must be going through."

"Did he ever talk about his past life?"

He thought for a moment. "No, I can't… Wait. One time he did mention his parents were both killed, I think, in a car accident maybe. Is that right?"

"Yes."

"He has had a tough life."

Bob looked away, as he whispered, "Yes, he has." Returning his attention to John, he said, "You are an important witness for us. Your testimony needs to be firm and just as we've talked today. We don't have much to work with here, and it's really important you testify exactly as we have visited today."

"That's not a problem. What I have told you today is the truth."

"Did you handle everything inside and outside the house in terms of repairs?"

"Yes."

"Someone said the lightbulb on the back porch was out. Did you know about it? That, of course, precluded anyone from determining if someone had slipped in the back door after Paul left that night."

"Yes, I knew, but I hadn't had a chance to fix it. It takes a special bulb and she only told me it was out the day before this all happened. That very same day, I bought the bulb to replace the one that had burned out. I guess, at least according to the cops, it wasn't a problem anyway because they said it didn't enter into the crime. I tried to replace it later, but they wouldn't let me near the house. I just took it back and got a refund."

Bob leaned back, and said, "Is there anything else you can tell me about the relationship between the two of them, or about what happened to her?"

"Not really. She was a good woman. She was a good customer of mine. She always paid me well. I am going to have to find *two* customers to take her place and replace the income she provided. I really, really hated to lose her."

They talked a few more minutes and then parted company.

On his way to see Paul, he figured John would definitely make a good witness. The problem with his testimony, however, was not so much about what he *would* say, it was about what he *wouldn't* say, and that was whom the actual murderer might have been. Unfortunately, the closer to the trial date they got, the more convinced he became that no one would *ever* know the answer to that question.

Chapter 24

Bob wanted to stop and visit with Paul one more time before going to the hotel to further discuss strategy with Jack.

He just squeezed in within the time set for visitation. Paul started smiling as he approached the window.

"Good to see you, Pops. How was the meeting with John?"

Paul's approach took Bob somewhat by surprise. It was the first time he seemed actually happy to see him since they had been reunited.

"Good. He seems like a nice guy, a likeable guy, believable—someone the jury will most likely listen too. He said he never heard a harsh word between you and Lynn. He told me you were about the last person on earth he would have expected might have done something like this. He will be a good witness for the purpose for which he's called, but…"

"But what…go on. Is there a problem with that?"

"The problem is that it's clear he knows nothing about the facts of the case. If we just had another witness or two that might be able to provide an alibi of some kind, of *any* kind—or that perhaps knew about another individual that had a problem with Lynn, then *their* testimony, along with the testimony of you and John, might be all we need. But we just don't have much to go along with what John has to say, other than you saying that you didn't do it,"

The smile quickly disappeared. "So, basically you are saying we have what amounts to a small chance in hell of winning."

"I've never changed my opinion from day one, Paul. We do have a chance, based on your testimony, but without anything to go with it concerning the specific merits of the case, we could have a problem. That's what I have told you from day one. Nothing has changed. Now that, however, doesn't mean we are going to lose. Just keep your chin up and we will keep plugging away."

"Did Jack come with you?"

"Yes. In fact, he's waiting for me now. We are going to basically brainstorm one last time and be ready to go Monday morning.”

“So, how far will we get the first day?”

“Most likely, not very far. We will start selecting a jury and that can take some time, as I have already told you. The Judge will probably want to visit with us first, and then we will start picking the jury.”

“Can I talk to you while all this is going on?”

“Yes. But we will have to keep it down. We will be able to whisper back and forth while the trial is actually going on. I would encourage you to ask me questions or offer your thoughts while the trial is proceeding.”

“Will we get any further than selecting a jury the first day?”

“We could get to the opening statements of the attorneys, but it is really hard to tell. I know how long *I* take under normal circumstances, but I know nothing about this Prosecutor and his style. And, of course, I have no idea how many of the prospective jurors might believe they have some type of conflict and don’t feel comfortable being on the jury. Those people take time and involve a lot of back-and-forth conversation between attorney and juror before the Judge can determine whether they should be dismissed. I had you go through the jury list, but we don’t have anyone to help us determine the relationship between jurors and Lynn. If she has a number of friends on that panel, it could take a long time before we sort it out. Just be patient. Jury selection is really an important part of the process.”

The officer said, “Hey, Paul. Visiting hours are up. I need to take you back to your cell.”

Paul stood and said, “Well, Pops, I guess this should be it.”

As Bob stood, he said, “I’ll see you either tomorrow or bright and early Monday morning.”

Paul hesitated.

As the guard said, “Come on let’s go,” Paul put his hand on the glass and left it there.

Bob reached out and placed his hand on the glass immediately across from Paul’s hand.

Paul nodded.

Bob smiled and said, “Until tomorrow.” As he watched the guard take him away, tears filled his eyes.

Bob drove around for a few minutes while he struggled to control his emotions. He didn't want to walk back into the hotel room and explain to Jack, or explain to anyone for that matter, why he was crying. It was certainly none of Jack's business and, in addition, his tears were an embarrassing sign of his own weakness. He wasn't about to try and explain that to Jack.

He walked into their hotel room just after eight p.m. As soon as he did, a wave of odor sweep over him. He closed the door behind him and turned around to see Jack in his underwear, sitting on the bed watching an obviously R-rated movie.

"What in god's name is that smell?"

"Let me finish this movie. Just a minute, it's almost over. It has just reached its climax, so to speak."

Bob stood directly in front of the TV and said, "What is the smell, Jack? Is it you?"

"Move."

"The smell?"

"Oh, I had room service bring up a sandwich and some spicy cheese dip of some kind. I'm thinking the dip didn't really agree with me. Now, move."

Bob walked to the window and opened it. The cold winter air quickly replaced the warmth of the room, causing Jack to look up at him and say, "What the hell are you doing?"

"You son-of-a-bitch, you stink up the room, to the point where it's not even livable, and you ask me what *I'm* doing? This remains open, until the smell is gone. Jesus, Jack what are you thinking about? You *know* someone else lives here too. It might be time you thought about someone other than yourself."

"Hey, I had to eat. What was I supposed to do?"

"If this happens again, we are getting separate rooms and you are paying for both of them. Just remember that."

An hour later, after the odor was basically gone and the room had once again warmed up, Jack said, "Did you talk to Paul? Do you think he's mentally ready to go tomorrow?"

"Yes. I don't think that's any longer an issue—at least not like I originally thought it might be. We discussed John's testimony and I explained how far I thought we would get the first and second days. I told him just to be patient and we would move slowly and methodically—we are in no hurry."

"You think he understands how tough winning might be?"

"Prior to today, I've tried to explain how difficult a task we have. But I backed off today and just tried to subtly explain that we have a tough road ahead of us. I don't want him giving up on us and I'm afraid he might do just that if he thinks all is lost. I believe he will be fine, at least until we get the verdict I am so afraid of getting."

Jack walked in the bedroom about an hour later. It wasn't long before Bob could hear him snoring.

He stood and walked to the doorway, quietly closing the door separating the living area from the bedroom. He pulled out a couple of extra sheets and made up a makeshift bed on the couch. He knew tonight he would need some sleep and he figured the odds of that happening were better on the couch than in that room, with that gas-making, snoring machine occupying the other bed.

His cell vibrated. It was Susan.

"Are you still up?"

Bob said, "Yes, I am. Obviously, you are too."

"I am. Is everything ready to go? Did you talk to that witness today? What about Paul? Is he ready?"

Bob laughed. "Whoa, are you as wrapped up in this as we are? I believe the answer to all of your questions was yes, I think...but I' m not sure."

"Will that guy make a good witness for you?"

"Yes. He won't win the case for us, but he'll make a good witness. What did you do today?"

"Oh, I cleaned, and…washed dishes…and…Actually I thought about you most of the day. I wish I were there—with you."

"I'll keep you updated as we go along. In fact, I guess I haven't had a chance to tell you, but I'll be home Monday night. The Judge had something come up. Maybe I can find a free moment tomorrow to slip over and see you."

"Great, great, I'll plan on it unless I hear otherwise from you."

"I better go, Susan."

"Okay. Bob…"

"Yes."

"I love you. You might as well know it. I love you. Maybe the phone isn't the best way to tell you that for the first time, but,,, I love you. So there. It's done. Now you know. I am really concerned about how all this is going to work out for you. So, I'll see you soon and we can discuss—you know—we can discuss what I just said."

He hesitated.

"Listen to me, Bob, before you run away after what I just said. What I said is how I feel and I'm tired of holding it all inside. I know you are conflicted concerning how you feel about us and I understand that. You are going to have to figure that all out yourself. Absolutely *no* one can help you sort out your thoughts concerning that particular issue. I can only speak for myself… and now, you know how I feel. I hope I didn't scare you away, but it's time it was said. I've held it in long enough."

"I understand. I do think this is something we need to discuss some other time. Let's defer discussing this issue until later this week, okay?"

"Sure. Yes, that's fine. What are we going to discuss? I mean, what's your position, when we—I mean what's…"

Bob laughed, and said, "Hey, just calm down. We are good here. I just don't want to discuss issues like this on the phone and especially tonight. Now, I need to go. I'll see you soon."

"Okay. Good luck."

"Thanks."

He terminated the call, then turned off the TV. As he tried to fall asleep, he thought about the conversation he had just concluded. She was most likely right—it *was* time to figure out a direction their relationship was heading and then proceed accordingly. But not now. Not tonight. He would go through witnesses and jury lists as he fell asleep tonight, just hoping somehow, he could come up with a new option which might convince the jury Paul was not guilty. Time was almost up. There was certainly a good chance that if something positive didn't turn up right soon, about a week from today and most likely one or two days each week for as long as Bob was alive, the only visitation he would have with his grandson, would be between jailhouse bars.

Chapter 25

What a night! The first time he looked at his watch it was a little after 3:00 a.m. He couldn't get comfortable, no matter what he did. Finally, about 6:00 a.m., he fell into a deep sleep, only to be awakened by Jack who walked into the living area shortly after seven.

Bob stood up and immediately began to mentally prepare for a long, tiring day. They arrived at the courthouse near eight-thirty, and after wasting fifteen minutes looking for a place to park, he told Jack he wanted him to stop in a no-parking zone, let him out and drive around until he found a space.

Jack reluctantly agreed. Bob was able to finally exit the vehicle and walk through the courthouse doors. As he approached one of the conference rooms, he noticed a guard standing nearby. Bob asked him if Paul had arrived. The guard answered in the affirmative, indicating he was already in the conference room waiting for his attorney.

When he walked in, Carrie was sitting with Paul. They stopped talking as Bob walked their direction. Paul stood, then reached out and took Bob in his arms, tightly embracing him.

He leaned back and said, "I haven't had a chance to do that since this all started. Thanks, Pops. I mean that. It doesn't matter how this turns out. You have gone above and beyond. I will be forever grateful for what you have done."

Bob, taken aback by the unexpected show of gratitude, said, "I wouldn't have done it any other way. I had to stop and evaluate the totality of the situation when I first heard from you, but in the end, this was the only logical option available. I would, without question, do the same thing again, if placed in a similar position. Sit down, sit down, let's talk."

As both sat, he turned to Carrie and said, "How long have you been here?"

"About fifteen minutes. I have been wanting to visit with Paul one-on-one for quite a while. Nearly all my visits with him have been when I was with you. But I really wanted to hear some of his thoughts without you around, which I was able to do, at least to some extent, here, this morning."

Paul said, "Not to change the subject, but how much time have we got before the trial begins?"

"Probably an hour. It is all up to the Judge. He will let us know when he's ready. And of course, all the jurors have to be accounted for too. They must either be here or be excused. What were you two discussing when I came in?"

Carrie said, "I was just trying to figure out how he survived when he left your house. He has an amazing tale to tell just concerning his ability to stay alive at sixteen and on the run, so to speak. That is really a story in and of itself—above and beyond his problem with Lynn's death and this trial."

Bob watched Paul as Carrie continued talking. There appeared to be a connection between the two of them.

Paul said, "Carrie are you going to report on that too? Do you think it's really relevant?"

"Yes, I do. I'm definitely going to cover all the legal proceedings until we have a verdict. And yes, that also includes your history from the time you left home until you got into trouble. I've already covered most of what has happened since then, up until today. So, if you have the time and wish to discuss it with me, I would like to go through those prior years with you too."

"Sure. In fact, I think I would probably enjoy it. At least during my time with you, I could concentrate on those questions and answers—just forget about the four walls surrounding me."

She smiled and said, "Great. Let's start on that later today, if that is okay with you."

"Sure. Once jury selection is over for the day, obviously I don't have much else going on so I will be available whenever you are."

Bob said, "Carrie, did you say you were from North Carolina?"

"Yes. I was born there, graduated from high school there and went to journalism school at NC State."

"How did you end up here?"

"I had quite a few offers, but this was the best one I got. So, here I am."

"Do you like it here?"

"It's a job. I've been looking for something in the television field. I have received a couple of offers. But the pay is so bad, I couldn't afford to leave the job I have. I am still looking around."

Bob said, "Have you looked at Nashville? They have TV stations all over the city. In fact, I have a good friend that manages one of them."

Carrie said, "Well, when this is finished and Paul is exonerated, maybe I will call on you to introduce us."

"I would be glad to."

Jack walked in and shut the door behind him as he said, "What did you say about Paul being exonerated? Did I miss something?"

"As usual, you are always about a step behind. No, we were just talking about jobs and stories—about anything to pass the time before we start the proceedings today."

As they waited for a knock on the door, Bob continued to watch the interaction between Carrie and Paul. It was apparent something was going on between the two of them. He wasn't sure…"

A knock terminated his thought process. The court attendant opened the door, and said, "The Judge would like to see the attorneys for a moment."

Bob looked at Carrie, then at Paul. They both looked terrified. He stood as he said, "And so it begins. Are you ready, Jack?"

They walked through the chamber's door and noticed George Jensen already there, waiting to get started.

The Judge said, "Good Morning. Good to see you both again." He extended his hand, which both shook as he said, "Be seated."

"Is everyone ready to proceed? Is there any chance of resolving this before we get started? Have the three of you discussed a resolution of the case?"

George said, "We have, Your Honor. At this point, I don't think there is much we can do. I made a couple of offers and they have been rejected."

Bob said, "Do you have anything else to offer?"

"Wait a minute. Do you all three want to discuss this one more time? If you do, don't do it in my presence. Go out in the hallway, or somewhere else. Anywhere, but in front of me."

George stood as he said, "Let's just walk out in the hallway a moment."

They walked through the chamber's door and into the hallway.

George said, "I can still go with manslaughter, but that's it. Does that work for you? I won't recommend a sentence. I'll let you argue that and just let the Judge rule."

Bob said, "Is that the best you can do, or can we discuss it?"

"That is the best I can do."

"He won't accept it."

"Do you want to discuss it with him?"

"No. I already know what he will say. Let's just go back in."

The three of them walked back into chambers and George said, "Discussions concerning a plea are over, Judge. The State is ready to proceed."

"Is that the case, Mr. Jones?"

"Yes."

"Okay. All the jurors are now accounted for. We will be in session all morning. Then as I told you, we will break around noon and not start up until tomorrow afternoon. Any thoughts or questions?"

The three attorneys indicated they had no other questions.

"All right then. Why don't the two of you go get your client. Take him in the courtroom. Once you are all seated, the court attendant will let me know, and we will begin."

Bob and Jack walked through the conference room door. Paul, wide eyed, and clearly on edge, said, "What now?"

"Let's go. It's time to pick a jury."

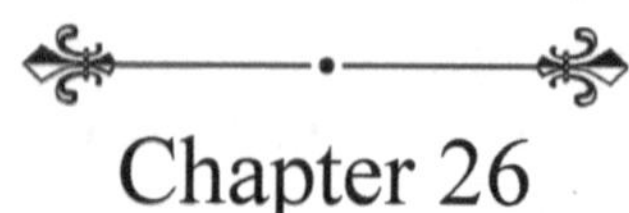

Chapter 26

Jury selection, during the limited time it was conducted, was unremarkable. Not one of those named as potential jurors, had a conflict of any nature with Paul nor were they acquainted with Lynn Baker. Before noon, they were able to reach the point where both parties were ready to select the jurors from those initially called and questioned, which would make up the final panel of twelve regular members and two alternates. Those selected, would listen to the facts and the evidence involving the case and come to a conclusion concerning the guilt or innocence of Paul Duncan.

At noon, all jurors were released and told to report for duty at one o'clock Tuesday afternoon. At that time, they would listen to opening statements by the attorneys followed by testimony presented by the State's witnesses.

It was near 4:00 p.m. when they reached Nashville. Bob took Jack to his office and he then drove to his own office hoping Charlene, even though it was near closing time, hadn't closed the office a little early for the day.

She was still at her desk when he walked in the front door. He nodded, simply said, "Hi" and walked on past.

Once in his office, he stood for a moment and looked down at the pile of phone messages he needed to handle in some fashion or another. As he sat down at his desk and started going through each message, Charlene walked in his office sat down and said, "So, how did you get along in Knoxville?"

"As well as could be expected, I guess. We finished picking a jury. The Judge wasn't available this afternoon so he let us go until tomorrow afternoon."

"I wondered why you said you were coming home. Actually, I still do. Why aren't you down there getting ready for tomorrow?"

"We *are* ready. There is really nothing else to do. We are as ready as we are ever going to be. Besides, it was time Jack and I were apart for at least a few hours."

"Oh really. Why is that?"

"Because I had reached the point where I could not stand to be with that old man another minute. We needed to go our own way for at least a few hours before the trial started."

She laughed before she said, "What's the problem?"

He leaned back in his chair, folded his arms, stared at her and said, "First off, he snores. I have earplugs, but they don't help much. I have no doubt people can hear him as they are walking down the hallway."

"I understand. Well, you can at least get a little sleep before it all starts tomorrow afternoon."

"That's not all. He stinks up a room quicker than a herd of elephants could. He's awful. I can't take it anymore."

Charlene, first smiled, then started to laugh.

"It's not really funny. Then he has this routine that he goes through every damn morning. Everything must be done to get ready for his day in precisely the same order. Breakfast must come at the appropriate time and scheduled between this thing and that thing. He needs to shave at exactly the correct moment in his schedule as he prepares for the day…he's anal—*about everything*—at least until he gets to the courthouse. I just had to get away. I slept on the sofa last night, but nothing can dampen the sound of him snoring."

As Charlene quit laughing, she said, "So what are you going to do with him?"

"He doesn't know it yet, but we are going to stay in separate rooms from now on. I will pay for half of his and all of mine, so he's not out any more money than he would have been if we had split the cost of one room. But that's one of the reasons I came home. Before we left, I slipped out of the room and went down to the front desk. I got it all set up without him knowing about it. When we go back down tomorrow, I'll tell him. In addition to making that change, I also wanted to just catch up on what was going on here, in the office. But, as far as Jack is concerned, it will be a whole new ballgame when we go back this time. I can get some sleep in my own bed tonight and then we can start over tomorrow."

"What time are you leaving?"

"Around nine. That should give us time to get there, go through a few issues with Paul and be ready to start the trial about one—that's when court is reconvening."

Charlene stood as he said, "Any messages I should be concerned about?"

"Not really. Oh, the one from Susan might be something to consider, but not be concerned about. She wanted to talk to you once you got here."

"I'll call her. I will probably be here an hour or two before we leave in the morning. I'll just see you then."

As she left, he punched in Susan's number.

"Hi, Bob. Are you here or still in Knoxville?"

"Here. I just got home. I have to be back tomorrow morning, so I'm not here long, but long enough to go through the mail and handle—handle another issue that came up."

"Anything serious?"

"No, no. It's more of a personal issue. I'll tell you about it sometime. It's not worth wasting our time discussing it."

She hesitated for a moment before she said, "I wish I could be there. It's really all I am thinking about anyway… wondering how you are doing, how the trial is progressing."

"I understand. It's coming along as well as can be expected. The jury is picked, and we are happy with its composition. But unfortunately, that could be the best part of the whole trial for our side. Opening statements and testimony start tomorrow. I'm afraid it won't proceed as smoothly as picking the jury did."

"How is Paul holding up?"

"He is really doing quite well. Our relationship has changed considerably since this all started. We have become close. Well, as close as one could expect in light of the fact he could end up in prison for a long, long time. He is guarded—he keeps himself under control, quiet, most of the time. And to be honest, so do I. But the relationship between us has really changed—for the better."

"Is that girl still writing the story—I think you said her name was Carrie?"

"Yes. It has been fun watching those two interact. There appears to me to be a little something going on between the two of them. Lately, she's been to see him without me being there. That didn't happen when they first met. I mean, they don't need me there, but it's just interesting that they are meeting together now, without me. And there's been a time or two they were discussing something they didn't want me to hear—they stopped talking when I approached."

"I guess they are both adults and they both certainly know the risk—the issues of becoming involved, even emotionally, with this trial and with the possible conviction hanging over Paul's head. You said you are happy with the jury?"

"Yes, I am. They are as good as we could have expected. They appear completely unbiased, unfamiliar with either Paul or the victim, and only slightly familiar with the facts of the case. Some of them read the articles Carrie wrote, but of course, that in and of itself didn't disqualify them. Those articles she wrote have most likely helped Paul since they aren't involved as much with the specific facts of the case, as they have been simply following a man in trouble, which was the purpose of her involvement from day one. Yes, I'm happy with them."

"You want to get a glass of wine somewhere? You want to come over here for a few minutes before you go home?"

"I can't Susan. I have way too much to do here. In addition, I'm so damn tired I can't see straight. I'll tell you the reason for that another time. I need to finish up here and go home—get some sleep. I'll probably not be back until this is over, but I will touch base with you every day if I can."

"Okay, Bob. Good luck."

"Thanks. I'll see you soon."

He terminated the call. Bob knew what she was waiting for, but he just couldn't force those words out of his mouth, not yet, not now.

The following morning, feeling refreshed for the first time in a week, he picked up Jack right on time. As he got in the front seat, Bob said, "Jack, we're going to make a little change."

Jack quickly turned toward Bob and said, "Now, you know I don't like change. I like a routine that's consistent and that's been proven over a period of time. You know..."

Bob smiled, turned to Jack and said, "Just shut up and hear me out. Oh, and before I go into details, you have no choice in the matter. The decision involving these changes has already been made, my friend—already been made."

Chapter 27

Four sat quietly in the conference room, waiting until the Judge was ready to proceed.

"So, how far are we going to go this afternoon? By the way, why did we have to wait until now to start? Wasn't my trial important enough to start on time? Why did we have to wait until this afternoon to start this thing?"

Bob looked at Paul and said, "Let me explain… *again*. This is the Judge's show. He decides *everything,* from the time you arrive in the morning, through the noon hour, up to and including the time you walk out of the courthouse. And that's true each and every day we are trying your case."

He stood and walked to the window. As he looked down on the street below, he continued his line of conversation as he said, "Nothing is done without his permission. No one does anything in his courtroom until you ask him if it's the right thing to do. You breathe if he says breathe, you hold your breath if he says hold your breath. He said we start at one today—so, today we start at one, period. No one asks him why. We simply start at one. And the process will continue that way every day we are in his courtroom." He turned to face Paul, smiled and said, "Does that help explain why we start at one?"

"Well, yeah, I guess. You were a little long-winded though. I got the idea a few minutes into your explanation. Do you go on and on like that when you're in the courtroom?"

Jack said, "Oh, my god yes. He is the worst I ever saw. I've seen judges die of old age before he finished a sentence."

Carrie started to laugh, as did Paul.

"Whatever. By the way Jack, you're the one that should be nervously babbling on and on right now. You are first up. You got the opening statement today. I get to simply sit back and critique you."

As Bob sat back down, he said, "You clean up pretty good, Paul.

You haven't been clean shaven since the day we reunited. You should make a good first impression on the jury and that's always a positive. You looked like hell that first day I saw you but you look presentable today—did Carrie get you to clean up a little?"

"No… no…well, maybe, yes." He looked at her, smiled and said, "She just made a couple of comments, but she said enough that I knew I probably needed to clean up a little more than I had planned. Now what exactly happens after the opening statements today?"

"It depends on how long both sides take. But I know Jack doesn't normally take long. He just expects the evidence to do the talking. Isn't that right, Jack?"

"That's correct. I won't take long at all. I'll concentrate on a couple of the facts, point out your complete denial, explain a little about the burden of proof and let it go. These opening statements never mean much anyway. They just give the jury a roadmap as to where we are going the next few days."

Shortly thereafter, a knock on the door indicated the Judge was ready to proceed.

Once seated in the courtroom, the Judge provided a short synopsis of the afternoon's session, indicating the jury would first hear an opening statement from the State, followed by an opening statement from the defense. He then asked State's attorney George Jenson to proceed with his opening.

Bob figured George would most likely outline his whole case, including a brief rundown of each witnesses' testimony and that is exactly what happened. He turned what could have been an interesting fifteen-minute explanation concerning the process and the facts, into an uninteresting, slow dissertation, which rambled on for over two hours.

They took a short break after his opening, anticipating Jack would take a similar amount of time. They didn't know Jack like Bob did. Jack would concentrate on a few points of law and then sit down. His opening would be short and sweet—far removed from the rambling, never-ending statement provided by the Prosecution.

After the break and after all were seated, the Judge said, "We will now hear an opening from the defense. Gentlemen, proceed."

Jack stood and as he walked toward the jurors, he said, "Good Afternoon, my name is Jack Raymond and I, along with my partner Bob Duncan, represent the Defendant, Paul Duncan. Paul is seated there a couple of chairs from the end of the table." He hesitated, before he said, "And by the way, he sits there as an *innocent man*."

He started to walk toward the end of the jury box as he said, "That's right, folks, he is an innocent man. The State in this case has charged him with murder, with *premediated* murder, no less. But as he sits there, unless the State has enough proof to establish, beyond a reasonable doubt, that he committed a crime, he remains an innocent man—that never changes."

"The State went through each of their witness's testimony. I'm not going to do that, because absolutely nothing we attorneys say to you is evidence. We can provide you with a basic idea of our position, and an idea what each witness *might* say, but nothing we attorneys say is proof or evidence in this case. So why, at this point, would we tell you what these witnesses may or may not say and waste your time and mine. The only evidence you hear that makes any difference at all will be that which comes from the witness stand, and which the Judge says you can, in good faith, use to determine the guilt or innocence of our client."

"Now, the State has a story to tell. They are going to put witnesses on the stand to tell a story that they hope, at the conclusion of all the evidence, will convict Mr. Duncan." He stopped and leaned against the railing surrounding the jurors and raised the level of his voice. "But the Defense has a story to tell too. If the only people you were to listen to were the State's witnesses, the trial would come to a conclusion quickly. But that's not the way it works. *Both* sides are given a chance to present witnesses and *we expect you to listen to our witnesses with the same amount of attention you pay to the State's witnesses.*"

Jack started to pace. "There were no eye witnesses to this crime. There is no one here to testify that can say they saw Paul murder anyone. *You need to keep that in mind.* The State's case is all circumstantial. *Keep that in mind.* The Defendant has emphatically stated he did not commit this crime and he will do so from the witness stand. *Keep that in mind.* No one the State presents as a witness in this case will *ever* be able to say, without doubt, the Defendant committed this crime. *Keep that in mind.*"

Jack looked up and down the two rows of jurors seated in the box, smiled and said, "Thank you for your attention. Once the evidence has all been submitted, I'll have a chance to visit with you again before you deliberate."

By now, because of the lengthy opening by the Prosecutor, the Judge decided to end the proceedings for the day. Since he had a morning conflict, they would begin with testimony from the State's witness's starting at 1:00 p.m. tomorrow afternoon.

As the four walked in the conference room, Paul turned to Jack, stuck out his hand and said, "Thanks, man. That was great. You did a great job. See, that's what I'm talking about. No one saw me do a damn thing. That's what I've been saying from the very beginning."

Jack shook his hand and said, "I wish that was all there was to it, my friend. Unfortunately, what I said in there amounts to very little. It's just a synopsis of how the attorneys for each side feel about their case and a little roadmap as to what is to follow the next few days. It's the *witnesses* you need to worry about. You'll understand once we start with the testimony."

"Well, I really feel like we got started on the right foot. I really do."

Bob said, "I hope you feel that way tomorrow Paul…after the State starts presenting their case. Now, we have a late start tomorrow too…the Judge has got something else he needs to do in the morning. So, we will just plan on seeing the two of you tomorrow noon, here."

That evening, after Bob and Jack had reviewed the testimony they expected to hear from the State's witnesses tomorrow and while Bob was lying in bed, trying to fall asleep, he thought about Paul—about how excited he was with Bob's opening.

What a shock he was in for starting tomorrow. Until the State completed their case, they would present witness after witness that would all point toward the same conclusion—that Paul Duncan was indeed guilty of the crime of first-degree murder. Unfortunately, Paul would not, at days end, be nearly as excited about the proceedings at the conclusion of testimony during the next few days, as he was today.

Chapter 28

“**O**kay, tell me one more time what's on for this afternoon?”

“Well Paul, the State is going to call both the medical examiner and the cop that investigated,” Jack replied. “I'm going to cross both of them when Jenson finishes.”

“Is there anything positive we can get out of either one of them?”

Bob said, “Nope.”

Paul smiled. “That seems overly pessimistic to me. Are you serious? Is there absolutely nothing we can draw from one of these guys that will help our case in some manner?”

“I am serious. No, they have nothing to offer that will help us. We just have to cross-examine them the best we can, take what they give us and get them off the stand. They will not help our case in any respect other than to reaffirm there wasn't an eye witness to the murder.”

Once again, came that dreaded knock on the door, which Bob had already come to despise.

After what had seemed an eternity of foundational questions designed by the Prosecutor to establish that Glen Majors was qualified to testify, they were now ready to proceed to the facts. Bob could already tell this case would take twice as long as it would have if someone else were trying it on behalf of the State. It appeared as though Jenson was going to try this case as if he had nothing else to do the rest of his earthly life.

“So, let me ask you—were you the investigating officer concerning the Baker murder?”

“I was, yes.”

“Were you one of the first on the scene?”

“Yes. I went as soon as her daughter called the station and said she had found her mother lying on the living room floor.”

“Tell us what you observed when you arrived.”

“The first thing I noticed was Ms. Baker lying on the floor. Her underwear—her panties, were lying on the floor away from her. She was naked from the waist down. Everything else in the living room seemed okay."

Was anyone else there when you arrived?"

"Just her daughter. One other officer had been there, but he left soon after I got there. The neighbor was standing outside the door of the home."

"What did you do then?"

"I covered her up. I then asked her daughter if she had any idea what had happened. She told me she didn't. She was terribly distraught. I had her go out on the enclosed porch, away from the scene. Before she left, I asked her if there were any cameras in or out of the house that might have filmed what happened."

"What did she tell you?"

"She said only on the outside of the home. I asked her if I could view them. She said I could."

"What did you determine from the video?"

"There were two cameras, but only one that was effective. It was the one in the front of the house. It showed the Defendant arriving midafternoon and leaving in a hurry, later in the day. He was the only one seen coming or going from the house during that time period."

"What did you do then?"

"The neighbor was standing there, and I visited with him for a moment."

"What did he have to say?"

Jack stood and said, "Hearsay, Your Honor. Let them call him as a witness if they wish."

"Sustained."

"Okay, based on information provided you by the neighbor, and based on the video, what did you do?"

"I arrested the Defendant and charged him with murder."

"When you arrested him and as he was booked, did you notice any unusual markings on his body?"

"Yes. He had a scratch on his arm. It was still red around the area, as if it had been recent."

"Did you talk to the bartender at the bar where he was arrested?"

"I did."

"Without going into the conversation with him, was his discussion part of the reason you arrested the Defendant?”

“Yes, it was.”

“Thank you, Officer Majors. You may cross-examine.”

Jack stood. “Thank you, Your Honor. Now, Officer, were any of the cameras within the house operational?”

“No.”

“So, no other individual was picked up by a camera inside the house committing this crime?”

“No sir.”

“And the outside camera in front only filmed him coming, then going, but no one else?”

“Yes.”

“Could someone have come in the house from some other entrance?”

“All of the windows were shut. They all had separate screens on them which, because of the makeup of the unit, would have been extremely difficult to replace. So, in my opinion, there was no way anyone could have gained entrance in that manner. The light was out in the back—it was pitch black in that area, so we couldn’t see anything concerning that entryway.”

“So, someone *could* have come through that doorway?”

“Maybe, but with all the other evidence we had, not likely.”

“That scratch on his arm could have come from something else other than her, couldn’t it?”

“Let’s just say the scratch was consistent with the other evidence we had. Yes, it could have come from some other source than her—but not likely.”

“The neighbor never saw what happened did he?”

“Nope.”

“No one saw what happened in that house that day, and certainly no one saw the Defendant murder Lynn Baker, did they?”

“No sir, that’s correct.”

“Nothing further.”

“Any redirect, Mr. Jensen?”

“Just one question. During the course of your entire investigation was there ever any indication of any nature, that someone else might have done this? Did you ever discover any physical evidence or have any indication someone else might have been involved in this crime?”

"No."

"Nothing further, Your Honor."

"This witness may step down. The State may call its next witness."

Bob knew the next witness would be the medical examiner. They had already discussed the fact that his testimony would not take long and the substance of his testimony would not necessitate any questions from Jack.

After extensive questioning concerning his qualifications to testify, Jenson said, "Did you recently have an opportunity to examine the body of one Lynn Baker?"

"Depends on your definition of 'recent' but yes, I did, yes."

"What were your observations?"

"You mean as to her cause of death?"

"Yes."

"She died of strangulation, same which occurred on the date in question. She had numerous scratch marks on her arms and upper body. It was clear from my examination she had been raped. Do you want to know about that too?"

"Yes, please continue."

"As I said, it was determined, because of a number of factors, that she, in my professional opinion, was raped. We did a test concerning DNA which came from her body. The DNA was that of the Defendant."

"Nothing further, Your Honor."

Jack stood and said, "How do you know she had been raped?"

"Hold on there, Mr. Raymond. Next time wait for me to give you the go ahead before you start your questioning. Now continue."

"Sorry, Judge. Sir, answer the question."

"To me, that was obvious. She was lying on the floor and there were numerous scratch marks on her upper body. Her underwear and pants were lying across the room. Again, it was my professional opinion, because of those factors, that she had been raped."

"You were able to uncover DNA that belonged to the Defendant, but not being there, you don't know that he raped her, do you? I mean they could have had consensual sex and someone else could have killed her, correct?"

"Not likely."

"But possible?"

"Unlikely—and that's all you're going to get out of me. Unlikely."

Jack sat and as he did, he said, "Nothing further, Your Honor."

A few minutes later they were sitting around the conference room, court having been adjourned for the day.

"So, I'm thinking that was not a very good day. Everyone else concur?"

Bob said, "I think I forewarned you that's how it was going to be, Paul. Tomorrow won't be much better, so just hang in. There are four witnesses tomorrow and none of them will help you. However, the good side of this is that they don't have any additional witnesses left, so they will probably rest after those four are done. Then it will be up to you and a couple of your friends to testify. But tomorrow will not be a positive day, I can assure you."

"Well, that would at least be consistent. I have had quite a few of those lately." He stood. "I'll see the three of you tomorrow. I'm ready to return to the sanctity of my cell."

Paul walked out of the room and Jack said, "He's losing hope. I don't blame him. I never had any from day one. We are in big trouble here, Bob. I guess we just press on, but I've never tried a case like this before—one that I knew I couldn't win before I started."

Bob stood. "Sorry I got you into this, Jack. Let's go have a drink and talk. Maybe when we are both about half-drunk, we can come up with something that might help."

As they walked out of the conference room door, Jack said, "Don't bank on it. We've already tried the liquor approach twice. Didn't work either time—doubt it's going to work this time either."

Chapter 29

The following morning, Jack and Bob walked in the conference room where they found only Carrie. She stood looking out the window, her back to the door. As she turned to see who had joined her, Bob could see she was crying.

He looked at Jack and said, "Take a walk."

"Excuse me. What the hell do you mean…"

Bob nodded toward Carrie. Jack took one look and said, "Got it. I'll be back in a few minutes."

Bob walked to her side and as he looked out the window, he said, "Everything okay?"

She wiped away the tears and said, "I guess."

"Are you concerned about Paul?"

She hesitated for a moment, then whispered, "Yes, I am."

"Have the two of you developed a relationship over the past weeks?"

"I guess so. I am somewhat confused about why or how this could have happened. I sure as hell didn't expect it to."

Bob smiled. "Sometimes that's just the way it works. We can't always plan our relationships and certainly, with Paul, with his history, how could you have ever planned this?"

"Leave it to me to fall in love with a guy who appears as though he's going to be convicted of murder. But you know, it just doesn't fit. I mean, that's not who he is. I know that from the short amount of time I've known him. He couldn't murder anyone if his life depended on it. Yet, here he is, and here…I …am."

She wiped away another tear, turned toward Bob and said, "Forget I said anything. I will be fine. I just…"

The door opened and Paul walked in.

"Morning. Where's Jack? Is he not coming today?"

Bob turned toward Carrie and whispered, "It will all work out. Believe me it will work out."

She smiled, then turned to continue looking out the window as Bob sat down by Paul and Jack walked back in the room.

"Are we all ready to go?"

There was a knock on the door as Bob said, "As ready as we will ever be."

Once all the foundational questions had been asked and answered, the Prosecutor said, "Now, Mr. Grand, you were a friend and an employee of the Defendant's, weren't you?"

"I was, yes. I've known him for about a year now."

"And what type of relationship did you have with him?"

"I worked for him in the landscaping business. I just did whatever he needed me to do whenever he wanted me to do it."

"Were you working for him last summer when Lynn Baker was murdered?"

"No. I had moved on by then. I had only been employed elsewhere a few weeks when I heard what had happened."

"During the time you worked for him, what can you tell us about the Defendant's temper?"

"Oh, under the right circumstances he could go kind of crazy and…"

"Objection, Your Honor. That question is improper. It's…"

"That's enough Mr. Jones. I agree."

While the Judge indicated to the jury the question was inappropriate and they shouldn't consider either the question or the resulting answer, Bob knew it was impossible for them to forget. Without doubt, they would consider the answer. The objection just wasn't made quickly enough.

"Let me ask you this sir, did he ever discuss his relationship with Lynn Baker?"

"Yes, many times."

"In what respect?"

"Well, near the time I quit, his conversation changed. Before, he was excited about her, about their relationship. But near the time she was killed, it changed. He didn't talk about it much and when he did it seemed to upset him. He said all she would talk about was him moving in and them getting married. That seemed to really upset him the longer it went on."

"When you say 'upset' him, what do you mean?"

"He would just say he was getting really tired of it and had reached the point he had even considered breaking off the whole relationship."

"So obviously the nature of the relationship had changed over the last few weeks prior to her murder?"

"Yes, considerably. The discussion we had about his involvement with her changed from excited, to him just becoming really frustrated with it all and considering ending it."

"Nothing further, Your Honor."

"Any questions, Mr. Raymond?"

Jack stood and said, "Yes, a few. Did he ever talk about killing her?"

The witness smiled and said, "No sir, he didn't."

"Did he ever talk about harming her in any way?"

"No sir."

"Did you ever see him, while you worked for him, hurt or harm a sole?"

"No sir."

"Were you shocked when he was charged with her murder?"

"Certainly."

"Why is that?"

"Well, because it wasn't something I would have expected him to do."

"Nothing further."

"Any redirect, Mr. Jensen?"

"No, Your Honor."

"Please step down, Mr. Grand. Next witness."

"The State would call Jim Arnett to come forward and be sworn."

Once the witness had taken the stand and answered all foundational questions, Mr. Jensen said, "Now, sir, it is my understanding you live next door to the home of the victim Lynn Baker, is that correct?"

Bob considered Mr. Arnett's age—the witness was clearly as old as he was, if not older. He made a good appearance. He was sharply dressed and appeared believable as he answered the Prosecutor's basic foundational questions prior to quizzing him about the specifics of the case.

"Now sir, do you still remember the day in question?"

Mr. Arnett smiled and said, "You mean because of my advanced age? Do you mean because people my age forget mighty quick?"

The jury laughed, as Mr. Jenson smiled and said, "No, not really. It's just a standard question I use with each of my witnesses to start with. Now, do you remember that day?"

"Like it was yesterday, yes I do."

"Please, tell us what you observed concerning the Defendant and concerning that day."

"Well, it was real late in the afternoon, I had opened my windows that face the Baker home. It was a nice day out, and I wanted a little fresh air in the house. It's only me in the house now, since my wife's death last year, so now it's up to me to do them things. As I sat back down, I heard a bunch of yelling coming through that window, so I walked over to see where it was coming from."

"Were you able to determine the source of the commotion?"

"Yes. It was coming from next door—from the Baker house."

"Could you hear the specifics of the conversation?"

"No. I could just hear the yelling that was going on—just the yelling but nothing specific. I knew whoever was involved was mighty upset, that was pretty clear."

"What happened next?"

"Well, I just sat back down, and I heard Lynn's front door slam shut. I stood up and walked to my window and I noticed that man there,". he pointed to Paul, "leaving the house in a hurry. I mean, he wasn't on the dead run, but he was moving at a rapid walk. He got in his pickup and drove away… quickly. Now, that don't mean he left in a reckless manner, nor nothin' like that, but he left in his truck pretty darn quick."

"Any doubt about your identification of the individual leaving the house that day?"

"None." He pointed at Paul. "That's him."

"Did you know him? I mean, have you met him before?"

"Yes. Lynn introduced us and I have said 'hello' to him many times since then."

"Judge, I have nothing further."

"You may cross, Mr. Raymond."

Jack stood and said, "Did you see or hear from Lynn Baker after that moment?"

"No."

"I assume you saw no one else enter or leave the house after that?"

"No."

"About what time did you hear him leave?"

"It was late afternoon…early evening maybe."

"Nothing further."

"Redirect, Mr. Jenson?"

"No, Your Honor."

"Sir, you may step down. Let's take our noon recess and then resume at one. Again, jurors do not talk about this case with anyone."

Once in the conference room, Carrie went to get sandwiches for everyone while the remaining three discussed the mornings testimony. Once they had finished eating, court resumed, with the first witness…Joe Bond…taking the stand.

After the witness had been sworn in, and all the general foundational questions had been asked and answered, Mr. Jenson said, "Now sir, you have already indicated you are a bartender at the Riverside Bar and Grill, and have been for some time, correct?"

"Yes."

"Do you know the Defendant, Paul Duncan?"

"Yes."

"How do you know him?"

"He's a frequent customer and has been for years."

"Do you remember the day Lynn Baker was murdered?"

"Yes."

"Were you working that day?'

"Yes. I worked from about four until midnight."

"Did you have occasion to see the Defendant, Paul Duncan that day?"

"Yes."

"Tell us about it."

"Well, he came in around seven and stayed…well, he stayed until he was arrested."

"Did you notice anything out of the ordinary that night, as concerned his demeanor?"

"Yes. He was agitated, upset, out of sorts, so to speak."

"Did he visit with you concerning the source of his agitation?"

"Yes. He said he had just come from Lynn's, and he was getting, in his words, 'goddamn tired of her marriage talk', Those were his words, not mine."

"Did he discuss that subject again before he was arrested?"

"Yes. That was all he talked about the whole time he was there. He was upset and it showed."

"Did you notice anything about his physical appearance?"

"Yes. His hair was all kind of messed up. And I noticed a big scratch on his arm. He had on a short-sleeved shirt, and it was a long scratch, red all around it. I wouldn't have noticed it under most circumstances, but he was there a long time and there was little else going on that night. So, I spent more time with him discussing his relationship with Lynn, and other matters, than I normally would— which is why I happened to notice the scratch."

"Nothing further, Your Honor."

"Cross-examine Mr. Raymond?"

"Yes, Your Honor. Mr. Bond, he never mentioned he killed anyone did he?"

"No. But he did say it got physical. I finally asked him about the scratch. He just said 'she's a fighter—it got a little physical.'"

"Nothing further."

"Redirect?"

"None, Your Honor."

"Ladies and Gentlemen of the jury, we are going to conclude testimony for today so myself and the attorneys can work on the instructions to the jury which we will use when the case is finally submitted to you. I'll see you at nine tomorrow, and we will proceed from there. Do *not* discuss the case with anyone."

Once back in the conference room, Bob said, "Paul we need to work with the Judge and Jensen on instructions. We are done for today. I expect tomorrow morning the State will rest. Your witnesses are scheduled to be here tomorrow and I doubt any of them will take much time to testify. I wouldn't be surprised if we might be ready to finish presenting our side of the case by late tomorrow afternoon."

"So, what did you think about what happened today?"

"I think it went as we expected it to. There were no surprises."

Paul smiled. "Pops, I'm not thinking that was a very positive comment. Was it that bad?"

"It went as expected. We'll give them your rendition of what happed tomorrow and then just keep our fingers crossed. I'll plan on seeing you here, tomorrow morning."

Chapter 30

Bob looked down upon the street below. Everyone was scurrying to get out of the cold winter air that was atypical for Knoxville, even during the winter months. He hurried through the front door of the courthouse earlier this morning, so he knew exactly how those walking on the sidewalks felt.

Bob turned to look at his three roommates and could feel the pressure that existed within each one. It filled the room and rightfully so. The previous few days had been difficult, to say the least. While today they would present evidence favorable to Paul, he was afraid their evidence was not nearly as persuasive as what they had already heard from the State's witnesses.

"Bob, what do you think…"

The knock on the door came midsentence. Jack stood and said, "Let's go. Time for us to present a little evidence of our own."

Doug Randolph presented a fairly unimpressive appearance. He was the first of two of Paul's friends, presented to the jury on behalf of the Defense. His hair was long enough to braid, and his cloths appeared to have been removed from a dumpster just prior to his appearance in the courtroom.

Once all of his foundational questions had been answered, Bob asked, "How long have you known the Defendant, Paul Duncan?"

"A couple of years, I guess."

"How do you know him?"

"I worked for him for about 18 months, and when I went on to another job, we remained in touch—we remained friends."

"How would you describe his demeanor? What stood out to you as far as his personality is concerned when you were around him?"

"He was a great boss. Really fair—about everything. He was fun to be around, and overall, he was easy to work for. After I quit working for him, we would meet up a couple of times a week and have a few beers together, just to talk about our lives, our jobs, different things."

"Were you aware of his relationship with Lynn Baker?"

"Yes."

"Were you aware that each of them seemed to have a different idea concerning the nature of the relationship?"

"Yes. She, from early on, wanted to get married—he didn't."

"What type of emotion did that seem to generate in Paul, if any?"

"He was dead set against marriage. He wanted to have a relationship with her, but not marry her."

"Did you ever observe him to lose his temper concerning this issue, or express any ill will toward her because of her thoughts of marriage?"

"Absolutely not. He just wasn't going to marry her, plain and simple. He wasn't mad, he wasn't upset, he just wasn't going to go down that path with her."

"Thank you. Nothing further."

"Any questions from the State?"

"Just one or two. When was the last time you saw Paul prior to the death of Lynn Baker, if you recall?"

"Probably a couple of weeks or so."

"Was there any discussion about their relationship then?"

"I don't remember."

"Do you have any idea what went on in that house the day she was murdered?"

"Nope."

"So, as far as you know, he killed her, correct?"

"Objection."

"Overruled. Answer the question."

He looked at Paul, then at the DA, finally answering, "Well, I suppose he could have, but there was no way..."

"Thank you. Nothing further."

"Redirect, Mr. Duncan?"

"No, Your Honor. We would call Rod McNamara to the stand."

As the witness was answering all the preliminary foundational questions, Bob couldn't help but notice how much of a difference the two prior witnesses presented in appearance. While the first witness presented a very poor general appearance, this witness was dressed in a suit and could very well have been mistaken for one of the attorneys involved in the proceedings.

"Mr. McNamara tell us your occupation."

"Banker. I work here in Knoxville at First National. I'm a loan officer with the bank."

"Are you acquainted with the defendant, Mr. Duncan?"

"Yes, I am."

"How?"

"Well, I have loaned him a little money, so I know him on a professional basis, and I know him socially."

"Okay, let's take those categories one at a time. You loaned him money through the bank?"

"Yes. When he first came to town, he needed a little money to get started and I loaned it to him. Then later, he wanted to expand and I loaned him additional funds."

"Has he ever missed a payment?"

"No. He paid off everything he owed us. He doesn't owe us a cent, and I can tell you I wouldn't hesitate to loan him whatever he needs…within reason of course. His payment record with us is perfect."

"How do you know him socially?"

"I've had a few parties at our home when both he and Lynn were there. Both were invited, and they came with each other."

"Would you consider him a friend?"

"Absolutely."

"So, would you say there were numerous times when you were around the two of them together?"

"Yes."

"What did you observe about their relationship?"

"Objection, Your Honor. What relevance does that have to anything? What difference does it make what he observed about their relationship at some point in time prior to her murder? This is all irrelevant."

Judge Strayer thought for a moment, then said, "I think the relationship between the Defendant and the woman he allegedly killed *is* relevant. I'll allow it. Please continue."

The witness smiled, as he said, "They were a fun couple to be around. He made her laugh, and believe me they laughed a lot. She was a few years older than him. She had come out of a disaster of a marriage and was looking not only for someone that was easy to be around, which he was, but it was also pretty obvious she was looking for a husband. He wasn't looking for a wife, and that did create a few issues. But the great majority of time, they were so much fun to be around. I just couldn't believe he had been charged with her murder. That is so far removed from what I observed about him as to literally be absurd."

"Did they argue about the marriage issue?"

"No, not while they were with us. She would throw out little hints about it. He would make a joke about what she said and they would move on. There was never one time, in all the time we spent with them, either one lost their temper. And to even consider him killing her, is just way beyond the Paul we know."

"Nothing further, Your Honor."

"Questions, Mr. Jensen?"

"Did he ever tell you what went on in that house the day she was murdered?"

"No."

"And you weren't there were you?"

"Nope."

"Nothing further."

"Call your next witness."

"We would call John Reed to the stand."

Once Mr. Reed was sworn and had answered some elementary, foundational questions, Bob said, "How long have you lived in Knoxville, John?"

"All my life."

"And as I understand it from your answers to my prior foundational questions, you do odd jobs around town, is that correct?"

"Yes. I've worked up a good clientele doing just that, of which Lynn Baker was one."

"How long did you work for her?"

"Probably the last eight to ten years."

"Did you have a good relationship with her?"

"The best. She was a good woman, and we got along well."

"Do you know the Defendant, Paul Duncan?"

"Yes. I didn't know him before he came to work for Ms. Baker, but I got to know him then."

"Were you friends?"

"Yes. We never saw each other off the job, but when we were both at Lynn's house at the same time working on something, we got along really well."

"What did you do for her?"

"If she needed some carpentry work done, or electrical work done, I would do it. I handled all those kinds of things for her."

"Looks like you work out a little, so I assume anything that involved physical strength that Lynn couldn't handle, you could, correct?"

"Yes. Whatever she needed me to do, I did. There was never a job she asked me to do I couldn't handle—other than the yard work. I don't handle that kind of work, and that's where Paul came in."

"What was your relationship with him?"

"We got to know each other through work. I never really saw him anywhere else."

"How was he to work with?"

"The best. He was easy to get along with, and his word was always, always good."

"Did you know about the relationship between he and Lynn?"

"Well, yes, it eventually became pretty obvious something was going on. They didn't try to hide it."

"Did you ever see him loose his temper around her, or vice-versa?"

"No. Now I heard them discussing that marriage issue once, and while they weren't arguing, it was a pretty strong discussion. You could tell they weren't on the same page."

"Anything come of that?"

He laughed, and said, "I happened to walk inside after it sounded like the discussion was over. He was kissing her. Lynn was a little embarrassed. Actually, it was kind of funny and a little touching to be honest. They fought, they made up, end of story."

"What was your reaction when you heard he was charged with her murder?"

Mr. Reed leaned forward in his chair, looked at Bob and said, "There's no way in hell he could have done what they say he did. Absolutely no way."

"Nothing further, Your Honor."

"Cross."

"Were you there the day she was murdered?"

"No."

"So, you have absolutely no idea what happened in that house that day do you?"

"No sir, I don't, but I know one thing that *didn't* happen—he didn't…"

"Stop right there. You already answered my question. Nothing further, Your Honor."

"Redirect?"

"No, Your Honor."

"Okay, ladies and gentlemen of the jury, we are going to recess until tomorrow morning at nine. Do not discuss the case with anyone. Court is adjourned."

Once they were back in the conference room, Paul looked at Bob, smiled and said, "You did good, Pops. You really made some good points."

"It is all up to you tomorrow morning, Paul. You can't lose your temper. You need to keep yourself under control. Don't yell at the Prosecutor. Remain completely under control or all the good we might have done today will go right out the window. We will see you here tomorrow morning."

Chapter 31

The courtroom remained deadly quiet while Paul Duncan continued to answer basic foundational questions prior to his testimony specifically pertaining to the day Lynn Baker was murdered.

Once Bob had finished with the basics, he took a deep breath and said, "Now Paul, tell the jury how you ended up in Knoxville."

The witness was dressed in a suit, clean shaven, hair combed. His physical appearance was impeccable, but Bob knew what Paul was thinking. He just hoped he could stop Paul from telling everyone what he *really* thought about this whole process before he finished with his testimony.

"I came here a few years ago from Kentucky. I considered moving to a number of different cities, but I just thought Knoxville was as good a place as any to make a living. I had not finished getting my GED. I figured when I did finish, I could continue my schooling right here at the university."

"Did you eventually get your GED here?"

"Yes. My next step was college. That is, until this happened."

"How did you meet Lynn?"

"She saw an ad which I placed in the paper and she gave me a call. I agreed to meet with her. Once we met and I found out what she needed me to do, I started working for her and continued to work for her, until…until she was no longer with us."

"How often would you go to her home?"

"About twice a week at first. Then after we started seeing each other romantically, we saw each other nearly every day, depending on both of our schedules."

"Did you ever argue?"

"Very seldom;"

"How long had you been romantically involved before she died?"

"Almost as long as I have lived here. She was one of my first customers."

"Amongst other things, did you travel together?"

He smiled. "We did almost everything together. We were in touch with each other an average of five or six days a week. I made an effort to visit with her every day over the phone if, for some reason or another we couldn't get together. The day just didn't feel right for me when we didn't have a chance to touch base with each other."

"Did you ever discuss marriage?"

"She did—I didn't. She would be the one to bring it up and if she did, normally it was a one-way conversation."

"Let's talk about the day in question. What was your situation that day—did you have to work or were you off? Tell the jury about that day, as best you remember."

"It was Saturday. Yes, I had to work that morning. We planned on getting together later that afternoon, maybe going out to eat that evening or going to a movie."

"Did everything work out as planned?"

"Up until late that afternoon it did. Then nothing worked out very well."

"So, you got there at about what time?"

"Around three."

"What happened then?"

"We talked, we had a couple of drinks, and later, maybe around five-fifteen, to five-thirty, we..." He looked down for a moment before he said, "We made love."

"Where at Paul? Where did that take place?"

"In the living room of her home."

"What happened then?"

"Once we were done, we were just sitting there having a beer and watching the news when she brought up this marriage issue again."

"Had she brought it up earlier that day?"

"Not that day, but recently she had brought it up a number of times."

"What had your response been to her thoughts about getting married?"

"I wasn't ready. I told her that a number of times. Most of the time she would just drop it when she could tell I wasn't interested in discussing it. A few of those times, we argued briefly about it, but that night, she was really wanting to push me into agreeing with her. I wasn't any more interested that night than I was any other night. I just wasn't ready."

"What happened then?"

"She started yelling at me. She had never done that before. I just decided I had had enough. I stood to go, thinking that might stop the discussion, but she just went on and on."

"So, I said, 'See you later. I need to go.' As I turned to leave, she tried to grab my arm. She had these long fingernails, and she didn't quite grab hold of me, but she did scratch my arm. It hurt. I quickly pulled away, and said, 'That's the last time that's going to happen, and that's a promise.' That was the last thing…I ever…said to her."

He looked away. When he reengaged in the conversation, he said, "I regret that situation more than anything I've ever done. The words we said and the way I left…I just wish we could do that all over again. I wish…"

"Did you go ahead and leave then?"

"Yes. I went to the bar and stayed until they came and picked me up."

"You could have driven a lot further than the bar if you had killed her, isn't that correct?"

"Yes. *If* I had killed her, I could have put a lot of miles between Knoxville and me before anyone ever found her. I would have been long gone if I had killed her."

"But instead, you stayed—you were setting on the same barstool when they came to arrest you, as you were when you arrived at the bar, correct?"

"Yes."

Bob hesitated a moment, took a deep breath and said, "Did you kill her?"

"No, I didn't. And I have no idea who did. She had many, many friends and not one enemy that I know of."

"Nothing further."

"Mr. Jensen, you may cross."

"Thank you, Judge. I have only a few questions. Now, let me get this straight. You were in the Baker home late afternoon and early evening on the day she died, right?"

"Correct."

"You had sex and then argued, correct?"

"Yes, that's correct."

"Your argument resulted in the scratch on your arm which she caused, correct?"

"Yes."

"So, all the factors pointing to your guilt are all correct with the exception of the fact that you killed her?"

"Well, I guess you could look at it that way."

"There's no question but what you were involved in a disagreement, concerning the same subject matter you had argued about time after time, right?"

"Yes."

"Did you just get tired of arguing with her—just get fed up with it all, did you?"

"Well, sure I was tired of it, but not tired enough to..."

"Did you go to the house that night with the idea in mind that if she brought the subject up again, you would shut her mouth once and for all?"

"Hell no, I didn't go there with that in mind. I never even thought..."

"You ever beat up any of your other women?"

Immediately, Bob stood.

Paul also stood, as he yelled, "What the hell are you talking about? I never beat up anyone. What are you..."

Bob said, "Paul, wait now, let me handle this. Sit down."

"But he can't get away with..."

"Sir, you do as your attorney says, or I'm going to find you in contempt and let you watch what's going on with a monitor in another room. Now, you sit!"

Paul looked at the Judge, turned toward Bob and said, "Okay, okay, I'm sitting down, but..."

As he sat, Bob said, "I would ask the court to strike the question concerning 'other women' and ask you to admonish the jury not to consider the question or my client's explosive reaction to such an unsubstantiated, improper question."

"I agree, council. The jury is hereby admonished not to consider the last question asked by the State, nor the response by the Defendant. Anything else, Mr. Duncan?"

"No, Your Honor, that's enough for me."

"Now are there any further questions on redirect?"

"Just a couple. Sir, have you ever been in trouble with the law concerning an assault of any kind involving any person, male or female?"

"No. I've never been in a physical fight with anyone, nor have I ever been charged."

"And once again, did you have anything to do with the death of Lynn Baker?"

Paul looked away for a moment, remaining quiet. When he looked in Bob's direction he said softly, "No, I didn't."

The morning session ended with Paul's testimony. The Defense had no more witnesses and the State declined to call anyone else for rebuttal. Bob figured that was because Jensen most likely figured they already had the case won—why take a chance with testimony from additional witnesses.

Back in the conference room, once they were seated, Paul said, "I screwed that up didn't I, Pops?"

"You did fine, Paul. I don't think anyone's going to condemn you for getting upset about the question you were asked. That was improper and the Judge made that pretty clear."

"So, what do you think?"

"I think you did a great job, as did your witnesses. Jack what are your thoughts?"

"To be honest, I'm not sure it could have gone much better. Paul, you told your side of the story, you got it all in the record, and it was believable. We couldn't ask for much more than that. Really, the rest is just up to the jury."

Bob said, "Carrie, would you mind going to get us a few sandwiches. We may as well all eat together before they take Paul back to his cell."

As she left the room, Paul said, "What are you guys going to do now? As I recall, you said after lunch, you were going to work on jury instructions, correct?"

"Yes. Probably a couple of hours will be spent on that I imagine. Then I need to work on my closing tomorrow."

"What are these instructions you talk about?"

"They are a list of a different rules the jury is to follow when deliberating. The Judge has already prepared them for us to review. Jack and I need to basically discuss them and make sure they are fair and that they explain adequately the law to the jurors as it applies to this case. We may want to amend or tweak one or two and we need to go through all that with the Judge this afternoon. He will read them to the jury right before we present our closing statements."

"When will that be?"

"Most likely tomorrow morning."

"And then they deliberate?"

"Yes?"

"How long do they deliberate?"

"Until they reach a unanimous conclusion or it's obvious, they are a hung jury and can't decide one way or the other."

"So, tomorrow morning this will most likely all be submitted to the jury and we start the waiting game, right?"

"That's correct. Hopefully, the wait will be well worth it, Paul."

Chapter 32

They sat in silence, waiting for a knock on the door which would signal the beginning of the final day.

"So, Pops, what are your thoughts? Are you happy with the way this all turned out? Did it all work out as you thought it would?"

"You know, the expert in this area of the law is him." He nodded at Jack. "What are your thoughts?"

"My thoughts are that we wouldn't be here in the first place if the Prosecutor's office thought they had a bad case. So, that gives you some idea what *they* were thinking when it all began. And I'm sure there has been nothing that has really happened since this trial started that has caused him to change his mind. To be honest, it appeared to me to be a tough case for us to win when we started, and nothing has happened to change my opinion. There has been no witness for us that have come forward and said 'I *know* he didn't do it *because*'…and that is exactly what we needed. I'm not saying all hope is lost, but not much has changed since our initial assessment of the case. The facts are as we always thought they would be."

"That's not very encouraging."

"Well, Paul, you asked, I responded. That's not saying we can't win. I just think we need to keep pushing and hope for the best."

"I know what happens if they find me not guilty, but what's the process if they find me guilty?"

An unexpected comment from Carrie drew all the attention, as she said, "Nope, not going there,"

She shook her head as she said, "We don't need to think about that at this point in time and we are *not* going there—not unless it actually does turn out for the worst. If it doesn't turn out well, there will be plenty of time to discuss the repercussions."

Paul smiled as he said, "I understand and I agree, but I just wanted to…"

"We are not going down that negative road at this point, Paul." She reached out and took his hand. "There will be time to discuss those issues if the worst happens. Today, it's all positive, period."

Bob smiled and said, "I agree. Now, one of the things…"

They all turned toward the door as the knock indicated the Judge was ready.

For over an hour they listened to Judge Strayer read the jury instructions to the jurors. Both parties had been given their opportunity to object to any of the instructions the Judge proposed. That process had been completed yesterday morning. So now, there was not a sound in the room while the instructions were being read—only the Judge's dull, monotone… for nearly an hour.

Once completed, the Judge told Jensen to go ahead with his closing statement, which he did—for nearly two hours. Near the end of his rambling, repetitive oratory, Bob leaned toward Jack who was seated next to him, and whispered, "I hope the jury doesn't base their verdict on length of closing remarks. If they do, we lose, hands down. My closing, pursuant to your advice, was to remain short and sweet. I have kept it that way."

Once the Prosecutor had concluded his remarks, the Judge took a fifteen-minute break.

They had only just sat down in the conference room and started to discuss Jenson's comments, when the bailiff indicated the Judge was ready to proceed.

Once seated, the Judge said, "Is the Defendant ready to present his closing statement?"

Bob stood, and said, "We are, Your Honor."

"Proceed."

Bob picked up one page of his copy of the jury instructions and walked to the front of the jury box.

"First of all, I want to thank all of you for being here, for performing your civic duty. It's hard to do—it is tough to break away from all you do on a daily basis and come here to do this. But you are appreciated. Again, thank you. I will be brief. My comments will not take up much of your time today."

"Now let's start out by determining what we can all agree on— what facts appear to be uncontroverted by either the State or the Defense."

"First of all, there is no doubt the Defendant and Lynn Baker were involved in a relationship. Of that, no one disagrees."

"Next, there is no question about the fact that Lynn wanted to get married—and the Defendant didn't. Certainly no one disputes that issue."

"No one could dispute the fact that the Defendant has never been in trouble before. Not one witness testified they were aware of any negative issues involving law enforcement and Paul."

"There is no doubt they were together that day. Nobody disputes that fact either."

He started to walk toward the end of the jury box as he said, "No one disputes the fact that she wanted to marry and he didn't. That had been the situation for apparently quite some time and everybody knew it."

"We have all been told there was a gap in time between the time this murder took place and the time the Defendant was arrested, as he sat quietly having a beer in one of the local bars. Nobody disputes that."

"There's no doubt he had a scratch on his arm. No one disputes it was there, or where it came from."

"Nobody disputes the fact that they had sex that day, late that afternoon. That was testified to by Paul."

"Nobody disagrees with the fact he worked for her and had for some time. That is agreed upon by everyone."

"He was in love with her. Everybody that knew them said the same thing."

"So, what is left? The only disagreement or dispute we have to consider is one single solitary issue—did he murder her. None of the other issues concerning their relationship or the facts of this case are at issue. There is absolutely nothing else to consider. So, let's discuss that issue and that issue alone, since there is no disagreement concerning all the other factors."

"First of all, I would point out the Defendant has been charged with first degree *premedicated* murder. That charge is absolutely *ridicules*. There is no evidence, *none,* that he went to her house that day to kill her or that he formed that intent while with her that day. You can dismiss any thoughts of that being the case, and I'm not even going to waste your time discussing it. That charge was, from day one, never even an issue."

"But, as you know from the instructions, you could find the Defendant guilty of murder in the second degree, which is murder that was *not* premedicated, as a lessor included offense, so let's discuss that charge. "

"There was no discussion at all about the Defendant's propensity for violence. Not one witness testified they had *ever* heard him raise his voice. Does someone just commit a murder like this without giving some indication of his propensity for violence—just out of the blue you murder someone? I mean, he has never been accused of assaulting someone, or losing his temper with a customer, or raising his fist in anger—*nothing. Nothing at all.* Then, out of the blue he murders the woman he is having a relationship with. That doesn't even make sense. You heard about this man's character, and there wasn't one word about him having a violent bone in his body."

"The only other charge the Judge will tell you to consider is manslaughter. And again, to find him guilty of any of the charges, you *still* must find that he took her life. And, here we are again—could he kill another living sole? Our response, as it has been from day one, is *absolutely not.*"

"Now, we know this marriage issue came up frequently between the two of them. How did they handle it—they discussed it and let it go. *Every time.* There was never a time when either became violent toward the other. They discussed the issue, maybe raised their voice a time or two, *but never* any violence of any kind."

"Consider his actions after he left her house. Were those actions consistent with someone who just committed his first crime and not only committed a crime, but committed a *murder? Immediately after committing his first murder, he simply goes to a bar he frequented many times and sat there until they arrested him?"*

"Now come on folks, use your own common sense here. You murder someone, then you sit and wait quietly for the police to come and pick you up? I know I wouldn't. I'd run like hell and never look back."

"Okay here's the bottom line, folks. You need to read instruction ten—the one I'm holding in my hand—really, really well. It provides that to find the Defendant guilty, the State had to establish his guilt *beyond a reasonable doubt.* That's the part of all these instructions that is critical—the phrase 'beyond a reasonable doubt.' That phrase is defined in the instructions, but to paraphrase it in just a few words, it means you must be *sure* he *is* guilty before you *find* him guilty. There's no guessing here, folks. And there's no '*do over.'* You must get this right the first time. You need to make sure each and every factor for finding him guilty is there, and if one isn't—if there is just *one* of those elements missing, you must find him not guilty."

Bob leaned on the railing separating the jurors from the rest of the courtroom.

"You see, Ladies and Gentlemen of the jury, there's a huge problem with the State's case. As he sat in this courtroom on day one and every day since then, he's not guilty. And at no point in time since he was charged, has the State ever established beyond a reasonable doubt he ever did anything wrong. Oh, they had plenty of facts to present to you, which they did, but the one major fact they couldn't produce, was the fact *proving* Paul Duncan murdered Lynn Baker. There's a good reason why they didn't—*because they had no facts proving he did.*"

Bob turned, walked to the council table and just before he sat, he said, "Ladies and gentlemen of the jury, we would ask you to find Paul Duncan not guilty. Thank you."

A few minutes later, they walked back into the conference room and as they did, Paul walked up to Bob and embraced him.

As he began to pull away, Bob said, "What was that for?"

"For believing in me, in who I am. Believing that I could never hurt anyone, let alone kill someone. Thank you for all you've done, regardless of the results."

There was a knock on the door and a law enforcement office walked in to return Paul to his cell.

As they walked away, Bob said, "I'll keep you informed, Paul. I'll let you know what's going on."

As the law enforcement officer closed the door behind him, Jack looked at Bob and said, "You did really well, Bob. Obviously, you can only argue what we have. You can't make up the facts. What do you think?"

"Want the truth?"

"Certainly."

"I think we're screwed."

Chapter 33

Once they had packed the car with all the items they had brought with them, Jack and Bob left Knoxville for Nashville. It would take time for the jury to settle in. They had no doubt a verdict would not be rendered this afternoon. Both would return early tomorrow morning and remain until the jury came to a conclusion or were unable to unanimously agree.

As they reached the interstate, Jack said, "Were you serious? Do you think we are in trouble? You think they will find him guilty of premediated murder?"

"Not really. At least, I hope not. As I told the jury and as you and I have discussed, there is just no evidence to support that charge. I think they would have to be angry with Paul about something that he said or did during the trial, for them to reach that conclusion. They all looked like they were listening and attentive today—no one appeared angry or distraught as I presented the closing. No, I don't think that charge has a chance. But I'm really afraid that they may find him guilty of one of the lesser included offences. What are your conclusions?"

Jack turned away for a moment, clearly deep in thought.

He took a deep breath, and quietly said, "Honestly, I'm afraid you may be right. I really believe they will find him guilty…I'm just not sure of which offense. I only pray to God it's not murder. We just didn't have a witness that could effectively address all the circumstantial evidence they had."

Bob looked at Jack and said, "By the way, you know your breath really stinks. Would you mind riding in the back seat. Good God!"

Jack said nothing, electing to sit in silence.

Bob eventually turned toward him and said, "What—no cutting, repulsive remark about me, my demeanor, my clothes—nothing?"

"I don't feel all that well. I have nothing to throw back at you today. But I'll make up for it later."

"That's a little unusual for you. Are you getting the flu?"

"I don't know. I'm going to the doctor later this afternoon. I'll see what he says." He turned toward Bob and said, "So, I suppose you will be going to see Susan tonight?"

"I might, Jack. I just might."

"So, how is everything going, Charlene? It seems like I've been gone forever. I suppose all of our clients are upset with me because I'm gone so much.

Charlene sat down in front of Bob's desk, and said, "You had a lot of calls. I put the messages there, on your desk. Most of them want you to return their call as soon as you can. You know, the Robert's case is set for trial next week. Are you going to be here?"

He put the messages he held in his hand, down on the desk and leaned back in his chair.

"Probably not. Better call Charlie Bradway and tell him I want a continuance. He owes me. He won't argue with you about it. Tell him to have it rescheduled sometime within the next month if he can, and then call whatshername, our client, and tell her it's been continued."

Charlene sat back and said, "You know I've had to continue a hell of a lot of hearings since you've been going to Knoxville. Do you want me to start turning prospective clients away?"

"Not really. Not yet anyway. I've decided I'm not quite ready to retire. I want to work a while longer. I am not sure how I want to structure it. But don't encourage anyone if they don't want to wait for me. Just let them go elsewhere."

He smiled, as he said, "You know, for the first time in quite a while I have family to think about. I like it. I am going to wait and see how this trial turns out and make all my permanent plans after it is over—after I know the outcome. So just do the best you can to keep everyone happy. I'll handle them and everyone else we have as clients, present and future, when I get a final verdict in Paul's case."

"Are you going back tomorrow morning?"

"Yes. I'll let you know when I'm coming home, but I know I won't be back before we get a verdict."

She stood, and smiled. "Are you going to see Susan tonight?'

"I am, yes. We are meeting for supper."

"Just so you know, she's called every day since you have been away."

"I'm not real sure how everything is going to work out tonight, but hopefully we will still at least be friends once the evening ends."

He terminated a telephone call, just as she walked in the front door. As she approached the table, he stood.

Before she sat, she kissed him on the cheek, and said, "You've been gone a long time."

He smiled as he sat, and said, "Not really. I mean, it seems long to me too, but it's only been a week or so."

"True. I guess it just seemed like a long time. I saw you on your phone when I walked in. Is everything okay with Paul?"

"Actually, that was Jack. When I left him today, he said he wasn't feeling well. I was just checking up on him."

"Is there a problem?"

"No, I guess not. He said he was feeling a lot better."

"You two are really close, aren't you?"

"Like brothers. In spite of all his idiosyncrasies and all I have to endure while virtually living with him in Knoxville, he's without doubt the best friend I have ever had. He would do anything for you—whatever you need him to do, he's always there. Would you like something to drink?"

"Yes. Whatever it is you are having is fine. I called the office about every day while you were gone, just to see how everything was going. What is your take concerning the trial, at this point in time?" She reached out and put her hand over his. "And, when are you coming home to stay?"

"Well, the trial is over. We gave closing statements this morning, and the jury started to deliberate near noon. I heard nothing from anyone this afternoon, and I'm sure by now they have all been sent home for the evening."

"So how did you feel it went—winner or loser?"

The waiter set her glass of wine down, as he said, "I am really not sure. I just don't know. The State got all their witnesses' testimony into evidence and so did we. They will never get a conviction for premeditated murder based on what they presented, but I think they anticipated that. I think they overcharged him on purpose anticipating the jury would just say that charge isn't going to work, but then compromise using one of the lesser included offenses, which they can do."

"I know you were worried about Paul testifying. How did he get along?"

"Actually, he did well. He lost his temper one time, but it was definitely for good reason. The question that generated his outburst was way out of line, and the Judge took care of it. I was proud of the way Paul handled himself and I told him so."

"Have you two bonded at all while all of this has been going on?"

The waiter approached the table to take their order. Bob waived him off indicating they needed a few more minutes.

"Yes, we have, we really have. He reminds me so much of my son. He is really a good kid. I hate to say it, but trying to raise him the same way I raised his father, was wrong. If I knew then what I know now, I would have changed my approach while raising him and maybe he wouldn't have run away."

"So, what's the situation with the two of you now? What is your overall plan as concerns Paul?"

"We have none. This verdict will dictate our future. If he is found not guilty, hopefully I can get him to follow me back here. If he's found guilty, I don't know what I'll do. The future, in that respect, is completely up in the air."

She smiled as she said, "And now for your final question of the night, where are you and I? Are we hanging there, 'up in the air' too?"

"You know, I love that about you. Right to the point. No messing around." He took a drink of his wine without taking his eyes off her.

"You're not getting by that easy. That was a nice compliment... I think, but I want an answer...please."

"Well, then I guess yes, we are probably up in the air too. I can't promise anything, Susan. I know I love being with you. I know there is no one I would rather be with." He smiled "And that includes Jack. I know this is the first time I have had family, other than my wife, for a long, long time. I think I need to get through the next few weeks with Paul. I need to just wait it out and see what happens with him, before I plan for my future—for *our* future. I promise as soon as this trial is over and Paul's future is clear, we will sit down and talk about life—about you and I. Just give me a little more time—please."

She smiled, and said, "You know, you are worth the wait. I'll give you the time you need to figure out what's happening with your grandson. But I can guarantee you once that trial has finished up, I'll be on your doorstep until you commit one way or the other. I need to know where I'm going too, Bob. I love our relationship, but I miss you. I want more out of our situation than a dinner date every week or so. I'll wait, but not forever. Does that suit you?"

"Yes. I agree with everything you just said. I too, love what we have, and I assure you I will be ready to move forward in one direction or another once this is all over. Just give me a little time."

"You got it. Now, let's eat. I'm starved."

Chapter 34

As he drove, Bob considered his time with Susan last night. Once they finished dinner, they had moved to the bar, where they remained until near 10:00 p.m. He kissed her goodbye and they each drove to their respective homes. He had considered going home with her, but he was tired. A good night's sleep in his own bed was imperative after the short nights he had endured while sleeping at the hotel.

Susan had been understanding, a trait he had observed many times when with her. She hadn't pushed him into a relationship—not yet anyway. He needed these issues—these issues involving his new found grandson—to come to a conclusion, one way or the other. Hopefully, it would be as he wished—a verdict of not guilty. But either way, the situation needed to resolve itself in short order— there were a number of people waiting to make life-altering plans based on how it all came to a conclusion. Certainly, one thing he needed to remember…

"Hey, where the hell are you, because you're certainly not in this car—you are certainly not driving this car—it's like *driving you.* You know, as bad as you are behind the wheel, you might want to keep your mind on your driving. Just a suggestion…one I'm sure you will disregard, but…"

"Jack. would you shut the hell up. If you're going to throw out nothing but bullshit, just keep it to yourself and let me drive in silence."

"What did you do last night? Did you go out with Susan? You know, we could have gone out together. If you would have said something, and *invited us,* we would have gone with you."

"We had a good time, by ourselves. I didn't want anyone with us, which is the reason you weren't invited."

"Whatever. What are we doing today? And explain to me why I'm going back to Knoxville. I mean, the trial is over."

"No, it's not. I have no idea what the hell is actually going to happen today…or tomorrow … or the next day, other than we *may* get a verdict. I want you with me until this is *totally* over. That means until we get a verdict—and…maybe longer."

"Whatever. So, after we check in, what then?"

"Did you go see the doctor?"

"Stay focused, Bob. What's the schedule?"

"Hell, I don't know. I thought we would go see the Judge first and find out if he has heard anything from the jury. Then maybe talk to the Prosecutor and get his thoughts concerning a sentencing recommendation if Paul is convicted. Did you see the doctor?"

"I may just stay in the room. None of those things are very important. I'll be close if you need me, but I am a little tired. I didn't get much sleep last night."

"Did that woman stay with you? Is that why you didn't get much sleep?"

"No, no. I was just up and down all night. No big deal."

"Did you go to the doctor? I'm not going to ask you again."

"Okay."

"Okay what?"

"Don't ask me again."

"You know, you wear me out. Don't talk to me the rest of this trip. If I need to ask you something, you can answer. Otherwise, no other conversation about anything."

"Okay."

Once settled in their rooms, Jack stayed behind, as Bob left for the jail. He wanted to visit with Paul and see how he was handling the wait.

Once they brought him to the visitation room, Bob said, "How are you doing? How are you handling the wait?"

"Do you go through this often?"

"What do you mean? Go through what often?"

"Waiting for a jury to come back. Is that something that during your years in practice you have done frequently?"

Bob smiled and said, "Yes, quite a few times. Not so much in criminal cases, but yes, I've been involved in civil jury trials many times. For me, they were gut-wrenching, even when there was nothing but money on the line."

"I have never been through anything like this personally, nor with someone else. I don't know how you do it, I really don't."

"Of course, this one is radically different from all the others I have been involved with. It's a criminal case, it's a murder trial, and it's you. All those factors just ramp up the pressure and the importance of the jury getting it right—concluding it with the verdict they should come back with. Have you thought about what you are going to do if you are found not guilty?"

"I have a few decisions to make, for sure. But the major question is what happens if they find me guilty. What happens then, Pops?"

"I'm going to visit with the Prosecutor today. We will see what he has in mind. He has been difficult to deal with through most of the proceedings, but maybe he will be easier to work with now, now that it's over. Again, not to press you, but what are your thoughts if they find you not guilty?"

"Just start over, I guess. I have no doubt my customers have all found someone else to handle their gardening and yard work, so my business is probably all shot to hell. I'm not sure what is going on between Carrie and I. We seem to have a lot in common, but I am just not sure what…So, as you can see, my life is pretty well on the edge no matter which way it turns out."

"Have you given any thought to coming back to Nashville with me?"

He remained quiet for a moment, then said, "I have, yes, I have. There are just too many variables in play here to come to any kind of a conclusion yet. But having you back in my life on a permanent basis would be something I think I would like."

"Well, hopefully the jury will make the right decision, and we can discuss that possibility at length. I need to go see the Judge and Prosecutor. I'll talk to you later today or tomorrow morning."

The Judge wasn't in his chambers. No one seemed to have any idea where he was. The Prosecutor was also unavailable. So, Bob decided to pay a visit to another member of Paul's 'team.'

He waited for Carrie in a small conference room. They had told him she would be but a minute. It had already been twenty minutes, but what did it matter? He had to wait somewhere for the verdict—this place was as good as any.

A quiet knock on the door and Carrie walked in, closing the door behind her.

Bob hadn't taken time to look at her—to really look at her—since this had all began. She had beautiful blue eyes—that was the first thing he noticed about her.

He stood, as she frowned at him, extended her hand and said, "Do we have a verdict?"

"No, no, not yet. I saw Paul a few minutes ago. He is holding up pretty well. I went to see the Judge and the Prosecutor, but never had a chance to talk to either of them. While I was thinking about what to do next, I thought I hadn't really had a chance to visit with you one-on-one. So, here I am. Do you have a few moments?"

"Absolutely."

She pulled a chair out, away from the table, then sat down next to him.

"How are you doing, Bob?"

"I'm fine. I hate the wait, but that's the stage we are at in these proceedings so I don't have a choice. That doesn't make it any easier—it's part of the whole process."

"What do you think they will do?"

"I really don't know. We are trying to prepare for all the contingencies. Are you doing, okay? You have been part of the process from the beginning."

"Well, from a professional standpoint, I couldn't be better off. This story has generated an incredible amount of interest. I have heard from everyone I know, and many, many people I don't know from all over the city. The story has piqued the interest of people in and out of Knoxville. So, in that respect, this could all be career-defining for me."

She looked away: he remained silent.

"Do you have family around here?"

"No, nobody."

"Have you ever been married? Do you have t an ex, somewhere? Any children?"

She smiled. "Are *you* writing the story now, Bob?"

He laughed and said, "Not really. Today, I just thought you and I had never really had a chance to get to know each other. That's why I'm here. I am not writing *anything* for *anyone*. I really didn't want to spend much time alone today, sitting around and wondering what the hell that jury's doing. So, here I am."

"I understand. My family is all away from here. I have never been married. I have no children. I am not in a relationship. And I'm in love with Paul."

Bob smiled. "I kinda had that last part figured out. I've seen how the two of you look at each other. I figured that was the case. You honestly have really become that close?"

"Yes. I've spent a lot of time with him. I know there's no way he would ever hurt anyone, let alone murder anyone. He's a great guy, Bob. You should be proud."

"I am. I'm not happy with all they are saying about him, obviously. But I'm proud he is my grandson. He has overcome a lot in his short life. Have the two of you made any plans? I mean, I know there's not much you can do to plan anything, until you know what the jury does. But have you made any plans, just in case they exonerate him?"

"You know he is thinking about moving to Nashville, right?"

"Yes, he did mention that."

"Does that bother you—how do you feel about that?"

"I would give up everything I have, for that to happen."

She smiled, and said, "And you know a few TV people in Nashville, right?"

"I certainly do."

"Well, if everything turns out the way it should, you might gain a son and his tagalong. Obviously, we have a long way to go yet before we can plan anything. But that's been the discussion between the two of us, just so you know."

Bob stood, as did Carrie. He embraced her, and said, "Nothing would make me happier than to have both of you close to me. Absolutely nothing."

Chapter 35

"So, are you just going to hang around here all day, or do you want to go with me?"

Jack sat down, put his feet up on the ottoman, looked up at Bob and said, "Now tell me again, where are you going?"

"You know, you have no memory left at all. I'm surprised you even remember who I am. We *just* discussed this."

"Okay, now it just took you longer to insult me about my memory, than it would have taken you to just tell me where you are going."

"You wear me out. You absolutely exhaust me. I'm going to see the Judge, then probably the Prosecutor, depending on what the Judge says. Then I want to go see Paul. Now, do you want to go or not? Because if you do, you need to get ready. It's already after ten, and I want to be sure and see all of them today. Of course, the jury could come in at any time too, and I want you there when they do. Now what's it going to be? You want me to wait for you, or leave without you?"

"Move over a little, I can't see the TV. Let's Make A Deal is on."

"That's it. I am out of here. I'll see you when I see you. Don't wait up."

"You know, this is a repeat. Why don't you sit down and watch it with me? It's the one where…"

Bob slammed the door shut behind him as Jack continued to speak.

Judge Strayer was in his chambers. Bob knocked on the door, and the Judge motioned for him to come in.

"Morning Bob, how you getting alone? Where is your partner?"

"Good morning, Judge. He stayed at the hotel. Do you mind if I sit for a minute or do you have other matters that need your attention right now?"

"No, no, I am just like you—I'm just waiting for this jury to come back."

Bob sat as he said, "Have you heard anything from them? Have they had any questions you needed to help them with as concerns a procedural issue, or any other type of problem that needed your attention?"

"No, nothing at all. I'm not surprised they've taken this long though. You gave them a lot to think about in your closing."

"I hope so. I just couldn't ever see the murder one charge as appropriate, I guess. That was really a concern. Of course, the whole case is a concern as far as that goes."

"He's your grandson, right?"

"He is, Judge, yes he is."

"As I hear it, he ran off when he was a teenager and this was the first you've seen him since then?"

"Yes. It has been a hell of a reunion, to say the least."

The Judge smiled as he said, "I can only imagine."

"What are they going to do? Any thoughts?"

"Hell, I don't know. Juries never cease to amaze me. I am thinking they will find him guilty of something. I'm not sure about murder one, but probably a lesser included."

"What if it's murder, but not premeditated? That's up to twenty-five years in prison, and it can be without the possibility of parole. Is that what you would sentence him to if that was the verdict? I'm just trying to ease the shock if he is found guilty and you have to sentence him."

"We just need to wait, Bob. First of all, I don't feel comfortable talking to you about sentencing options with the Prosecutor not being present. I would want the State's recommendation, as you know. And we will also have other, procedural issues to handle before I sentence him. Lots of factors in play. But I will tell you if that's what the Prosecutor recommends, and that's what the other data I normally review, recommends, then I wouldn't hesitate to send him up for twenty-five, with no possibility of parole. Now, we are, at this point, far away from that happening, but I would just tell you I wouldn't hesitate to do that if that's what the recommendation was."

"I understand. I just wanted your take on it." He stood as he said, "I'll leave you alone. Thanks, Judge. I will see you when we get a verdict."

As he turned to walk away, the Judge said, "Oh, Bob."

He turned toward the Judge and said, "Yes, sir."

"You and your partner did a hell of good job with what you had to work with. You did all you could do. You can't make up the facts. You did well with the hand you were dealt."

"Thanks, Judge. I just hope it was good enough."

"George will see you now. You can go on in."

"Thanks."

Bob stood and walked through the door into the office of George Jensen. "Morning, how are you?"

George stood, and said, "Good, Bob, have a chair. How can I help you?"

As he sat, he said, "I just wanted to visit with you a moment about the criminal charges against Paul and your thoughts concerning sentencing if he is found guilty."

"Little premature, isn't it? After all, he could be found innocent. I don't think that's likely, but he could be."

"You know, I have no idea what they will do. But I do want to soften the shock a little with Paul in case they do find him guilty. If he's found guilty of either murder one or just the general charge of murder, what kind of recommendation would you make concerning his sentence?"

"Oh, I don't know. It would depend on a lot of factors, I guess. You know, there would have to be a presentence investigation prepared for the Judge to review, and I would probably key off that."

"I know as well as you, that your recommendation would carry a lot of weight. Let's say he was found guilty of the general charge of murder. Let's say they throw out murder one and find him guilty of the charge of murder. What would your recommendation be?"

"Well, first of all, that is where I do think the jury will end up. That is what I think their verdict will be. And if that happens, I would probably recommend a sentence of 25 years, with no possibility of parole."

"You're kidding. That's the max allowable. Do you really feel this case warrants that stiff a penalty?"

"I'll tell you what I think. I think he murdered a good woman that the community respected and that a lot of people knew and liked. And I think that a lot of people are looking closely at what the District Attorney General's office does with this guy. Your little newspaper friend has made this a high-profile case, and yes, if they find him guilty, regardless of the recommendation in the presentence investigation, I'll recommend the max."

"Those newspaper articles were not my idea. We had nothing to do with that at all. So, you are going to hold that against him? The fact that the local paper followed the case is part of your consideration in what you would recommend? Do you think that's fair?"

He smiled, and said, "Oh hell, I don't know. I just know that for whatever the reason I have twice as many people asking me about this case, then any other case I have ever handled. So, if he's found guilty, I'm going to make sure the punishment more than fits the crime. I'm just trying to be upfront with you here, Bob. That's just the way I look at it."

Bob stood. "You know, letting something not even relevant to the case dictate your recommendation is bullshit. That's how I look at it. But, one thing about it—you have been full of it since the case stated and you are at least consistent. I will give that to you—you are consistent."

Bob turned and walked out the door without another word.

"Morning, Pops. I didn't think you were coming. I waited for you most of the day and just finally came to the conclusion you weren't going to make it. I just figured you were working on something involving the trial and I would most likely see you tomorrow. Any news concerning the jury?"

"No, not really. But I'm thinking we are probably getting pretty close to a verdict. The jurors, I'm sure, have about had their daily lives interrupted enough. I would imagine we will hear from then soon, one way or the other."

"You think they are having trouble coming to a unanimous conclusion?"

"I really don't know. I talked to the Judge earlier today, and he hasn't heard a word from them. Sometimes, juries will let the Judge know they're having trouble coming to a conclusion. That has not happened, so I'm thinking we will hear from them soon."

"If they can't decide, then it is tried again, right?"

"If that's what the Prosecutor wants to do. I just talked to him a few minutes ago. Based on my conversation with him, I don't have much doubt he'll want to retry it."

Paul looked away as he said, "How long will it take to get it back in court and retried?"

"You know, I really don't have any idea. I imagine another six months or so."

He looked at Bob, then said, "Okay. If that's the way it is then that's just the way it is. Is that what you went to talk to the Judge and Prosecutor about?"

"No."

Paul hesitated, obviously waiting for a follow-up response. When hearing none, he said, "Okay, why *did* you go see them…any particular reason or just to have coffee."

Bob smiled. "No coffee with either of them. I just wanted to get their take on what sentence they might be considering if you are found guilty—and by that I meant guilty of the general charge of murder."

"Hmm. Did they tell you what they were thinking?"

"You really want to discuss it, or should we just wait and see what happens before we go into that?"

"No. What did they say—both of them?"

"They indicated they would both probably look at 25 years, most likely without the possibility of parole. That's just what they…"

"Holy shit. So, after all they heard at the trial about the real facts of this case, they are still looking at the max?"

"Yes, I'm afraid so."

"I just figured…when they heard the whole story…I just figured…

"Hold on now, Paul. That is *if* they find you guilty."

"I know that. I understand that. It's just that…"

He thought for a moment, looked up and smiled at Bob, stood and said, "Better go. Thanks for all you've done, Pops. I need to go. I'll see you what, maybe tomorrow?"

"Yes. Yes, I'll be here tomorrow. Now, Paul, don't get so discouraged you…"

Paul interrupted as he said, "Gotta go. I'll just see you tomorrow."

Bob watched as he left the conference room. Maybe he shouldn't have told him about the conversations with the Judge and Jensen. But unfortunately, that was the reality of Paul's future. He hadn't lied or sugar-coated the situation to Paul since they were reunited. He wasn't going to start now. Hopefully, the jury would just find him not guilty and all these other issues would become moot. Hopefully, *that* wasn't all just wishful thinking.

Chapter 36

Bob tossed and turned all night as he considered the conversations he had with the Judge and the Prosecutor. It wasn't that he hadn't laid awake many other nights doing this very same thing, but that was at a time when the 'problem' and its ultimate conclusion, seemed so far away—so far into the future. This was different. Now, this *situation* was only hours away from a conclusion and that *conclusion* could in deed quickly turn into a living hell for his grandson.

He finally ended the battle and climbed out of bed.

Once he had dressed and finished an abbreviated breakfast, he returned to their hotel floor and knocked on Jack's door.

As Jack opened it, he said, "What are you doing up so early?"

"It's not early. It's almost nine-thirty. Did you just get up?"

"Yes. It was a long night." He left the door open, and turned to walk away.

Bob walked in, shut the door, and said, "You probably better get cleaned up. They could call today and I want you to go with me if they reach a verdict."

Jack dropped down on the couch, and said "It won't take me long if they do call. Why do you think it will be today?"

"Human nature. They have been cooped up with each other long enough, and the weekend is approaching. They're not going to want to have this 'problem' on their minds while relaxing this weekend. They will come to a conclusion today or tomorrow."

"What are you going to do this morning while we wait?"

Bob sat down and said, "Just watch TV with you, I guess. I don't have much else to do."

"I'm not really sure I can handle being locked up in this room all day with you and no one else. You sure you can't maybe find something else to do in a while—maybe go to a movie, walk out on the street for a while, roam around in the..."

Bob said, "Just relax. Believe me, I will grow tired of your bullshit in about fifteen minutes and be more than happy to go somewhere else. You want a cup of coffee? I'll fix one for you in that coffee machine if you want me too. I see you haven't used it yet. Was it too complicated for you? You know, all you have to do is…"

"Yeah, yeah, fix the coffee. Maybe doing that will shut you up."

Bob's phone buzzed. He answered, but all he said was, "Thank you."

He stood. "Get dressed. The jury came to a conclusion. They've reached a verdict. We need to go…*now*."

As they walked in the courtroom where Paul was already waiting, he couldn't help but notice a large number of people sitting in the bench seats apparently also awaiting a verdict. He quickly concluded that the Prosecutor was correct when he had mentioned Carrie's articles had generated a large amount of interest in the case. As each day passed, the number of spectators had grown. Today the courtroom was nearly full. Lynn's daughter had been there every day and was in fact, seated in the front row today.

Bob and Jack sat down on either side of Paul.

"Are you ready for this?" Bob whispered.

"I don't think I have a choice."

"Nope."

The Judge walked in the courtroom and everyone stood.

"Please be seated. In a moment the jury will be brought back in. It is my understanding they have arrived at a verdict. I do not want to hear a sound from any of you once the verdict is read. Just keep quiet, or I'll have you escorted from the courtroom. Bailiff, bring in the jury."

The bailiff left the room and shortly thereafter, he led the group of twelve into the courtroom, where they took their seats in the jury box.

Judge Strayer looked at the panel, and said, "Mr. Foreman have you arrived at a verdict?"

An older gentleman seated in the front row of jurors said, "We have, Your Honor."

"Please hand it to the bailiff."

The Foreman handed it to the bailiff who in turn handed it to the Judge.

The Judge read it to himself then said, "The Jury, in the case of State versus Paul Duncan does hereby find the defendant Paul

Duncan, guilty…of the charge of murder in the second degree." Bob heard a couple of people behind him, say, "Yes."

He couldn't think. He couldn't look at Bob. There was a deafening silence as everyone in the court room, in their own way, accepted the final conclusion reached by the Jury.

Judge Strayer looked at the Foreman and said, "Is this your true and correct verdict in the matter of State of Tennessee versus Duncan."

The Foreman stood and said, "It is, Your Honor.

The Judge then thanked the jurors for their time and sent them home. Most all the spectators with the exception of Lynn's daughter, stood and left the courtroom.

The Judge waited until the courtroom cleared, then said, "Mr. Duncan, you have been found guilty of the charge of murder in the second degree. I am hereby ordering a presentence investigation which the court can use for sentencing purposes. I want it prepared and provided to all attorneys of record no later than one week prior to sentencing. I will check the schedule and set it by subsequent order of court. Do any of the attorneys have any questions?"

None of the attorneys indicated they had questions for the Judge.

"Folks, court is hereby adjourned until sentencing. You attorneys, of course, will all receive a copy of the presentence investigation and we can discuss it at sentencing. Court is hereby adjourned."

Bob turned to Paul, and said, "Paul, we need to discuss…"

"Look. I really feel like being alone…all alone. I am going back to my cell. I'll just talk to you later."

He stood, and as the deputy came to take him away, Bob said, "I'll be there in a few minutes. We need to talk to you about where we go from here."

Paul never turned around, but he did nod his head.

Jack said, "I'm going to the bathroom. I'll be back in a few minutes."

Carrie, who was sitting in the first row of seats for onlookers, stood and walked up to Bob, taking the chair where Paul had previously sat.

"Bob, are you going to be okay? This has to be a horrible result for you."

As he turned to look at her, he could tell she had been crying.

"I need to go see him. He can't lose hope. He can't just give up.

He's got to know…"

As Bob started to sob, she put her arm around his back, and said, "You need to hang in there. You did all you could do for him. It could have been worse. It could have been murder-one, and that would have been a total disaster."

"I know, but…"

"What's the next step? What can we do now?"

"I don't know, I'm not sure…I"

Jack sat back down, and said, "You and I need to visit for a moment."

"Jack, I figured we would at some point, but I wasn't coming into the bathroom to do that. Carrie, let me kick things around with Jack, and I'll let you know. Are you going to see Paul?"

"Yes," she said as she stood. "But I need to write this story for a few minutes first. Then I'll go be with him."

"Okay."

As she walked away, Bob said, "Jack, what are your thoughts?"

"Well, I think we need to have the record transcribed, then review it—maybe there is a mistake or two the Judge made that would provide grounds for appeal."

"Should you and I back off—get someone to represent him that handles appeals all the time, rather than trying to tackle this one ourselves?"

"I think that is a good idea. I know a guy that does nothing but appeals. I'll give him a call shortly and see what he says."

Bob said, "Once we get that presentence investigation, I assume it will make a sentencing recommendation, and we can take it from there."

"Why don't you go talk to him. Tell him we are working on the next step. I don't think I should be there. You handle this initial conference with him between grandfather and grandson, not between lawyer and client. I think that would be best. I can visit with him after your initial conference."

Bob stood. "I agree. I better go now. I'll just meet you back at the hotel later today."

He watched as Paul slowly walked up to the visitor's window. As he sat down, he never looked up.

"Paul, I'm sorry."

He made no effort to acknowledge Bob's comment.

"We need to talk, at least for a moment."

He never looked up.

"We need to talk about where we go from here."

Slowly, he looked up at his grandfather and said, "Really. Does it *really* matter? I mean, we discussed how much longer I would need to be in here if I lost. What else is there to discuss? I lost. I'm in here for a long time, no matter what we do now. There is really nothing more to discuss. We have said it all."

"Don't give up, Paul. Please don't give up yet. We are looking into an appeal. I'll most likely ask for a new trial. There are lots of things going on that might help get you out of here. Don't quit on us. We haven't quit on you, don't do that to us. We will figure this out together. Carrie is hanging right in there, too."

"Where is she?"

"She will be here shortly."

"I would *really* like to talk to her right now. I need to know if she is hanging around or if she's…off to another story."

"I don't think you need to doubt her, Paul, I really don't."

"I don't know what to think about anything. I need to go. I'll talk to you tomorrow."

He stood, as Bob said, "I understand. I'll see you in the morning."

He watched as the officer escorted him back to his cell, clearly discouraged… and as broken as Bob.

Chapter 37

"Are you ready to go?"

"Yeah, I guess. But this just seems so silly. We go back to Nashville today, then back here tomorrow. Why don't we just…"

"Just stop! I told you we had an appointment tomorrow morning with that appeals attorney in Nashville. If you don't want to come back here the next day, I'll pack the rest of your stuff up for you and bring it home once I am ready to leave here. Now, let's go. We need to stop and see Paul for a moment, before we leave town,"

Bob heard him grumble quietly to himself as he walked away. He would try to encourage Jack to stay in Nashville when he returned tomorrow. That decision would certainly be up to Jack, but there would seem to be no reason for him to return. When he drove back tomorrow, he simply wanted to visit at length with his grandson and talk briefly with the Prosecutor. He could certainly do that without Jack.

Once they arrived at the jail, Bob asked to see Paul. They waited until an officer told them he didn't wish to see anyone today. The officer said Paul told him to tell them to come back some other time. He just wasn't interested in discussing the case today.

Bob understood. Hopefully, as they figured out the best direction to proceed from here, he would become more engaged in the process and the depression created by the verdict would, at least to some extent, disappear.

Upon reaching Nashville, he took Jack home. As he dropped him off, he told him he would pick him up tomorrow precisely at nine. Their appointment with the appeals attorney was at nine-thirty. He didn't want to be late.

"Now, again, you be ready to go. I don't want to get you up, help you dress, and push you to the car. I do *not* want to miss this appointment and you are crucial to the conversation. You're the criminal lawyer, not me."

"You know, you take a thousand words to say what most people say in ten. You absolutely drive me crazy. I'll be *up,* I'll be *ready.* Now, go on, get out of here."

"I drive *you* crazy. I drive *you* cr…"

Jack slammed the car door and walked up his sidewalk, ignoring all of Bob's comments.

Fifteen minutes later he was seated in his office, going through phone messages and reviewing files that had been left on his desk by Charlene.

She walked in his door with another open file. "Are you ready to try that Andrews case next week?"

"What day?"

"Friday."

"I will be ready. As I told you, we'll go back down tomorrow morning, if Jack wants to go. If he doesn't, I'll go anyway. Paul wouldn't see us this morning, but I'll make sure he does tomorrow. I'll take Carrie with me when I go see him. That will insure he sees me."

"Are they that close?"

"It appears to me they are, yes. Why don't you have Andrews come in early next week. I'll make sure I'm here. Set up his witnesses for appointments with me early next week. Prepare subpoenas for those he doesn't think will show up on their own. When you call to set up appointments, just briefly go through the essence of their testimony, will you—so I have some idea what they're going to say before I interview them."

"Not a problem. So, you never did say what the next step is with Paul. Appeal?"

"I think so. We are to meet with Johnson, that appeals specialist tomorrow morning. We will know a lot more then."

"Should I count on you being in the office more often now? I mean, you have recently been in Knoxville almost full time. Are you going to start being in the office, say three days a week from now on?"

"I'll tell you what. I meet with this guy in the morning. He will tell me what I need to know about this whole criminal appeals process. Then you and I can talk about it at length. Today, I'll be in this afternoon, so bring in whoever you think I need to talk to. I'll be gone tomorrow."

"Got it." She turned to walk away, then stopped as she reached the door and said, "Susan called. She said to remind you of your date tonight. You are meeting her at the restaurant, right?"

"Right."

"At seven, right?"

"Yes. Yes, that's right. Thanks for the reminder."

She walked in a little after seven. He had already been there for thirty minutes, but at the bar…just because he really needed a drink. At seven, he moved to the table, ordered another Manhattan and ordered her a glass of wine.

As he stood, she kissed him and said, "Welcome home."

He smiled as he said, "Thanks. It's not really the way in which I wanted to return home, but thanks anyway."

She took a drink, and said, "Tell me what happened. I don't know much about the procedure involving a case like this."

"Well, the courtroom was full of people. That newspaper writer I told you about, is good at what she does. There were many readers that were there for the verdict. They found him guilty."

"First things first. You mentioned that writer…do you think Paul and her are involved?"

"I know they are. I am not really sure what's going to happen to their relationship now—now that he's been found…guilty."

"Okay, so what is the next step in this process?"

"Most likely an appeal. Jack and I meet with an attorney in the morning that does nothing but criminal appeals. He is really good at what he does, and we're going to just generally pick his brain tomorrow. An appeal is most likely the only remedy we have."

"What is your chance of success?"

"Hell, I don't know. But based on my limited experience, it appears to me we don't have much of a chance. To me, there were few mistakes during the trial upon which the State Supreme Court could overturn the verdict. I think we are really in trouble, but I'll let the guy we are seeing tomorrow tell me what he thinks before I come to my own conclusion."

"Does Jack have any thoughts about it?"

"He feels pretty much like I do. Our chance of success is limited."

"How did you two working together work out?"

"Great. He's so easy to deal with. He has his issues, as do I, but we got along great. I relied upon him all the way through the process."

Later, as the conversation about Paul began to subside and they completed their meal, Susan said, "Are you home now for a while? What's your schedule?"

"I am heading back to Knoxville tomorrow noon with Jack then home on Friday for the weekend. Then, most likely back and forth to Knoxville as I try to take care of Paul down there, and take care of a couple of cases here, which should have been tried months ago."

"Hmm. It doesn't sound like there's much time in that schedule for us, Bob. Is there? I mean, is there any time for us, or is this schedule, without me in it, going to just continue on and on and on?"

"No, of course not. I just hit the highlights of my week. That's not all I'm going to do. I'll have some time in there for you."

"So, you mentioned the *highlights* of your week, without mentioning me at all. How should I take that? Sounds like to me I'm not much of a part of your life, whether you're trying a case in Knoxville or not. Is this insane schedule of yours ever going to end?"

"Yes, I think so—I hope so. The trial is over, and we are down to his appeal. Of course, I'll need to go see him frequently in jail, and if his conviction is overturned, I'll have to return to try the case. But there is time for you. I'll have time to see you next…Well, I'll have time…Let me look at my schedule at the office and see…"

"You know, I don't *want* to have to be sandwiched in. I don't want you to have to look at your schedule and find 'a place' for me like you do your clients."

He reached out and took her hand. She pulled it away. "Look, Susan. I do care for you, I really do. But I just can't make all this go away. It's not that easy. I have Paul. I have my commitments at the office. I have personal day-to-day activities I have to stay on top of and that need attention. I'm sorry, but this is just a crazy time in my life."

"You know how much I care for you, right?"

"Yes, yes I do."

"And I think you would agree I've waited quite some time for you to place me in your priority list along with Paul, your office and Jack."

"Yes, you have. I agree."

"Okay, I've gone about as far as I can go. I need you, Bob. I need you not only to love me, which I think you do, but to be here, to be with me, you know like other couples. You seem to say one thing about us, but then you do or say another. I think we should just forget about each other until you are able to commit more to us than you're willing to now."

"But I *do not* have a choice. I can't do anything other then what I'm doing. Look, I don't want to lose you. I have finally come to that conclusion. I do have a life to live. And I have finally quit feeling guilty that I have someone I care about. I loved her. That will never ever change. But I can love again, and I am in love with you. I have finally reached the point where I can accept that and move on with you. So, I finally reach that point in my life… and then you run out on me? Don't do this. Just hang in there with me a while longer."

She stood. "When your schedule can finally include me, let me know. If I'm not busy, maybe we can spend some time together." She started to cry. "But Bob, I've had enough of this craziness. Let me know when you are ready to commit your time, your life to someone else other than your clients, Paul, Jack, Charlene, whoever. I'm sorry. I really am. But I'm done unless and until you are really ready to commit."

She walked out the door, while he sat stunned. He had another drink as he considered all she had said. When he left, he thought about calling her, but decided against it. He would give her a day or two and call her Friday when he came back to Nashville. A call now would most likely just be more of the same lecture he had just endured.

Bob sat in Jack's driveway waiting for him to make an appearance.

He honked a couple of times, but with no results. As he sat, he continued to think about his evening, his *abbreviated* evening, with Susan. He thought about calling her later this morning, but again, just decided to wait until he returned home tomorrow.

He honked again. Maybe tomorrow he could take her out for supper and…

Where the hell was he? Bob slowly opened his car door and slammed it shut. He was most likely still sleeping. He told Jack how important it was he be ready to go when he arrived to pick him up. It wasn't the first time he had overslept and he had no doubt it wouldn't be his last.

He knocked on his door but heard no response. He tried the doorknob, but the door was still locked. He looked through the window in the door and the living room was dark.

Bob knew where he hid the key. He walked to a planter full of flowers that sat on the top railing of his porch, dug down in the dirt and pulled out the key.

He cleaned it up as he walked back to the door, then inserted it, opened the door and walked in.

Not a light was on.

He walked through the living room and into the kitchen, but it too was dark. Certainly no one had been in the kitchen this morning.

He yelled out his name, but again, received no response.

Bob walked to the stairway, yelled out his name, and hearing nothing, started to walk up the steps. Once he reached the second floor, he again yelled out his name, but again no response.

Only one of the doors on the floor was open. Bob assumed that would be Jack's bedroom. He yelled out his name as he walked, and as he reached the open door, he looked in. Jack was still in bed, but when Bob called out, he never moved.

"Oh my God, no." He walked to his bedside and felt Jack's arm. It was stiff. He tried to find a pulse, but could find no trace of one.

He pulled out his phone and called 911. He told them about his friend. He told them that he had no doubt Jack was gone, but they should come as quickly as they could.

Then he sat down….in the only chair in the room….and cried.

Chapter 38

It was one of *those* Sundays in middle Tennessee—rainy and cold—when it was best to just remain indoors.

Bob sat alone, in his office, He had been looking out his window for the past hour, doing nothing but remembering the friend he just buried. He was one of the pallbearers. Jack had never appreciated cremation. Even the word itself, made him wrinkle up his nose. He wanted a traditional church service—a traditional burial. And that was exactly what his son gave him.

He wiped a tear away as he thought of all the time they had spent together. At a time in his life when he really needed Jack, when he figured his life had ended with the death of his wife, he was there for him. When his grandson was charged with murder, Jack gave up his own personal lifestyle to drive to Knoxville and remain, day after day, far away from his livelihood and his own lifestyle.

The thought of going through the coming weeks and months without him was almost unbearable. He had other friends, he had other acquaintances, but none shared the relationship they had shared. The two of them had gone through all life could throw at them—together. They had been through the death of both of their wives, the birth of their children and the death of Bob's child. There really had not been an aspect of life…or death…they hadn't gone through together.

"I figured I would find you here."

He hadn't heard Charlene when she entered the office or walked down the hallway. He jumped as she spoke, then swiveled around to face her.

As she sat down, she smiled, and said, "Sorry. I didn't mean to scare you. Were you lost in your thoughts of him?"

"Yes, I was. You, of all people, know how close we were. Did you go to the funeral? I didn't see you there, but I wasn't looking for you either. I was trying to just focus on what my responsibilities were during the funeral."

"Yes, I was there. It was a nice service. You did a great job. What you said was really personal—obviously from the heart. To lose your wife and now your best friend within a year of each other—well, that has got to be tough."

He looked away and said, "And then there is Paul."

"But his cause is not lost yet. Did you ever talk to the appeals attorney? When you left here late Friday morning you hadn't had a chance to visit with him."

"I was able to contact him late in the day Friday. I told him what happened, and we scheduled a phone conference for late Monday morning."

"Good. I was on my way home and the reason I dropped in was because I wanted to talk to you about Monday. Will you be in or out? Did his death affect your schedule? I figured if it did and I did find you here, maybe we could talk for a moment, and you could tell me if there's anything I should be doing over the weekend for you to prepare for Monday."

"I'll be here. We will just plan on the same schedule we discussed before Jack…before…Jack's death."

She leaned forward in her chair as she said, "Bob, I am so, so sorry. If there's anything I can do for you during the next few days, just let me know."

"I will. I'm fine. I'll get through it…I'll get…"

He wiped a tear away, as he swiveled around in his chair, now facing the window.

"As you can imagine, I'm not real sure of anything right now. I'll just see you on Monday."

Once she left the office, he once again reviewed all he had been through during the past year. Maybe when he talked to the appeals attorney on Monday, he would just turn everything over to him—just let him handle it all. How could he possibly help anyway—he hadn't handled an appeal of any kind in years. He could just pay the bill and let him handle…

His personal phone rang. He looked at caller ID and quickly answered. It was a collect call from the Knox County jail, which Bob accepted.

"Paul, is this you?"

"It is Pops. How are you?"

"I'm…fine. What's going on? Is everything okay with you? Are you alright?"

"Well, yeah, kind of, but as you can imagine, it's a little difficult to be really *'alright'* when I've just been convicted of murder. I mean, looking at my life as a whole, other than the fact I am locked up in jail and have just been convicted of murder, I'm doing quite well actually."

"Did you hear about something that is going on in your case? Are you feeling okay? You never call me."

"No, no, everything is as it was the last time I saw you. I just wanted to tell you I'm sorry about Jack."

He hesitated for a moment before he said, "How did you find out?"

"Carrie. She monitors everything that happens in Nashville, partly because of her work and partly because about everything that goes on in Nashville is of interest to her. She saw a little article in the paper about a long-time Nashville attorney passing away. Because of you, she read it and realized who it was. She told me."

"Yeah, well, not a good situation I'm afraid Paul. I was the one that found him. We were getting ready to go see that appeals attorney, and I was to pick him up. I knocked on his door and went in when he didn't respond. It was…awful. I just can't believe he's gone."

"Clearly, you two were really close. It was like you both knew what the other one was going to say before they said it."

"We were friends forever. Yes, we were close."

"You are having a bad week."

"It has not been the best."

"Are you discouraged?"

Bob hesitated, cleared his throat and said, "A little, yes."

"Obviously, there is little I can do to really help. But you need to hang in there. You and I… *we*, will get through all of this. I can only imagine how you feel losing your wife and your best friend in the same year. But you need to hang on, and hang in there with me. We Duncan's, those of us left anyway, need to stand together, stand tall, and all that other shit that people say to someone when they need to step up."

Bob laughed and said, "You know, that is what I have been saying to you, in my *own* way, for the past three to four months. Guess it's only fitting that you throw it right back at me."

"Again, I'm sorry about your loss, Pops. He was always good to me—helpful in every way. I just don't want you to get discouraged about all of this and think all is lost, because it's not. We got each other, no matter where the hell I'm living—whether it's in state prison, or there in Nashville or here in Knoxville." He hesitated. "I need to go. I'll see you whenever…"

The line went dead.

"Paul, Paul…"

The line had gone dead during other prior calls involving the two of them. This time it was no surprise.

He turned around to watch the rain. My how the situation had changed. Now, it was Paul that provided the comfort, the pep talk. That in and off itself was enough to fight the battle with just a little more resolve.

His phone rang again. This time it wasn't a prisoner in the Knoxville jail.

"Hi, Susan."

"Hi. I didn't have a chance to talk to you at the funeral. I was hesitant to call you at all, not knowing if you were perhaps spending time with Jack's family."

"I left right after we went to the cemetery. I felt it was time for them to handle family matters without me around. I have been with them since Friday. I just figured it was time for me to move out of the picture, at least for a while.:

"You did a good job at the service. Inspiring words to say the least."

"Jack made those words easy for me. He was one of a kind. I'll miss him."

"I am sure you will. I just wanted to tell you how sorry I was. How is this going to affect the case with Paul?"

"I don't think it will affect it much. We will be in appeals court and the attorney we were going to see Friday morning will most likely handle that. By the way, I just got off the phone with Paul. He called me. He said he was sorry to hear about Jack's death and then told me to 'hang in there.' He told *me*, to hang in there and *he's* the one just found guilty of murder. I was overjoyed he called."

"That's great, Bob. It sounds to me like your relationship with him is really coming around. I'm happy for you, I really am."

"Would you like to…would you like to meet somewhere for supper this evening?"

"No, I don't think so. I need a little time to think everything through Bob, and I need to do it without you. I said some things maybe I shouldn't have said the other night. I just need to think about where we are in this relationship of ours—what the bottom line might be for both of us. I just need to clear my thoughts for a while…without you with me, I might add."

He remained quiet for a moment then said, "I understand. You know, all these things that are keeping us apart are going to come to an end soon. This isn't the new norm for me, I'll tell you that. I think you just need to have a little patience as concerns us, and…"

"I agree. And while I am trying to figure out where I'm at *and* where you're at, you need to have a little patience with me. Give me some time too. I have never been good at making quick decisions especially when the subject that's part of that decision is standing right in front of me. Just give me a little time. Are you okay with that?"

"If that is the way it has to be and that's what you are most comfortable with, then yes, I'm fine with that. I just hope you don't take long to come to a conclusion. I already miss you."

"I understand. Again, I am sorry for your loss. I'll be in touch."

Chapter 39

"**D**avid, how are you?"

"Before we go any further, Bob, let me express my condolences concerning the passing of Jack. I am so, so sorry. I know you two were close friends for many years."

"We were, yes, we were."

"Was he working on the case you and I are discussing today?"

"Yes."

"Would you rather I come to your office? Is there paperwork you want me to review, or is the phone going to be good enough for now?"

"Yes, this is fine. I just wanted to briefly discuss what the current situation is. If then you believe the case is worth your time and effort, we can get together and go through the paperwork. Does that work for you?"

"Certainly, that's fine. However you wish to proceed. Now, it is my understanding he was charged with murder one, but found guilty of murder in the second degree, is that correct?"

"Yes."

"What about the record, Bob? Was it clean? Were there mistakes made by the court as concerned allowing exhibits or testimony into the record that shouldn't have been allowed? Was there anything that stood out to either you or Jack?"

"To be honest, no, there wasn't. But then, we weren't looking at it in that respect, at that time. I mean, sure if there was something obvious as concerns the testimony, we objected, but the great majority of the time, I felt the Judge just did what he should have done."

"That was Judge Strayer, right?"

"Yes."

"You know, I've worked on a couple of appeals in cases he handled at the trial level. He doesn't make many mistakes."

"That is why I need your expertise in this area—to look at everything and tell me what we should do."

"Have you asked that the record be transcribed yet?"

"No. I wanted to talk to you about all this before I made a move."

"I hate to ask this Bob, but how is he going to pay for the cost— and by that, I mean the cost of preparing the transcript and my fees?"

"I haven't told you all the story, David."

"Oh really. What, might I ask, did you skip?"

"He is my grandson."

David hesitated, then said, "The Defendant is your grandson?"

"Yes. So, I will be paying all the bills. And I will most likely just stay out of the way, rather than try to help you. He is broke. I really want the best in this field handling his appeal. I don't want someone that's court appointed and that we don't know, to handle this. It is too important to me."

"I understand. Why don't you get the court reporter started on typing the transcript. Then let's you and I get together next week and go through the specifics, if that works for you."

Charlene walked through his office door and stood in front of his desk.

Bob put his hand over his phone and whispered, "I'll just be another minute."

"Okay, I'll wait."

"David, I'll do that. Thanks for the help. I'll be in touch next week."

As he terminated the call, he looked up at Charlene and said, "Well, this must be mighty important for you to wait in front of my desk while I'm finishing as important a call as that was. What's going on?"

"Probably nothing, but do you know someone by the name of Carrie Thompson?"

"Nope."

"She says you do. Does she have something to do with Paul? She mentioned his name during the conversation."

Bob smiled, and said, "Oh, okay, *that* Carrie. Yes, she works for the newspaper in Knoxville. She has been writing stories about Paul's case and has been involved from the beginning. I really think Paul and her have a budding relationship going on but neither of them say much to me about it."

"Okay, well anyway, she called. She said she needed to talk to you. I tried to discuss details but she said she needed to talk to *you.*"

She handed him the message. "I told her I would give this to you right away. I don't know her, but she seemed on edge. She wanted to make sure you got the note as soon as possible."

"Hmm. I wonder if something has happened to Paul. I'll call her right now. Thanks."

As Charlene walked out of his office, he punched in Carrie's number.

She answered immediately.

"Hi Bob. First off, I'm so sorry about Jack. I know how close you were. He was always so kind to me…and to Paul."

"Thanks, Carrie. It has been a long day today—I talked to him almost every day of the week, especially while we were working on Paul's case. The day seems a little empty without him."

"I'm sure it does. Okay, now for the reason I called. And to be honest, this is probably nothing, but I felt you should know."

"Certainly. Go ahead."

"Well, as I continue writing these articles for the paper about Paul, the story gathers quite a following. I started out with no comments, or thoughts from anyone for the first few articles, to where now I have lots of mail every week. People also follow a special page I set up on Facebook. That following has really grown in numbers too."

"I know you've told me about that a couple of times—about how so many people are now following the story."

"Well, it's not unusual for people to call the station and want to talk to me about the case. I learned early on not to answer any of them, or return any of their calls. Most of them are not favorable for Paul. I don't listen to that garbage anymore. I know he is not guilty and that's the end of that."

"I assume that just basically goes along with the job you have, at least to some degree."

"Oh, it does, but nothing, and I mean nothing, has generated the interest this story has. And while I take none of the calls, nor return any of them, I do look at who called."

"Yeah, I'm sure some of them are lunatics. I'm sure you learned early on not to return phone calls to those you don't know."

"That's for sure. But, that said, yesterday I got a call that interested me."

"Who was it from? What did they want?"

"It was from a pawnbroker by the name of Carl Williams. He runs a pawnshop right outside Knoxville. He has been following the story. He knew Lynn. They had a common interest in antiques and old artifacts of all kinds. They had even done a little business together.”

“What did he want? Did he have some information about the murder?”

“No. But he did have a little information about Lynn—about the way she handled her life and about the old antiques in her house.”

“Did you call him back?”

“Oh yeah, I called this one back. He told me a guy came in the other day with some items that were pretty rare and he recognized them. There were three or four things that he recognized because they were unique and worth quite a bit of money.”

“What was the guy doing? Was he wanting to pawn them?”

“Yes.”

“So why did this catch his attention”

“Because the last time he saw those items they were in Lynn Baker’s living room.”

“Okay. Well, okay. Were they that unique he could identify them as being hers?”

“Yes. One of the vases had a small scratch along the bottom. He mentioned it to Lynn when Carl and his wife were in her home for a social gathering and she asked him about its value.”

“How did this guy get them? Did she give them to him?”

“Carl said something to the guy about that, and the guy got a little jumpy… you know, a little nervous, and just mumbled something like ‘Yes, she gave them to me.’ Well, according to Carl, she never sold nor gave *anything* to *anyone*. He tried to buy some of her items in the house, but she would never sell anything. I called her daughter and asked her about that too. She said Lynn never *gave* anything away either. She wouldn’t even give anything to *her*. She was almost to the point of being a hoarder.”

“So, did Carl take those items”

“The guy pawned them. Carl still has them. But as soon as he had them in his possession, he called me. I told him to hang onto them no matter what.”

“I wonder how this man got hold of them if she never gave anything away.”

“Yeah, so do I and I really think we should find out.”

"I agree. Okay, the trial I had scheduled for later this week was continued and is rescheduled for next month. I have some appointments I need to take care of this afternoon, but I can leave late today and be there this evening. Why don't we just meet at the jail tomorrow morning? Can you call Paul and tell him what you've just told me?"

"Certainly."

"You know, this probably doesn't mean a lot. I assume the guy has a perfectly logical story, but I think we need to pursue it. I mean, it almost looks like the guy was desperate for money, but wanted to hold on to those items until there was a conviction in her murder case, before he did anything—which makes you wonder when he got them and how he got them. This is all probably just wishful thinking—that maybe *he is* the one that murdered her and took those items. But who knows. We definitely need to follow it up. I'll just see you in the morning."

"You know, I wouldn't have thought that much more about it, until I finally asked Carl who it was that pawned those items."

Bob leaned forward in his chair, as he said, "Why? Who was it?"

"It was that guy that did all those odd jobs for Lynn and who testified for Paul at the trial. It was John Reed."

Chapter 40

"**S**o, what are you doing here today, Pops? I didn't think you were coming back until the weekend."

"Carrie called me. I am just waiting for her to get here. She told me…there she is now."

Paul smiled and said, "Hey. What a great surprise. I didn't expect *either* of you and I got *both* of you. Now, what's going on?"

Bob said, "Carrie, go ahead and tell him."

"Okay, here's the deal. Carl Williams called me. He runs a pawn shop near the outskirts of town. He has been following my articles, which is why he called. He said John Reed came in the other day and pawned items which he knows belonged to Lynn."

"How did John get them?"

"We are leaving here to discuss that very issue with him at length, but Carl said John told him they were given to him."

"Given to him! She never gave anything away—nor ever threw anything away. Her basement and the building out back were full of items that needed to be tossed long ago. She never gave anything to anyone."

"That is what we have been told. We are going to see Carl right now. We'll come back when we are done with him."

Carrie said, "Carl, nice to meet you. This is Paul's grandfather, Bob Duncan."

"I've read about you, Mr. Duncan, in those articles Carrie has written. She did a hell of a job. Everyone I know waits for the addition of the paper that has the next article about the trial in it. Really well-written and very complimentary about you, too."

"Thanks, Carl. Now, tell us about John. Have you dealt with him before?"

"Yes. I know very little about him other that the fact that he is broke most of the time. He brings things in here to pawn and most of the time I don't think much about it. Oh, there has been a time or two I wondered where something came from, but there's never been a time when he brought me something that I was able to determine it was hot."

"But you felt this time was different?"

"Yes, this time it *was* different. I knew Lynn. I knew her well. We bartered back and forth many times. We have been in each other's homes. She was a good friend and customer. I dabble in antiques as well as run the pawn shop, and antiques were what she loved. I knew where that one vase came from the moment I saw it."

"So, did you ask him where he got it?"

"I told him I knew where it came from. I told him that right off the bat. He then said she gave it to him one day for some extra work he did for her, which she felt was really done well."

"Did you talk to her daughter about it?"

"Yes. In fact, she came here, to the shop. She looked at the vase and confirmed that all the items he brought in here *appeared* to be Lynn's but the only one she could identify for certain was that vase. She also confirmed Lynn was a kind and good individual, but she was about as far away from a *giving* person as you could possibly be. Once she got it, she kept it."

"Paul confirmed that with us too."

"So, what are you thinking happened here?"

Bob said, "You know, it's interesting he would pawn those items right after Paul was convicted for her murder. I mean that just looks strange. Of course, we know he is lying about those items being gifted to him too. And if they were stolen by him while she was alive, she would have surely called the police—there would be a report on it."

Carrie said, "This doesn't smell right. What do you think, Bob?"

"Maybe we should see if we can get in to see the Prosecutor. I wonder if he would be interested in these new facts."

"Let's go find out."

Ten minutes later they were sitting in the reception area waiting to talk to Mr. Jensen. His office door opened and he stepped through as he said, "Well, we meet again. What do you want? I hope it has nothing to do with that guy we just convicted of murder."

Bob stood and said, "Sorry, but it does. Do you have a few minutes?"

"What for? The case is over."

"Just humor us for a few minutes, will you?"

He smiled, and said, "Why not. I have literally a few minutes to waste and that's all...*period*. Come on in."

As they sat, George looked at Carrie and said, "So, I finally get to meet the writer. You did a hell of a job."

"Thanks."

"I thought there were a couple of times you were way hard on our office, but I let it go. I never said anything to you, even as badly as I wanted to. You know, you brought a lot of people into the courtroom with those articles, many of whom were second guessing us and our office all the way through the proceedings. I wanted an opportunity to tell you I really didn't appreciate your negative, antagonistic approach, not for one minute. Thank you for the opportunity to tell you. Now, what do you want?"

Carrie leaned forward in her chair, and said, "Now you listen to me, you..."

Bob quickly stepped in and said, "Carrie, hold on here. Just take a deep breath. Remember what we are doing."

She quickly turned toward Bob, then looked at George and said, "I didn't mean to cause a problem for you, or your office."

Jensen smiled and said, "Thanks. That's big of you. Now what do you two want? I got a lot of ground to cover this morning and you are both in the way."

Bob said, "George, we just found out that a witness at the trial, recently pawned some items that belonged to Lynn Baker. We have also come to the conclusion Lynn Baker wouldn't have given anything away if her life depended on it. We believe they were taken from her home and that the man who took them might have murdered Lynn right before he took them."

"Really. Who is the guy?"

"His name is John Reed. You probably remember him. He testified at the time of trial. He did odd jobs for Lynn."

"But he wasn't there the night she was murdered. That would have been a little tough for him to do—that is, to murder her and take her items—if he wasn't there."

"We are thinking he *was* there. We're not sure how he got in and out, or when he was there, but there's definitely something wrong here. The guy also waited until the trial was over before he pawned the items, thinking, I assume, that there would be no further investigating since

Paul was already convicted."

Jensen leaned forward and said, "So, we got your grandson in the house at the time she was murdered, he admitted they had sex, then he got in an argument with her. He had scratch marks on his arm, he was seen leaving her house at or about the time she was murdered, the jury convicted him, and now you want us to devote more manpower to the case to determine if he's guilty in a case where he has already been *found* guilty. *Is that about the gist of it?*"

Bob leaned forward and said, "The gist of it is this—Paul didn't do it. It's too bad these additional facts came out now instead of before the trial. It appears to us John was somehow involved."

Jensen stood. "Okay, what the hell do you expect us to do now? Our job is finished. We prosecuted and convicted the man that committed the crime."

Bob stood, and leaned over Jenson's desk. "I expect you to do your job. You have new facts here that perhaps indicate you convicted the wrong man. Now, do your damn job. Figure out what's going on here. Help us out."

"We are done, Mr. Duncan. We *did* what we were supposed to do. This trial and this case is over. We are not going one step further. Now, the two of you need to get out before I call security."

Bob looked at Carrie, who was still seated. "Come on, let's go."

She stood and as she did, she looked at Jensen and said, "You haven't heard the end of this—not as concerns this case or as concerns the articles. And, you asshole, if you think I put the heat on you with those prior articles, you just wait."

He laughed. "Just tell the truth, missy. You know what happens when you slander someone."

"Oh, they will be truthful. Just be sure and read them. Because you are sure enough going to want to know what they said so you can defend yourself, you worthless son-of-a-bitch. "

"So, what happened?"

Carrie said, "It went well with the pawn broker. Not so well with the Prosecutor."

"What did the pawnbroker have to say?"

"Just what we already told you. He feels the same way we do— that somehow John is involved in all this."

"So, then you went to see Jenson?"

"Yes. We told him what we had found out, and he just basically kicked us out of his office. I told him to be prepared for the next round of articles. I told him if he thought those prior articles were negative as concerns their office, wait until the next few."

Paul said, "He wouldn't listen at all? I mean, how could it not appear to him as though something's not quite right? I would have figured he would at least do *something*—maybe not reopen the case again, but do something to figure this out."

"Nope, not a damn thing. By the way, your grandpa is a bad ass. I thought he was going over the top of his desk to get to him."

Paul smiled. "Runs in the family. So, what's next. What can we do now?"

Bob said, "You know, Carrie, that cop I talked to the first time I came down here seemed really nice—and helpful. I wonder if we could get in to see him. Maybe he would be willing to help. I don't think either you or I should confront John."

She stood. "I agree. Let's go see if he is in and if he will talk to us. One thing about it. No matter how our conversation goes with him, it can't be as bad as the conversation we just had with Jenson. That son-of-a-bitch is a real piece of work."

Chapter 41

As Bob called the police station, for the *third* time, all he could think of was that small glimmer of hope in his grandson's case. He had called for Officer Majors twice. No one would take a message. They all told him to call back later. This was the third time he had called back *later*, and if this didn't result in success, they would drive to the station *without* making an appointment.

A few minutes later he walked in the visiting room, smiled at Paul and said, "I got him this time. He told me to come to the station…. now. He told me he would take time to visit with us about the case, but, after I briefly explained what we were doing, he told me not to be optimistic—the case, as far as their department was concerned, was over. I didn't tell him many of the specifics. We will see what he thinks when we tell him everything. Let's go, Carrie."

"Paul, we will see you as soon as we finish with him."

Officer Majors was waiting for them when they arrived. He ushered them into a small conference room and, as they sat, he said, "Okay, what's going on? You didn't tell me many of the details other than you had some interesting facts that involved Paul's case, and which indicate someone else could very well have been the murderer. What have you found out?"

As they sat, Bob said, "Do you know Carl Williams?"

"The guy that runs the pawn shop on the outskirts of town?"

"Yes, that's him."

"I know who he is, but that's about it."

"Well, it seems, he was a long-time friend of Lynn Baker. They socialized, and even did some dealing back and forth. He called Carrie the other day and told her that one of the witnesses at the trial, John Reed, had brought in some things to pawn—vases and things of that nature—that he was certain belonged to Lynn."

"How did John get them?"

"That's the point. In talking to him along with Lynn's daughter, and in discussions just a few minutes ago with Paul, it has become clear Lynn never gave *anything* away. He wouldn't have had the money to *buy* these items. He was broke, which was why he was pawning them."

"And he did this *after* Paul's conviction?"

"Yes. Not only was the fact that he had the items in his possession somewhat confusing, his timing in pawning the items also seemed strange to us. He waited until there was a conviction concerning her death before pawning them—making sure the alleged murderer was identified *and* convicted before he pawned the items."

"Have you been to see Jensen?"

"Yes. To put it mildly, he basically kicked us out of his office. He said the case was over and he wouldn't even consider looking into it any further."

"So, what do you want from me?"

"I thought about just confronting Reed. But, upon reconsideration, I don't think that is the thing to do. I will if I have to, but I am just not sure I should be confronting a guy, who might in fact be the one that actually killed Lynn."

"No, you need to leave him alone. I'll do it. I have a little time this morning. I could run him down and ask him how he got those items—just see how he reacts."

"Should we wait here or come back when you call us?"

He thought for a moment. "I think you should come back."

"Certainly. I'll give you my cell number, and you can give me a call when you are on your way back to the station."

On his way to see Paul, Bob called David Williams. David's secretary put him through immediately.

"Hi David, this is Bob. Have you read any of the transcript from my grandson's trial yet?"

"Yes, I have. I took a look at the testimony of some of the State's witness."

"What are your thoughts?"

"I still have a considerable amount of testimony to read yet, but Bob I have to be honest. I have seen absolutely nothing upon which to base an appeal. Now, I do have most of the transcript to read yet, but I can tell you if it continues to read as it has so far, you better not rely on an appeal to get him off. I hate to be the bearer of bad news, but those are my thoughts as of now."

"To be honest, that's no surprise. Just keep me informed."

Bob terminated the call and waited for a call from Officer Majors. It came a couple of hours later. He wanted Bob to meet him at the station whenever he could get there. Bob called Carrie and told her to meet him at the station as soon as she could.

Once they were both there, Officer Majors escorted them into a conference room.

As they sat, he said, "Well, I don't have very good news for you. I found out through his wife, where he was working. Once I met up with him and told them why I was there, he told me in no uncertain terms those items were a gift from Lynn. I asked him why he waited so long after her death to pawn them, and he said he didn't need the money until then. I asked him about being involved in her murder and of course, he completely denied it."

Bob leaned back in his chair and said, "I guess those are the responses I expected. And of course, we are still fighting the issue of no one else being seen going in or out of the house during that time period. Even if we can show he took those items, we can't put him there at the time of the incident."

Glen looked away for a moment and remained silent.

"Right, Glen? We can't put anyone at the scene other than Paul."

Glen thought for a moment, then said, "You know, I always liked Paul."

"I guess I didn't know you even knew him."

"He did some work for me, at our home. We wanted his ideas concerning a small flower garden my wife wanted to put in, so we called him. His recommendations were great."

As he turned to face Bob, he said, "I never really felt he committed the crime. I mean, from what I knew of him, and about him, I just never felt he had it in him to hurt anyone, let alone a woman he really cared for."

Bob could tell he had something on his mind—something was bothering him. He had dealt with enough of life's characters that it wasn't hard to tell that Glen was bothered about something.

Bob said, "Did you have any other contact with him while this investigation was going no?"

"No, I heard all about it though. And when all those parts started to fit together as easily as they did, I wouldn't say there might have been a rush to judgement around here, but that's the way it appeared to me. There was literally nothing I could do about it, even in light of some of the issues that bothered me. Those that were involved felt they had the right man, and that was the end of it. Of course, that was all confirmed when he was convicted."

Bob leaned forward. "When you say, 'nothing you could do about it', what do you mean? About what?"

"I have a few issues in mind, concerning the case, that I really feel we should discuss."

"I don't understand. Like what?"

"I need to figure out how to handle this before I do it. I don't think it will be a problem, but I need to think this through first."

"Why can't we discuss it now? I will say nothing to anyone other than what you tell me to say."

He stood. "Nope. I can't do it that way. I need permission first. I don't think there will be a problem, but I cannot take a chance. I need permission. Why don't you come back here about ten tomorrow morning?'

Bob stood, as he said "Okay, if that is what we need to do that is what we'll do. We will see you here tomorrow at ten."

They brought Paul to the conference room, where he sat down as he said, "What happened? Did they talk to John?"

"Yes."

"I assume he admitted nothing."

"That is a valid assumption. I didn't expect him to admit, I guess. I was hoping he would, but I didn't expect him to."

Paul leaned back in his chair and said, "So, is that it? Are we done? Another dead end?"

"You know, I am not sure. The officer acted somewhat strange about this whole deal. He said he needed to think about something and he wanted us to come back tomorrow morning. He absolutely wouldn't say anything concerning what he had in mind. So, we are going back tomorrow morning."

"I wonder what that's all about. By the way, did your attorney friend look over the transcript?"

"He has looked over some of it, yes."

"Need I ask if he has found anything that might help, or are we done there too?"

"Just don't ask. He is not done yet, but let's just leave it at that."

'Yeah, just another dead end. You don't have to tell me."

"It is not over, Paul—not until we have followed every avenue we can follow. Let's just see what happens in the morning."

"Yeah, yeah, I understand. It's just that…"

Carrie said, "Bob, are you ready to leave?"

"Well, yes, I guess I am, why?"

"I need a little time with Paul alone. Do you mind?"

Bob smiled and said softly, "No, no I don't mind at all. I'll head back to the hotel. Do you want me to pick you up tomorrow morning?"

"No. I will just meet you there. I'm not sure where I may need to go after we are done with Majors and I might as well have a vehicle with me so I don't have to go back to work to get it."

He stood. "I'll see you there at ten. Paul, hang in. I am not sure what's going on but whatever it is, apparently Glen needs permission from someone to let us in on it. I'll see you tomorrow."

Chapter 42

It seemed the night lasted forever. He had been unable to fall asleep and watched TV until well after midnight. Once he turned it off, he tossed and turned until he finally sat up, got out of bed and made coffee in his room.

Bob now waited patiently in one of the police station conference rooms. Carrie was late. Officer Majors, who had placed him in the room, left him alone while he 'checked on a couple of items.'

Finally, just as he was ready to search for Officer Majors, the door opened and Carrie walked in. As she closed the door behind her, she said, "Sorry I'm late. Have you had a chance to talk to him yet?"

"No. He put me in this room and then left. That was a half-hour ago. I assume he hasn't forgotten us. You know, I was awake damn near all night thinking about what he said to us yesterday—wondering what this conference today was all about. So, if I get a little short with him, you have my permission to tell me to shut the hell up and just take over. Were you able to settle Paul down after I left yesterday?"

"Yes. He was fine after we talked a bit. He gets that way. The best way to handle him is talk it out. I figured out a long time ago that was what works best for him."

They both turned toward the door as Officer Majors walked through, closing the door with one hand while holding an iPad in the other.

"Good morning."

Bob said, "Good morning again, Glen." He glanced at the computer and said, "Well, this is already interesting. What has changed as concerns this case, that now necessitates the use of a computer."

As Glen sat, he said, "Just forget about the computer for a moment." He placed it on the table, and said, "Before I show you what I want to show you, I need to explain something."

"That sounds a little ominous."

"Now, I just want to premise what you are about to see, with this in mind. You know, when this all happened, the facts concerning Paul's involvement in the crime were not complicated. By that, I mean that the facts were pretty damn obvious."

He paused for a moment, cleared his throat, and said, "Now, I know I don't have to explain to you what the facts were that resulted in us charging Paul with the crime. They were right out there for everyone to see. In general, he was seen leaving the house. They were heard arguing about something. He was scratched up. There was no one else seen coming or going from the house, and, of course, law enforcement had, as a result of testing, determined the two of them had been sexually active."

"Certainly, we are aware of all the issues having just tried the case. So, what's new? Go on."

"Well, all of those issues were the basis for arresting him, and they formed the basis for his conviction. So, there was never a doubt, from the time we started investigating the crime, through the jury's verdict, who did this. It was just a matter of getting it all into evidence and convicting him."

He paused.

"Go on. So far, you have told us nothing we don't already know."

"So, what I am saying is that there was never any exculpatory evidence of any nature and if there had been…if there had even been quite a bit of exculpatory evidence, it would have had to have been damn convincing or it would never had made a difference—at least not to the officer's involved—or to a jury."

"Okay, okay cut to the chase here. *Is* there exculpatory evidence no one considered? *Was this a rush to judgement?*"

"I just wanted to premise what you are about to see, with the mindset of the officers working the case at the time. There was never any doubt in anyone's mind about Paul's guilt—every shred of discernable evidence pointed in Paul's direction."

Bob leaned forward and said "We," and he pointed toward Carrie, then at himself, "get it, we really do. Now would you please quit apologizing for whatever it is you are going to show us and just move on."

"Okay, somewhere along the way, did you hear about a camera in the back area of the house?"

"I remember hearing something about one, yes."

Carrie said, "I do too. But there was something about a light being out so you could see nothing. I never thought anything about it, because we were all told by the officers it showed nothing"

Bob said, "We asked for it in discovery and were told it was useless and of no consequence. We let it lie based on their statements"

"At the time of the incident, someone with the department looked at it and told all of us there was nothing to see. So, I let it go, until one day, when I was reading about his trial, and I just decided to take a look for myself."

Bob moved forward in his chair, and said, "Is there more to it than that? Does it show something we should have known about?"

"It really didn't show anything when it was first viewed, that fit in or would have helped either side. At least that was the conclusion reached by the officer that viewed it. But now that we have an idea someone else really may have been involved, I want you to look at it."

He opened the iPad, and said, "Okay, before I show you this, you need to know that the camera was situated on the roof of the small storage building she had behind her house where she kept a few of her antiques. The camara faces downward and toward the back of the house."

"Is there a light for that area?"

"No. And that's the other thing. You know, it was John that was supposed to fix that light. He didn't. As a result, it's all dark, dusk until dawn, which I'm thinking now, might have been done on purpose. Just watch."

Initially, there was nothing but a dark screen. But after a few moments, one could barely see some movement in the shadows. Clearly, something was moving. It was too dark to even tell if it was human, but there was definitely movement.

Glen said, "Okay now let me move it ahead in time."

He advanced the data about twenty minutes and then again, slowed it down. As they continued to watch, there was additional movement, but as before, it was impossible to tell who or what it was.

Glen pulled out the flash drive out and said, "That's the end of what it shows during that time period, but clearly something was going on there."

Bob sat back in his chair, and said, "Someone lied to us."

"No, no I don't believe that was the case at all. At the time, all the evidence pointed directly at Paul and the jury convicted him. There was and is no way to tell who that was or even if it was human. For all intents and purposes, they had the right perpetrator, and he was charge and convicted. It was only after I, just on a whim, took a second look searching for something on the film that might be advantageous. Only now, after we know John has some of her possessions, does the movement become significant. *But even now, you really can't tell if the movement is a human being.*"

Bob leaned back, took a deep breath, and said, "I guess all that is interesting, but it still doesn't get us our killer."

"You're right, but it does fit together pretty well with what you now know about John. Could that movement have been him?"

An hour later, they were sitting with Paul and explaining what they just viewed.

"Paul, I really don't know where we go from here. I just feel pretty certain someone went in that house after you left. I mean, it appeared maybe the door was opening and someone…It is just so hard to tell, but it appeared to me, maybe because it's what I want to conclude, that someone went in there after you left, after it was dark."

"Where do we go from here?"

"I'm not sure, I guess. Obviously, we need more than we have right now though."

"So, do we just wait and see if seething else turns up?"

"Probably. You know, the officers should have given us that video. Now, maybe we couldn't have done anything with it, but they still should have given it to us."

" Would it have helped at the time of trial?"

"Want the truth?"

"Always."

"Probably not. There were just too many other factors against you."

"Okay, let's say that somehow, someway, we determine someone else was in there after I was. Legally, is there anything we can do about it?"

"I've never had anything like that come up before. I don't know. Jack could have probably laid it all out for us. I think we need to get to the point where we have enough to tell them that, without doubt, you are innocent. We certainly are not there yet. Let's worry about the procedural aspects of it, when we have the facts to support your innocence. We need to sit tight and see what happens now. Carrie and I will both keep digging based on these new facts."

Carrie said, "You know, Bob, I don't think I should write about what we now know—not yet anyway. We could scare Reed right out of the area."

"Good idea."

"Paul. don't worry about the process, at least not yet. Let's keep our ears open and see what happens next."

"Carrie, keep your readers updated, but I, like you, think it's a good idea not to release these new facts. I need to go back to Nashville for a few days. Hopefully, maybe something else will turn up. Stay positive, Paul." He stood. "I'll be back in a couple of days."

Chapter 43

“What is going on in Knoxville? You were here and you said you were staying, but then you left in a hurry. Now, you are back, but your phone message early this morning said you may be gone as soon as tomorrow. I’m having trouble keeping track of you.”

Bob just sat down and started going through his messages when Charlene walked in.

“First of all, do I have anything in court the rest of this week, or next?”

“No. I had everything continued…again. But I can tell you, I am starting to meet with a grumble or two, not only from attorneys, but from judges. I don’t know how many more times I am going to be able to continue some of these hearings. What’s going on now?”

Bob looked out the window for a moment, before turning toward her as he said, “First of all, I am sorry for putting you in this position. I can guarantee you it’s not going to last much longer. I believe if I can spend just a little more time in Knoxville, we will be finished one way or the other. Here’s what is going on. One of the police officers had Carrie and I come in and when we got there, he showed us a video that was taken from a shed Lynn had out back of the house.”

“Why is that relevant now? Why would that mean anything at this late date? The trial is over. What significance is the video now?”

“From what I saw, not very much. It was dark and all it really shows is what looks like a shadow of something or somebody. It looks like maybe someone could be opening the door to the house, but it’s just so dark it’s hard to tell…there is absolutely no way you can make out who it is or if it is even a human.”

“So, it is of no help?”

“Hell, I don’t know. As I say, it appears to me that maybe someone is trying to open the door and then about twenty minutes later opening it again. But like I say, it is so dark, it’s really impossible to tell what’s going on.”

"Did you know about the video at the time of trial?"

"No."

"Shouldn't you have been told about it, whether relevant or not? Isn't that something that should have been provided to you?"

"Probably. But there's not much we could have done with it at the time of trial. There was no way we could identify whether the movement was even human. But yes, I'm thinking they should have provided it anyway."

"Even if it couldn't help you, correct?"

"Probably. Maybe. Hell, like I told you, I don't know. The State probably should have provided it but it most likely wouldn't have helped. Now, after the trial is over, and we know this other guy is pawning items that belonged to her, it starts to fit together, but we didn't know about the pawning business until after the trial was over. SO…"

"It's still not enough, is it?"

"Get David Williams on the phone for me, will you?"

"Certainly."

A few minutes later, Charlene let him know David was on line one. "David, how are you? Have you had a chance to review any additional portions of the transcript?"

"Yes, I have. I'm afraid I haven't come up with much. I am almost finished and unless there are issues with the instructions to the jury or in closing statements, or unless something happened near the end of the trial I haven't yet read about, there's really not much here to appeal."

"I was afraid of that."

"You know, I just continually look for mistakes—for errors the Judge made during the trial—but there just aren't any that justify an appeal. Now, I can proceed if you wish, because there are a few issues the appeal's court might just take a long look at, but I just don't think they are serious enough to warrant overturning the verdict. "

'Let me ask you this. I have recently discovered some new information which the police had, but which we were never told about. At the time of trial, it might not have been of any value, but we have now discovered a new party of interest and this bit of information might implicate him. Was it incumbent upon law enforcement to provide us with everything before the trial started, whether they determined it was worthless or not? I mean, maybe we should have pushed harder at the time, but they indicated when they provided us with what they had, that they had no more relevant information. We believed that, and to be honest, at the time, it was most likely worthless to all of us anyway. Even now, it may not be worth anything, but, is that appealable.?"

"Good question. If it had some value before the trial, it might have been, but knowing it could provide no useable evidence at the *time* of trial, makes it an interesting issue. I'll have to take a look at that."

"Don't bother. We don't have enough, even *with* that, to establish anyone else might have committed the crime."

"You will want to review in depth, Rule 29 which allows you, under certain circumstances to have a verdict set aside. Now, it doesn't sound like you have enough yet to use it, but keep it in mind. There are some timelines set for when a motion concerning that issue must be filed, but you are still well within those timelines. Just don't get caught with your pants down and miss it."

"I understand. I'll have you help me with it if and when we feel it needs to be pursued. But clearly, we don't have nearly enough yet. Thanks for the advice, David. I'll be in touch."

A few minutes later, Charlene peaked around his doorframe, and said, "I'm not sure what I'm supposed to be doing with Susan. I don't hear much about her around here anymore, but she is on the phone. Are you...do you...want to talk with her? Should I put her through, or do you want to call her back...or..."

"I'll take it. Thanks, Charlene."

"Susan, hi, how are you?"

"I am good, Bob. I just thought I would see how the trial was progressing. Any news?"

"Not really. We are just trying to pick up the pieces. We are still doing some investigating. I got some interesting news yesterday concerning some information we weren't provided before trial, so I'm working on that angle at the present. But there isn't much positive news concerning Paul. How are you?"

"Oh, I am fine." She hesitated. "I miss you."

"I miss you too. Is it time we get together and discuss where we are going from here? Do you feel uncomfortable in discussing the issues we both seem to have?'

"I just feel sorry for you...and for Paul. Is there any hope left in the case as concerns getting out of all this and out of jail so you can really have a relationship with him? This is all such a shame."

"We are working on something now, but it's a longshot. We need more than what we presently have. As of now, no, there's not much hope. I take it by avoiding my question you aren't interested in getting together."

She hesitated. "No, I'm not. I am concerned about you. I am concerned about your relationship with your grandson. But as of now, I just need a little more time to determine what I want out of the rest of *my* life."

"I understand. Neither one of us are spring chickens. We both need to make sure the decisions we are making now are the right ones—decisions that will be beneficial for the life we have left."

"Let me know if anything changes, Bob. Thanks for the update."

Bob terminated the call. As soon as he did, Charlene came in, sat down, and said, "Do you two have problems? You always seemed to get along so well. It's none of my business, but you both seemed like a perfect match for each other."

"I have to many issues pulling me in too many different directions. She wants more out of me than I can offer. She needs time to figure out exactly what she wants to do with her life at this point in time and I am giving that to her. Now, moving on from my personal issues, what's going on from your point of view?"

"I'm just trying to move a few more hearings down the road for you. So far, no problem. Oh, and someone by the name of Majors called. I know we don't have a client by that name, but he wouldn't tell me what he wanted. I knew you weren't taking any more clients, so I just set the message aside. Do you want it?"

He sat up and moved forward in his chair, as he said, "Go get it right now."

"Oh, okay, hold on."

Officer Majors had indeed called and wanted Bob to give him a call when he was free.

"Glen, this is Bob Duncan. What's going on?"

"Oh, I just think there's something else we should probably discuss, I thought about it all night. I reviewed everything that happened in this case since the verdict and came to the conclusion we still need to talk. I think you should come see me when you are in town the next time."

"Is it important enough for me to drive down right down, or can it wait? I have a lot going on here. I could come down near the end of the week, if that works for you."

"No, you need to come sooner than that."

"Okay…well then what about tomorrow morning? Will that work for you?"

"I'll make it work. I'll see you in the morning."

Bob terminated the call, and as soon as he did, he called Carrie. They agreed to meet at the police station around ten. She asked him what the meeting was about. Bob told her Majors had additional information for them and apparently it was important enough he didn't want to wait until next week to discuss it. Carrie told him that was all she needed to know and would meet him tomorrow morning.

Chapter 44

As Carrie walked into the conference room, Bob smiled and said, "This is getting to be second nature. I get a phone call from the cops, I drive to Knoxville, I meet you here."

As Carrie sat down beside him, she said, "Do you know what's going on?'

"Not a clue. Glen just told me he thought about something all night and wanted to meet us here to discuss it. He never mentioned any of the particulars."

"I wonder if it involves something else the cops forgot to provide us."

"I guess we will soon know."

As Carrie started to respond, Glen walked in the room.

"Morning. Sorry I was so vague about the reason I needed to see you, but I felt I should explain this in detail and in person, rather than over the phone."

"What is it that was so important?"

As he sat down, he said, "Well, there is another aspect of this case I need to discuss with you. I had to, once again, get permission from my boss to talk to you about it. He wasn't in favor of it. He insisted the case was over. But I convinced him it was the right thing to do.

He finally changed his mind and agreed with me. "By the way Carrie, if you ever end up writing about this aspect of the case, I want you to remember, we were under no obligation to explain these different issues to you after the trial ended. No one would have been the wiser. We know what I have been discussing with you could cast us in an unfavorable light. But I want you to know that if the circumstances surrounding this case came up exactly the same again, it would most likely result in us handling the case in exactly the same manner as we did this time."

"Okay Glen, there you go again—apologizing before you even tell us what it is you were going to tell us. Now, could you please just move on?"

He leaned back and said, "You know, they took that sample from Lynn and determined Paul had sex with her not long before she died. That all came up at the time of trial. That was all part of the evidence."

"Yes, old news. Do you have some *new* news for us?"

"I do, yes, I do. The test they did to confirm Paul had sex with her that day, also confirmed she had recently had sex with someone else."

Bob leaned back, looked at Carrie, then at Glen as he said, "What the hell does that mean?"

"Lynn had sex with someone else around the same time period—either before or after Paul did. The doctor wasn't sure which."

"Did they get DNA concerning both samples."

"Yes."

"Who was it—did they ever determine that?"

"They have no idea. They, of course, were able to determine the one sample belonged to Paul. They were *not* able to match up who the other sample belonged to."

"So, they ignored the other sample and just used Paul's?"

"Again, it all fit together with the rest of the evidence, The fact that one of the samples belonged to him, was all that mattered. Whether she had sex with someone else before he killed her made no difference to us. Besides, they had no other suspect—they couldn't match it up with anyone. And with the overwhelming evidence they had against Paul, they didn't feel they needed to."

Bob sat quietly as he evaluated the situation.

"No one ever questioned the results. Even if we would have *told* you she had sex with some other unknown individual, it wouldn't have made the case against Paul any less compelling. Should we have held off charging him because someone else had sex with her that day? No, I don't think so."

"But you still could have told us about the other sample."

"It didn't matter. It wasn't evidence in this case. It didn't diminish the department's thoughts that Paul murdered her. But now, with the pawnshop issue, and with the shadowy figure, if that's what it is, outside her back door, I felt obligated to let you know someone else's DNA was detected."

Bob said, "Well, I suppose we could discuss the issue of whether we should have been told, all day. I mean, I somewhat understand why this was done this way, but I'm not sure it was the *correct* way. Regardless, it still doesn't put us much closer in determining who the other sample belongs to."

"With the facts we have now though, we *know* Reed had some of her property. In addition, we have concluded that most likely that was a human figure outside her back door. Let's move on with this additional information."

"I'm thinking before we do anything else, we must determine who the hell that sample belongs too. I think if we do, we just might be able to figure this whole thing out. At that point, then maybe we could figure out what to do with Paul's conviction and move forward against the other guy—the guy who appears to me to be John Reed."

Bob looked away for a moment, then turned toward Glen and said, "So, where do we go from here?"

"I don't know. I called the hospital and asked to talk to the individual that did the testing. They are discussing the case as we speak. I should have an answer for you as to what's going on later today. Are you staying here overnight or going back to Nashville?"

"Definitely staying here."

"Okay, why don't you meet me here tomorrow morning, same time, and I'll see if I can get an answer for you concerning the next step."

Bob and Carrie both stood. "We will see you here tomorrow morning at the same time." They stood and started to walk away. Bob stopped, turned around and said, "By the way, Glen. Thank you. How ever this might turn out, if it hadn't been for you, we would have never come this far."

"Let's just see where this all goes. We haven't come to many other conclusions yet other than the fact that Paul has been convicted. Let's see if we can turn this whole thing around—get Paul out of jail and Reed in."

"I hope so—I hope that is the result."

Bob tuned toward Carrie and said, "Do you want to go with me to see Paul, or are you going back to work?"

She smiled. "I've been with him most of the morning. I need to go to work. I'll see you here tomorrow morning."

As Bob came to a stop in a parking space not far from the jail, he called David Williams.

"David, we have another issue that has just came up."

"What is it?"

We just found out that when they checked Lynn for sexual activity, they also found someone else's DNA other than Paul's. They didn't feel it mattered because it was unidentifiable and they already had the one that killed her in custody. So, they never told anyone about the other sample. Would that, along with the issue involving the video, help us concerning a Rule 29 motion?"

"Do they have anyone in mind as concerns the other DNA sample?"

"*We do now.* But all of this has come up after the conviction."

"That's fine. I think *now* we have a shot with the motion. So, what are you doing?"

"The officer helping us is talking to the individual that tested the DNA to see where we go from here."

"Just keep me updated. I'll check on the time limitation issue concerning the filing of the motion, but I'm thinking we still have plenty of time to file. You know, you could perhaps wrap this all up if you could determine whose DNA it is. Perhaps everything would then resolve itself."

"Maybe. Nothing has gone smoothly in this case, as you know. We are just taking everything a step at a time. I have no idea how the hell we will ever match up that new sample with someone else. I'm going to talk to Paul and find out what his thoughts might be. I'll contact you later today if I have any more news."

"Good luck."

A few minutes later, Paul said, "What are you doing here? I wasn't expecting you."

"I've got some news."

"Good news, bad news, what kind of news?"

"Glen called us down here to discuss another issue involving the case."

"Again? You two should be good friends by now. This is getting to be a daily event."

"Lynn had sex with someone else apparently the same day she was murdered."

Paul leaned back and said, "Oh, I don't think so."

"They found someone else's DNA besides yours."

"You have to be kidding. That makes absolutely no sense. There is no way she was having a relationship with anyone else other than me."

"It *does* make sense if she was *raped* by whoever killed her."

"I don't... I can't... that...who's DNA is it? Have they figured it out?"

"Not yet. Whoever it belongs to isn't in the system. They have no idea-- which is why they never said anything about it—that and the fact that all the other evidence pointed toward you anyway."

"Why did they tell you now?"

"Because one officer felt it was the right thing to do. It now seems to all of us, to be way, way more than a coincidence that Reed pawned items that belonged to her, *and* there is definitely a shadow at the back door in the video, *and* we now have this DNA issue."

Paul leaned forward and ran his fingers through his hair, as he said "I can't believe they didn't tell us."

"It really wouldn't have mattered anyway. What were we going to do with someone's unidentified DNA? Maybe we could have used it in our closing argument, but we had nothing to go with it, and they had all that evidence against you."

"So, now what.?"

"Glen is checking with the folks at the hospital to determine exactly that. We meet with them again in the morning."

"How are we ever going to match the sample?"

"I'll know more in the morning. I'm going to the hotel. It's been a long day. I'll see you tomorrow after I've talked to Glen."

Chapter 45

As Bob got dressed the following morning, he couldn't help but wonder when, and actually *if,* his life would ever return to normal. The trips back and forth were taking their toll. It took him hours to fall asleep last night and this morning, it took most all the energy he had left in his body, just to get out of bed, as he apparently faced another day of chaos.

He figured if he was still forty, the days might have been somewhat easier. But at his age, each day seemed to take its toll. Hopefully somehow, someway, Glen would tell him there was now indeed an end in sight.

As he walked into the conference room he said, "Morning, Carrie. How long have you been waiting?"

"Not long, maybe ten minutes. I'm excited—ready to go. For the first time in a long time, I really think there's a reason for some hope."

Bob sat down, and said, "Maybe. I'm still somewhat skeptical but we'll see. By the way, that was another great article today. I am really thankful your boss has allowed you to carry on reporting about Paul's situation rather than ending it all with a verdict."

Glen walked through the open door as he said, "Morning. I agree. That was a good article. Thanks for bringing everything up to date and not writing it in a manner that depicts the police department as the bad guys."

Carrie smiled and said, "I just wrote the truth Glen, nothing more, nothing less."

As he sat, Bob said, "Well, as you can imagine, we are a little anxious after yesterday. What did you find out?"

"To be honest, not much. First of all, I asked them to retest that second sample and make sure there was no match."

"Good idea. What did they say?"

"They told me the test never fails—it is one hundred percent accurate. It is not a match with anyone in the system *period.*"

"Well, that is certainly not a good start to the day. So, is there anything else we can do?"

Glen leaned back, and said, "Well, since we have an idea who *might* have done all this, if we could get a bodily fluid sample from Reed, we would at least know about him. Beyond that, I have no idea where we could look. It's either him, or we will most likely never know who it was."

"Then we need a sample from Reed to help figure this all out, right?"

"Exactly."

Bob smiled and said, "Great. How soon can you get that done, so we know one way or the other/"

"I wish it were that easy, Bob. We can't just go ask for some type of bodily fluid from him. He will certainly know what's going on and he doesn't have to voluntarily consent at all. We have already convicted someone of this crime. If he finds out we really believe he might have been involved, I have no doubt he'll run, and we will never know."

"Are you serious? You can't get a sample by just asking? If you can't do it that way, how the hell are we going to get one?"

"Well, it's not going to be easy. We have to figure out how to get our own sample, without him knowing about it."

"Have you done this before?"

"Yes."

"How has it been done in the past?"

"The easiest way is to get a glass or cup the individual drank from and test his saliva. That's the easiest way we have found to do it."

"And I assume it would be insanity to think you could just walk up to his house and ask for something he recently drank from?"

"Correct. The way I did it one other time was that I followed him until the guy went to a fast-food place and then I got the cup he drank from. It didn't work out because there was no match, but the process worked."

"So, can you do that?"

"No, I can't. I've been told not to work on this case. As far as we are concerned, it's a done deal. They don't want me spending anymore of the department's time on a case in which the guy we feel committed the crime, has been convicted. They are allowing me to visit with you. But for me to go out and actually work the case—well, that's not going to happen."

"So, who is going to do it? *Someone has to do it.*"

Glen said nothing.

Carrie looked at Bob and said, "It's up to us."

He looked at her, then at Glen. "Is that right? *We* have to do it?"

"If you want it done, you have to do it. I can initially advise you to get you started, but the bottom line is you are going to have to do it yourself."

Bob looked at Carrie, and said, "Can you do this with me? I don't want to do it by myself. I need someone to help me."

"I'll have to ask my boss. But yes, I'm willing to do it. I just need to get his permission."

Bob thought for a moment, then said, "Okay, if that is what we need to do, I guess, conditioned upon her employer's approval, we can try. But, how the hell should we start?"

"Well, if it were me, tomorrow morning I would park down the street from his home. I would then follow him to wherever he is working and go from there. Maybe he'll drink from a cup at work and throw it away. Maybe he'll go to a fast-food place and eat, then toss a cup there. Just play it by ear and see what happens. You are going to be out in public the whole time, so there's nothing he would be able to do if he catches you. But I have no doubt if he murdered Lynn and he figures out you're up to something, he will run and our opportunity will end."

"What do we do with the cup if we do get a sample?"

"I will get you a plastic baggie. Just grab the cup by its base, put it in the baggie and bring it to me. I'll take it from there."

Bob looked at Carrie, and said, "Are you okay with this? Do you understand everything he is telling us to do?"

"First, let me call my boss, and we can go from there."

An hour later, Bob sat on the other side of the glass as he explained to Paul what was going on.

"You and Carrie are doing this? You know, I don't much like this. I'm afraid it could be dangerous. If he ever gets wind of what you are doing, please remember—he's apparently already killed once."

"There is no other way. Carrie got permission from her boss to go with me. Glen absolutely can't be involved. It's just the two of us."

"When do you start?"

"Tomorrow morning. We are going to be down the street from his house early morning and follow him to his job. Hopefully, he'll have one to go to. Once we get there we will just watch and figure it out from there. If he doesn't have a job lined up, we are just going to have to wait until he gets one."

"What if he is employed, but he goes home to eat? What if he takes his meal to work with him?'

"Then we'll have to figure out something else. Hell, Paul, I have no idea what I'm doing. Neither does Carrie. But according to Glen we got to get a sample, and this is at least a starting point."

"If you do get one, you take it to Glen, he takes it to the hospital, they check it out, and if it's a match we have our killer, right?"

"Well, I hope it's that simple, but as far as we're concerned, he's the killer. This is all new territory for me, but if it is his DNA, for all intents and purposes yes, he is our killer. I'm just winging it, Paul. According to Glen, this is the next step we need to take, and that is just what we are doing."

He stood. "I better go. I'll talk to you sometime tomorrow, unless the son-of-a- bitch shoots me." He smiled. "If he does, then I'll most likely not be back."

"I don't like this one…"

"I know, you already told me that. It is the only way. I'll see you sometime tomorrow and let you know what happened."

Chapter 46

Bob watched out the window of his hotel room as the sun slowly inched its way above the horizon. The dark of last night had little impact as concerned his desire to fall asleep. He had remained awake most of the night, worried about those activities scheduled to begin in a matter of hours. It was going to be a beautiful spring day—one he would have enjoyed had he not had so much on his mind.

He picked up Carrie at six-thirty, which was their pre-arranged time. He knew it wouldn't take them long to reach John Reed's home and they wanted to be in place by seven. Knowing John worked mostly for individuals, rather than businesses, he figured his customers would not want his type of outdoor activity taking place in and around their home much before seven.

Both continued to hope John had a job to go to—that he wasn't out of town, or that he wasn't sick and would not be going to work today at all. *If* he didn't go today, they would return each and every morning until he did.

They didn't have long to wait.

At seven-thirty, John drove his truck out of the driveway and down the street away from them. Bob had preferred Carrie drive, so she drove his vehicle, staying a good distance behind, but close enough to observe everything he did.

A few miles and on the other side of town, he pulled into the driveway of a home that had just been constructed. As they pulled over to the curb and parked, Reed grabbed his tools out of the back of his pickup and walked behind the house, taking his water jug with him.

Carrie and Bob carried on a continual conversation, discussing the weather, her job and Bob's profession, until they finally just ran out of subjects Then both remained quiet for a while, until Bob cleared his throat and said, "If you don't mind me asking, how close have you and Paul become?"

Carrie smiled. "That was subtle."

"Sorry. I have been hoping to find a little time alone with you, for quite a while—to talk about the two of you. I guess I just figured while we were waiting, now would be as good a time as any to do just that. We are most likely going to be here a while anyway…waiting until he leaves to eat somewhere around noon. Hopefully, he didn't bring his lunch with him and he will go to some restaurant so we can do our job."

He hesitated, then said, "Do you mind talking about Paul—about your relationship?"

"No, not with you."

As she looked out the window, she said, "We are really close. We spend a considerable amount of time just talking about life…about relationships—*and* about *our* lives after this mess is all over with. It's tough. We just don't know when he will be released, if in fact he ever is."

She turned toward Bob and said, "We do know one thing. We are going to give our relationship a chance if he does get out in the near future. We have reached the point now where we honestly believe we have something good going on and if we get the chance, we are going to give it all we got."

"Have you discussed what your future plans might be if he is released? And if so, do you mind sharing them with me?"

"No, I don't mind. We have talked about the future, and really, the only thing he is insistent about is that he live close to you."

Bob turned away. He knew emotionally he was on the edge anyway—he was about to cry, and he really didn't want her to see that.

As he used his sleeve to wipe away the tears, she said, "He knew running was a mistake. If he had to do it all over again, he would never, ever even considered such a drastic solution to the problems he felt he was having living with you and Jean."

Bob quickly gained control of his emotions, as he said, "Does he have any idea what he wants to do with his life?"

"He has considered law…of becoming a lawyer."

Bob evaluated her response, but before he could answer, she said, "You know, he is really well read. He knows a little about a lot of things. For not having an advanced education, he's really a smart guy. I have trouble keeping up with him. You should be proud"

"I just hope I get the chance to spend time with him—more than just a few minutes a day. What about the two of you? What are your thoughts about your relationship if he doesn't get out?"

"We are going to just take it day-by-day. Hopefully, that won't be a problem. We know we enjoy the same things in life. We feel we are really compatible, but obviously until he gets out, we are not going to come to any conclusions whatsoever—about anything. That verdict almost ended what we had. We were both getting pretty discouraged anyway. But now, with all that has gone on since, we have at least a little hope. I guess we will just have to see where it all goes from here."

They both remained quiet. A few minutes later, the two of them began discussing all matters other than her relationship with Paul. But near noon, Bob interrupted her, and said, "Thank God. Here he comes. I am assuming he didn't bring his lunch with him. I just hope to hell he's going somewhere to eat and not going home for the day."

As he drove away, he drove in the opposite direction from which he arrived and away from home. "Looks like we don't have to worry about him going home. Now, I just hope to hell he's driving to a restaurant."

As Carrie continued to follow him, the golden arches of McDonalds came into view. They both watched as he turned in the parking lot and slowly looked for a place to park.

As they approached the restaurant, Bob said, "Just turn in. Thank God. This should work perfectly."

He turned to Carrie and said, "Now let's see whether he eats inside or out." They pulled into a parking space on the other side of the building, but where they could view the outside eating area. Clearly, the restaurant was packed, but there were still a few open seats in the outdoor area.

Soon after they parked, John walked out the door with food in hand, He quickly found a table where he would eat by himself and away from others also seated outside.

"Okay, what's the plan here, Bob?"

"We will just hope he finishes his drink outside, not in the truck and that he throws his cup away in the garbage container near him— that one right there."

They watched for a full twenty minutes, while John slowly ate his burger and fries, washing it all down with whatever it was he was drinking.

About a half-hour later, he stood, gathered up all his garbage and walked away.

"You want to go or do you want me to?"

"Bob, you go. I don't think I could stomach going through that garbage."

As he got out, he said, "If he shoved it down into the container, we are screwed. I'll never be able to separate out which one was his unless it's lying right on top."

John walked to the garbage container, and started to pull the top off. But just as he removed it, one of the employees walked up to him, asked him to move away, then dumped all that was in the container into another larger container. Bob stood there and watched him walk away.

As he got back in the car, he said, "Okay, that's not going to work. Besides the fact I would have ended up fighting the employee over the garbage, there must have been a hundred other cups in there with his. I am not really sure I could have picked out his if I had actually had the opportunity. We need to move on to plan B."

"And that was to…."

"Let's follow him and see what he does after work. Are you okay with that?'

"Yes. I've got all day off work to do this if need be."

"It is going to take all day for sure, because he's most likely going back to work. That will take all afternoon and then I'm just hoping maybe he goes to a bar before he goes home. Maybe we can figure something out there, if he does."

They waited through the afternoon hours, but once it was quitting time, they watched and followed as he drove straight home, locked up his pickup for the night and went in his house.

A half-hour later, Paul sat down on the other side of the glass and said "Well, what happened? Did we get the job done?'

"Not even close. I did enjoy my time with Carrie though. That was by far the best part of the job."

Paul smiled. "She's incredible. I am just glad I had a chance to meet her. What happened? Were you able to get a sample from him?'

"We got nothing. We followed him. He went to McDonalds, got something to eat and I tried to get the cup. But it was in a container with a lot of other garbage. The employee came and took it away before I could find it and pull it out. I'm not really sure I could have located the right one anyway—to much other crap in there besides his cup. We are going to try again tomorrow. Hopefully, this time it will work out better than it did today."

"What makes you think it will be any different tomorrow than it was today? It sounds to me like if you continue using the same plan you're using, it's going to be way too difficult to make it work."

"We got a little different approach planned for tomorrow. I need to go. I knew you would be anxious to know about today. It didn't work the way I had hoped it would. But tomorrow is a new day. That girl of yours, Carrie, she's a pretty smart kid. I don't think one would ever want to underestimate her. She came up with a new idea. Now, I need to go. Carrie and I are going out for supper. I have to clean up. Don't want to be late, you know."

He winked, stood, turned around and walked out the door.

The next morning, he picked her up a little before seven. As Carrie got in his car, Bob said, "Good Morning. That was good food last night. Thanks for taking me there. Are you ready to roll."

She smiled and said, "Glad you enjoyed it. Now, if this idiot will just cooperate, our partnership should have a very, very successful day."

John proceeded to the same worksite he did the day before. All morning, they talked…and watched. Near noon, he got in his truck and drove to the same McDonalds, where he once again parked, got his food, and sat down within the outside eating area.

Today however, as he started to eat his meal and after he had taken a long drink of whatever was in his cup, he was interrupted by his cellphone.

"Mr. Reed, this is management. We need to talk about your order and about the amount you paid us. Can you come back in for just a moment?"

John said, "What the hell's wrong with what I paid you? I don't understand. How come caller ID don't show you as McDonalds? It's showing some guys name on it."

Bob said, "Our business phone is in use. I had to use my personal phone. Now will you please step inside? I don't have all day and if you don't resolve this, you're not eating here again."

Bob watched as he angerly slapped his phone shut, stood and

walked back inside. As soon as he stood, Carrie, who was standing nearby, started toward his table. As he continued walking away, Carrie grabbed his cup and walked in the opposite direction.

Once the car door slammed shut, they were on their way as Carrie carefully placed the cup and its contents, in a plastic baggy.

Glen walked in and said, "So, what happened yesterday?"

"Nothing."

"Okay then why are you two here? Did something go wrong?"

"No, it didn't. The reason we are here is not to explain what *didn't* work right yesterday, but to give you what *did* work right today. That baggy contains John Reed's drink. Not one individual touched that straw, but him. It came right off his table after he took a drink. And he drank it through the straw, which should be just full of his DNA."

"You are kidding. Great." He stood. "You two want to discuss anything else, or can I take this and get it tested?"

Bob said, "Go, go. We got some good news to pass on to our prisoner. We'll be around when you get the results. I need to head back to Nashville shortly, but you got my number. Call me as soon as you know anything."

Glen smiled, and said, "Believe me, you will be the first to know."

Chapter 47

He had reviewed litigation files until he simply could not review one more factual situation involving either *him* against *her* or *her* against *him*.

Bob swiveled around, toward the window, closed his eyes and leaned back.

Even though he had jumped out of bed with the best of intensions, now some four hours and fifty files later, he felt like it was time to go back to where he started early this morning—maybe sleep just a little longer.

As he sat there, he considered all that had happened during the last number of months and wondered how he had survived all the turmoil. His friend Jack hadn't, although hopefully his death had more to do with other issues than the pace of life Bob had subjected him to, once he found out about Paul.

But beyond Jack, he wondered how he had survived all that had happened since that phone call from Paul. He found it hard to believe he had endured all he had, considering his age. Was it worth it? Certainly! Without a doubt! At that time, he had reached the point where he was ready to make a life-altering decision—a decision that would have most likely resulted in never knowing the grandson he so loved, but whom he thought was most likely gone forever.

Paul had saved him. Now, Bob would continue to do everything in his power, to save Paul.

What would he do if they couldn't get that conclusive test result they needed? And even if they did get the results, could they, at this late date, do anything to set aside the jury verdict? The answer to both those questions could literally be determined within the next few hours.

"Hey stranger. How's everything going?"

He slowly swiveled around, as he said, "Morning. Thanks for coming in on a Saturday."

Charlene said, "I had nothing else to do, but clean the house and separate two screaming teenagers. It was a break for me to come here. How is everything in Knoxville?”

“Fine. We are just waiting for some test results. I am not really sure when I will have to go back or if I will have to back at all. But I wanted to discuss some of these files today, in case I need to leave here early Monday or so.”

“I can tell you this, Bob. You are either going to have to withdraw from representing a few of these people, settle their cases, or try them. There are a few of your clients that aren’t happy at all. And to be honest, they have a right to be upset. We have babied some of them along for quite some time now and they are tired of it.”

“That was a mistake I made when all these issues with Paul began. I should have realized when I took his case that it would consume me… and of course, it has. Do we have anything set for trial next week?”

“Just the Jenkins case. It’s set for Thursday.”

“Okay, I should be here most of the week, regardless of what happens with Paul’s case. I’ll look over Jenkins today. I will make some notes for you concerning what to do, but let’s plan on trying it. Call the opposing attorney, whoever it is, I can’t remember—and tell him we are ready to go. If he has any last-minute offers, he better be disclosing them right quick.”

“Okay. Bob, how are you? I mean, you look so tired. This has to be taking its toll on you. Are the issues involving Paul nearly over?”

He smiled and said, “You know, I really didn’t think I could look any worse than I did before Paul came into my life. Whoa was I ever wrong. We’ll see what happens in the next few days. What’s going on now will decide the next step all of us take in his case. Right now, we are just playing a waiting game.”

Charlene left his office shortly thereafter. Bob finally arrived home near 6:00 p.m. His eyes were tired from reviewing files, but he felt it was easily his most productive day since Paul’s ordeal had begun.

As he started to pour some scotch in a glass that already contained ice cubes and a small shot of water, his cell rang. He looked at caller ID and he quickly said, “Hi, Susan. How are you?”

“I’m good, Bob. I had asked Charlene to let me know when you returned to Nashville. She called me this afternoon after she had left the office.”

Bob laughed and said, "The two of you seem like you are getting pretty close."

"I guess we are at that. You want to have some supper together tonight or have you already eaten?"

"No, I haven't and yes, I would love too."

A short time later, they were each seated with a drink, as Susan said, "So, I suppose you are wondering why, after our time apart, I called this meeting."

"I was a little curious, yes. The last time I talked to you, I wasn't sure if I would ever hear from you again."

She smiled and said, "I wasn't sure you would either."

She remained quiet, but he was determined to let her lead the way. She had called the meeting…she could continue as its moderator.

"Okay, Bob here's the deal. I was having a real problem not having time with you. But it took my time away from you to figure out that having very limited time with you, was way better than having no time with you at all."

"To be honest, Susan, at that time, I was having some issues of my own—you know, some guilt issues concerning Jean, concerning the woman I lived with and loved so much all those years. I needed a break too. I needed to figure out what to do with those feelings about her and with the guilt I was feeling about being with you."

"What did you finally conclude?"

"I just finally decided I needed to move on. It was without a doubt what she would have wanted me to do, and, to be honest, that was what I would have wanted for her. Before you came along, I had those moments when I was trying to figure out where my life was going. And to be honest, I had virtually made up my mind—it was going nowhere. Then came Paul. He changed everything. He cleared my mind. Once I found him, I knew I had to end all the self-pity. I concluded I needed to live those years I have left with as much enthusiasm as I did when Jean was alive. She would have had it no other way."

He hesitated as he took a drink. Finally, he said, "And you know, that also applies to my time with you. I know, without a doubt, exactly what Jean would have wanted me to do when it came to some other woman. You have become an important part of my life, even though we haven't seen much of each other lately. For quite some time, I just wasn't sure what to do. But I know now—I know what I want and I know where my life is going. A good part of that 'life' I hope now includes you. But exactly what happens from here on isn't really up to me anymore. Now that you know how I feel, the ball is in your court."

She looked away for a moment, and when she reengaged, she said, "You know, Bob, I was wrong in my approach to our relationship. I should have never put such pressure on you. I came to that conclusion while we were apart. I know now that I was dead wrong and that *any* time with you was better than none. I'm sorry. I should have never ever said what I said, or did what I did to separate us. My time spent without you in my life has been awful… and I'm sorry."

"Don't be. I understand. You know, we're both walking down a path neither of us have walked before. Let's just enjoy our time together. And by that, please understand, our time together will be significantly increased as soon as Paul's ordeal is over. Once we know what is happening with his case, maybe you and I can plan a little better–spend as much time together as we both want to."

"Sounds perfect to me. Now, no more of 'where we have been.' 'Where are we going'—that's the question. What is the story with Paul?"

"I'm just waiting to hear from one of the officers with the Knoxville Police Department that is working on his case. We are waiting for test results. If they come back like I hope they do, we have a chance. If they don't, I'm not sure what the hell we are going to do. One step at a time. Now, what have you been doing since the last time we were together?"

They talked through a couple of more drinks, two steaks and a shared dessert. When they were finished, he drove home, where he parked his car. He got in her car and for the first time in a long while, he voluntarily spent the rest of the night in someone's bed other than his own.

Chapter 48

He sat back and looked at all the paperwork he needed to review and which now completely covered his desktop. How far removed this morning was from yesterday morning. At this time yesterday, he was enjoying a home cooked breakfast in Susan's kitchen--eggs, bacon, toast…

"Hey, boss, I just got a call from that attorney in the Jenkins case. He told me just to have you call him back, but he said he thinks we may be able to settle. He said he talked to her first thing this morning and he thinks we may be able to resolve everything without a trial."

Bob smiled. "That is really good news. I would love to get that one out of the way and avoid spending the rest of the week preparing for trial. I could go ahead and just concentrate on all the other files that need attention, but aren't quite so pressing."

A few minutes later, as he cleaned up office work which he should have completed days ago, Charlene informed him Susan was on line one.

"Morning."

"Hi. How's your morning going?"

"Let me explain it this way—it's one hell of a shock after yesterday morning with you. I can tell you without hesitation where I'd rather be right now."

"I'm not even going to ask. I am just going to assume that you would rather be with me."

"Valid assumption."

"Can you meet me for lunch, sometime around noon?"

"I doubt it. I'll probably just have Charlene pick me up something and eat right here. I am starting today to cut my work load. I just can't work at the same pace I have been working. And honestly, I don't want too. It is too much. I have to many other places I would much rather be, and people I would rather be with, than the clients whose names are on these files."

'I understand. I'll just talk to you later this afternoon."

As he terminated the call, Charlene walked in and said, "You have a call from Paul on line two."

"Morning, Paul. Everything okay?"

"I'm not sure. That's why I called. Have we heard from the cop yet? Did they have a chance to determine if John is the one?"

"I haven't heard anything. To be honest, they really haven't had much of an opportunity to do the testing yet. I am sure they don't test over the weekend, so they would have only had a limited opportunity to test on Friday, after we gave him the cup and straw."

"I have been thinking about what you did. You took quite a risk, both of you. If he would have seen what you did, he could have figured out what you were doing and took off—left the city."

"I know, but what choice did we have. It was that or nothing. Glen made our options pretty clear."

"I understand. I'm just proud both of you had the courage to do it."

Bob smiled. "You know, one positive issue that has come from all of this is that I was able to really get to know Carrie. She is a good soul. She has been fun getting to know."

Paul hesitated for a moment, then said, "I have to get off. I'll wait to hear from you."

"I have no idea when I'll hear from Glen. I'll certainly let you know the moment I do."

Bob met with clients the rest of the morning. He ate lunch at his desk, as he continued to read all his notes from prior days and review the files of all those cases he had ignored the past few weeks.

Shortly after two, Charlene let him know Carrie was on the line.

"Hi, Carrie. How's my partner in crime?"

"Bob, Glen just called. They have the results of the test. He wants to see us whenever we are available."

Bob leaned back in his chair, as his heart skipped a beat. "It's going to take me a little time to get out of here. I'll be there as soon as I can. Where do you want me to pick you up?"

"Just call as you approach Knoxville. I'll drive to the station and meet you there."

He quickly cleaned up a few lingering issues that he simply could not put off any longer. He then left the office, went home to pick up some of his personal effects and started the drive with which he had become so familiar.

As he approached the city, he called Carrie and told her he was on the outskirts of town and would be at the police station in a matter of minutes. She told him she would see hm there.

Carrie was waiting in the conference room when he arrived. As he walked in the room, she stood and hugged him. As they sat, he said, "Have you talked to Glen yet?"

"No. They just escorted me in here. I haven't talked to anyone yet."

Just as the last word left her mouth, Glen walked in closing the door behind him.

He turned around, and said, "We got the results."

Bob said, "Good or bad?"

"About as good as it gets, at least for the two of you and your friend in jail. It was a match."

They both sat in silence as it sunk in. Then Bob looked at Carrie and started to smile. He grabbed her hand, and said, "Thank God, thank God. There's no doubt?"

"Absolutely not. It's a perfect match."

"So, what now?"

"I have had a chance to talk to my superior officer after I contacted Carrie and told her we had the results. We are going to charge him with Lynn's murder. He did it. There's no doubt in anyone's mind, at least around here, that it was him. He could say anything I guess, but with the pawn shop owner's testimony, with the shadow in the video, and with the information concerning the test results, we feel we have him right where we want him."

"Okay, with that in mind, what can be done as far as Paul is concerned?"

"I really don't know. As it stands now, he has been convicted. But surely there is a way that can all be thrown out. I am just not sure, but I suggest you contact the Prosecutor's office and see how they want to proceed."

Bob looked at Carrie and said, "I suppose we will have to deal with that jerk Jensen again."

"Surely his attitude will change now that he knows the truth."

Glen said, "Actually, until we get a conviction or Reed admits what he did, there is still someone convicted of the crime. And until that is somehow wiped out, Paul is still a convicted murderer. I know Jensen has been a problem for you to deal with so far and to be honest, I wouldn't expect that to change."

Bob stood. "It will be interesting to see what happens when Reed is confronted. Will you let us know?"

"Yes. It will probably be later tomorrow or so before we apprehend him. I'll give you a call and let you know what's going on."

As Paul reached the window he said, "What are you two doing here at this time of day? Visiting hours are almost up."

Carrie said, "We have a little news for you."

"Oh really. What's that? What's happened?"

Bob smile and said, "The two samples were a match."

Paul hesitated, smiled and slammed his fist down on the small shelf between him and his conference room window. Just as soon as he did, he looked at the guard, and said, "Sorry, sorry, I just got some really good news. Won't happen again."

As he turned to face Bob, he said, "You have got to be kidding me. Perfect match?"

"Yes, according to Glen. We just came from the police station."

"So, what now?"

"Tonight, they are going to confront him, then arrest him. Once they tell him what all they have against him, the next move will be his."

"What about me? What happens to me while all this is going on? Do they release me?"

"I doubt it. You are still on the record as a convicted murderer. It's going to take a little time, but let's just see what happens when he's confronted."

Paul looked away and remained silent.

"Take it easy now, Paul. We still must go through the hoops. We'll see what happens tonight, then I will go see Jensen tomorrow to figure out how he wants to handle this. One step at a time, just like it has been from the very beginning."

"I know, but..."

"Just keep your chin up. This was a big step. We would have been lost if the testing hadn't turned out the way it did. We are still in the game, and that being said, we still have to play strictly by the rules. The rules right now indicate we need to hear what he has to say in response to those test results and the other evidence we have uncovered."

Bob stood. "Time for us to go. Visiting hours are about up anyway. We will know more tomorrow. I'll see you as soon as I know what he had to say for himself."

Paul stood, and smiled, "Thanks—to both of you. Sorry I turned a little negative. I'm just so anxious…so anxious to get…"

"We both know that, Paul. Now just relax. I think we are close. Just hang in there. We will see you tomorrow."

Chapter 49

Bob looked at the pile of files lying on the table across his hotel room. He had grabbed the first one of many about an hour ago, then just as quickly closed it and threw it back on top of the pile. He had brought them along with the best of intentions in mind. But those 'best intentions' had suddenly hit a wall and he had reviewed nothing since.

Just as he got ready to pick up one of those files, his phone buzzed. Caller ID indicated it was Glen.

"Morning, Glen. What's going on? Did you find Reed last night?"

"We did, yes. Why don't the two of you come in when you have time? I will be here all day. We need to discuss a few things."

"Certainly. I will call Carrie right now. Hopefully, we can both be there within the hour."

Bob called Carrie. She agreed to meet him at the police station. She was busy at the moment, but made it clear that nothing was more important than Paul's situation. She further indicated she would be there as quickly as possible.

Thirty minutes later, both were seated in the conference room, waiting for Glen to make his appearance.

They stood as he walked through the door.

Bob said, "What going on? Good news, bad news, no news—what's going on, Glen?"

They all sat as Glen said, "Okay, here's the deal. We found Reed and brought him in to discuss Lynn's murder. At first, we told him nothing, only that we felt he might have been involved."

Bob said, "And I assume he denied that emphatically."

"Yes, he did. But, to be honest, what surprised us is that he didn't ask for an attorney. At that point, we weren't surprised he denied what we were accusing him of, but we were surprised he didn't ask for an attorney. That would have stopped everything and ramped it all up into a new, much more difficult situation. But he didn't ask for one, so we slowly fed him just a little more information and a little more of what our thoughts were."

"How did he respond?"

"Well, we told him we knew he had taken Lynn's antiques without authority. We told him we knew from reliable sources that Lynn never gave anything away and that he *had* to have taken them without her authority."

"Did that change his mind? Did he admit anything?"

No. He continued to insist she gave them to him. So next, we told him that we could see someone going in and out of her house after Paul left. We showed him the video. He said he couldn't tell who it was, but he finally admitted it looked like someone was going in and out, but that it was impossible to tell who it was."

"Did he ask for an attorney then?"

"No, he didn't. We were holding our breath though; I can tell you that."

"So, what about the DNA?"

"Okay, so we told him someone else had sex with Lynn around the same time Paul had—maybe a little earlier or maybe a little later. He, of course, emphatically denied it was him, until we told him about the DNA match. He wanted to know how we got his DNA to test against the sample they had from Lynn, and we told him. We did not tell him who it was that got the sample from him, but we told him we had it and it matched."

"I assume then he screamed for an attorney?"

Bob said, "I'm sorry. What?"

"No, he didn't. He wanted a moment to think, alone…and we gave it to him." Glen smiled. "When we came back in, he admitted everything."

"Say again."

"He admitted everything. He said it was dark in the back area because he had intentionally not changed that light bulb. He raped her, he murdered her, he stole her vases. Apparently, the two were having a few issues. He was mad because he wanted some of her items and he killed her to get them. He had previously seen Paul's car in her driveway. He waited until he was gone and it was dark."

Carrie said, "Then this is all over?"

"I don't know. I guess. We know now we have the right man He has admitted it, and he actually signed a written confession, I really don't know, legally, where Paul's case goes from here. I guess that's up to the

Judge."

Bob looked at Carrie, smiled and said, "What a relief. Thank God. Now, I guess we best go see Jensen and find out what his thoughts are about letting Paul out of jail."

Carrie said, "I have a bad feeling about working with him on anything. I don't think he cares much for either of us."

Both stood, as did Glen.

Bob put his arms around Glen and said, "Thanks. Thank you so much for all you've done. Thanks for having faith in him…and in us."

Glen hugged Bob and said, "It was all worth it. We got the right guy now. Good luck from here on. Based on what you've told me about Jensen, you are going to need it."

They had been waiting to see George Jensen for over an hour. Finally, his office door opened. George waived at them to come in.

As Bob sat, he said, "Have you been in contact with the police department—specifically, Glen Majors?"

"Yes. Actually, his commanding office called me. It sounds like there's been a new development."

"Yes, there has been. The guy who actually committed the crime—the one who actually killed Lynn Baker, has admitted it."

"Good. That's good. Why are you here?"

"What's it going to take to get Paul out of jail?"

"Oh, hell, I don't know. Get the law book and read it."

"Is there any way you can have him released pending further proceedings—maybe talk to the Judge, tell him what's happened and ask him to release Paul until this is all sorted out?"

"Nope. File your paperwork and we will look at everything then. Just do your job Mr. Duncan, do your job. Once you have filed, I'll talk to you about it, but not until. Even if there was something I *could* do at this point, I will not move on with it until you file the appropriate paperwork. Now, is that all?"

Carrie said, "No, it's not all. Are you saying you know the wrong man is in jail and you'll do nothing to help us get him out, knowing he shouldn't be there—knowing that he should not have been there for months now?"

"Correct. Not until the paperwork has been filed." He stood. "Now, if that's it, I have other people to see yet this morning."

They both stood as Carrie smiled and said, "Thanks for all your help all the way through this process Mr. Jensen. Be sure and read tomorrow's paper. There will be lots of information about you in my article."

Jensen smiled and said, "Now sweetie, you watch yourself. Nothing but the truth. You know what a libel suit can do to a paper's credibility."

"Let me tell you something you bastard. You better hope I don't tell the truth. But I will—you know I will. And in the end, the truth will be what leaves you without a job. I can assure you I won't quit until everyone knows how you handled this situation…knowing an innocent man is locked up, and failing to raise a finger to help him. I can assure you without doubt, that the story will be fully explained, truthfully. Hopefully before this is all finished, your ass will be out of this office and your new job will be shoveling shit out of a chicken house… or not working at all, which is as it should be."

She turned and walked out of the office.

Bob smiled and said, "Oh my God, I can' think of anything worse than having her on the other side of something I did. Good luck Mr. Jensen, good luck indeed."

Later, Bob called David Williams.

"David, Bob Duncan. You got a moment?"

"I do. What's going on in Paul's case?"

"We have someone in custody that has admitted everything. He went in the house after Paul left, he stole some of Lynn's possessions and then he murdered her."

"You are kidding? You must be ecstatic. I am so glad to hear that."

"Oh, but now, we are dealing with this Prosecutor who won't raise a finger to help us get Paul out of jail, until we file the appropriate paperwork. Now, you mentioned something about a Rule 29 motion. Specifically, what does that involve?"

"Well, in your situation, it is basically just a motion that's filed after a conviction, which asks the court to set aside the conviction, based on situations like yours where the defendant was wrongfully convicted."

"Does that set him free?"

"Yes."

"Is that the only relief that is available?"

"At this point, yes. At least, that's how it appears to me."

Bob thought for a moment, then said, "How soon can you get it filed?"

"I can have it ready by the first of next week. It will take a little while to get it before a judge, but I think that can be expedited, based on the circumstances. I assume the Prosecutor, knowing the situation, will work with me on it."

"No, he won't. He's a total jerk. Go ahead and get it filed as quickly as you can."

"I'll have it filed by the middle of next week."

"Okay Paul, we've got some really good news and some news that is not so good."

"Good news first."

Bob said, "Law enforcement picked up Reed to talk to him, and he admitted everything—he admitted he murdered Lynn—he admitted everything."

Paul hung his head and when he looked up, he smiled and as he wiped the tears away, he said, "I can't believe it. You mean I can get out of here? You mean this nightmare is finally over?" He stood. "Can I go now? Can I just tell them I'm not guilty, they got the guy that did it, so let me loose?"

"No. I said I had some news that's not so good. It's not that bad I don't think, but it's not good."

He sat back down, as he said, "What now?"

"The Prosecutor isn't working with us at all. He wants us to file the appropriate paperwork, then have a hearing. He wants it all done by the book. I also talked to his boss. He said he would have to abide by whatever Jensen said. So, until the paperwork is filed, until we have a hearing, and until the Judge dismisses the case, if he even *can*, they are keeping you right where you are."

"When is the hearing?"

"I have my attorney friend David preparing the motion as we speak. You need to know this situation doesn't happen very often. The rule we are filing the motion under is not designed to do exactly what we want, so we will just have to see what the Judge wants to do. But you have been exonerated, Paul. Now we just have to wait for the hearing and see what the Judge wants to do."

"So, while it has now been determined I did nothing wrong, I'm still sitting in jail for God knows how long."

"Patience. Just hang in there a little longer. Hopefully, when it is set for hearing, the Judge will come to the right conclusion. Don't lose faith—we are one hell of a lot closer to getting you out of jail now, then we were last week. Don't lose faith, Paul. Not now. Not when we are *so close…so close.*"

Chapter 50

"So, David, where are we concerning the motion? Did you file it? I know you told me yesterday you were getting it ready to file. Did you get it done?"

"I did, yes. Now we can sit back and relax for a bit. It's up to the Judge to set it for hearing. I don't think, because of the subject matter alleged in the motion, it will take long for him to do that."

"Are you planning on being at the hearing, or do you want me to handle it? I have never, ever been down this road before. I've never filed a motion like this, so I have no idea what to expect."

"As soon as I get an answer from Jensen, I'll review it, then go through it with you. But I really believe you can handle this. It's pretty straight forward. Read the rule. It pretty much sets it all out."

"I know, but…"

"Don't worry about it. Once I get his response, I'll let you know and we can discuss it then. By the way, you are right. He's a dick. I'll call you when I hear anything."

Later that afternoon, he called back.

"I just wanted to tell you I got his answer. He basically just denies everything and says the conviction should stand. He goes on to say that if the conviction is overturned, then the most the court should do is grant a new trial and try the case all over again. He says even if we show the jury the video, and introduce the DNA results, it should still be retried."

"He's going to remain a true son-of-a-bitch to the very end, isn't he? Are you filing a response?"

"No. Enough has been said. Let's wait until we get the order from the Judge setting it for hearing and go from there."

Later that afternoon, Charlene told him David had called while he was with a client. He wanted him to return his call.

"David, what's going on?"

"I got an emailed copy of the Judge's order setting our motion for hearing. He set it for next Wednesday. Before I clear my schedule why don't you take a look at what you need to establish at the hearing and determine whether you can do it yourself. I really think you can handle it even with your limited experience in criminal law. The facts are clear and you know what you want the court to do. I just emailed the order to you. If I were in your shoes, I would do as you have basically done since Jack died—just handle it yourself."

The three sat quietly, waiting for the Judge to walk through the courtroom door. Bob had decided to handle the hearing. He was extremely apprehensive. Hopefully, he wouldn't misspeak or make a verbal mistake that resulted in the court ruling against Paul. He would never forgive himself if he did.

Everyone stood, as the Judge walked in. He sat down, and said, "Be seated everyone."

He looked at Bob and said, "Are you ready to discuss your motion, Mr. Duncan?"

Bob stood and said, "Yes, Your Honor."

"Please proceed."

"Judge, the motion pretty much speaks for itself. But to discuss the basics of it, first of all, the State failed to provide a video to us which appeared to show movement in the back of the house during the evening in question. That movement could have been deemed to be someone entering and leaving the home after Paul left."

"Secondly, the State failed to provide information concerning the fact that the victim had sexual relations with another individual at or about the time she was murdered. That information proved extremely beneficial in the final analysis. The DNA belonged to an induvial that ultimately admitted he killed Lynn Baker, and it too, should have been disclosed."

The Judge said, "Even though it appeared it wasn't useful to anyone at the time?"

"Certainly. That issue was for *us* to decide what we wanted to do with the information. The State and specifically the police department had no right to determine, unilaterally, what we *could* use and what we didn't need."

"It's my understanding someone else has now admitted they committed this crime, is that correct?"

"Yes. He has, in fact, signed a full confession."

"You know, normally a new trial is the remedy if a motion of this nature is sustained. In fact, I'm not sure I can do anything *but* grant a new trial."

"How silly that would be, Your Honor. The man is innocent. It's just that simple. And to leave him in jail and go through another trial concerning a crime he clearly did not commit, would seem to be a terrible waste of everyone's time. It just doesn't make sense."

"Thank you, counselor. Mr. Jensen, do you want to join the discussion."

George Jensen smiled, and stood as he said, "Yes, Your Honor. We have resisted their motion to set aside the conviction, but if you do grant the motion., we would just ask that you allow them a new trial, as the rule provides."

"So, what's your position concerning not providing them with the DNA material, or the video?"

"Well, Your Honor, it was really worthless at the time. We figured we had the killer, and you really couldn't tell who or what the shadows were in the video. The DNA sample could not be tied to anyone, and since it appeared there was no one else in the house during that time period, it wasn't relevant anyway."

"Let's just stop the flow of crap, Mr. Jensen. The bottom line is they were entitled to that information, weren't they?"

"Well, I guess...maybe they were. But even if they were, it doesn't appear you can do anything but grant him a new trial based on the failure of the State to provide that information."

The Judge smiled, looked at Jensen, and said, "You know, I can pretty much do whatever I want to do—I can do whatever I deem appropriate, now can't I?"

"Yes sir, I guess you can."

Jensen sat down, as the Judge shuffled through his paperwork. He finally looked up at Bob and said, "Here's what I'm going to do. First of all, I agree with the Defense as concerns the substantive issues raised in the motion. And I agree some relief should be granted."

Again, he rustled paperwork.

"You know, to retry this case is a huge waste of everyone's time. And really for you Mr. Jensen, to even propose this case be retired, to me, is ludicrous. He's not guilty, plain and simple. There is absolutely no reason to set this case for trial again, only to have the Judge dismiss it. And to be honest, Mr. Jensen, I find it appalling that you would even suggest that as a solution."

He looked at Paul and said, "Paul, I'm sorry you've had to go through this process and spend so much time behind bars for something you clearly didn't do. I assume you've lost your business and most everything else during the time this has been going on. But now, I'm going to do what I can to remedy at least part of that problem. This case is DISMISSED and this Defendant is hereby released from custody. Good luck, son."

He then turned to the Prosecutor and said, "As for you, Mr. Jensen, I want to see you in chambers before you leave the courthouse."

Everyone stood as the Judge left the room. Once through the door, Paul turned to Bob and threw his arms around him. He continued to hold him as he said, "Thank you. Thank you. I don't know what else to say other than…thank you."

As Jenson started to walk away Carrie looked at him and said, "What did you think of the article today, George? Did it suit you?"

"Go to hell!"

"Hey that's really cleaver…and so original, GEORGE."

She started to stand and follow him into the Judge's chambers but Paul grabbed her sleeve and held her back.

They sat back down, as Bob said, "So what's next, Paul? You have your whole life ahead of you. What's next?"

"Can I go with you—I want to stay near you if I can Pops. I'm not sure what I'll do. I got a lot of things in mind, but I was afraid to seriously consider them, thinking if he left me in jail, I would be disappointed once more. I would really like to go home with you."

Carrie smiled and said, "Well Bob, so would I. You got room for one more?"

"I got plenty of room. By the way, I talked to my client, the one that manages one of the TV stations in Nashville. He definitely wants to talk to you. I let him review some of your articles. I've saved all of them."

"That sounds. great. I still need to give them notice here, but then I'll pack up and move to Nashville. Paul, are you okay with that?"

He leaned over and kissed her, then smiled as he said, "First kiss. Yes, I'm really okay with that."

He then turned toward Bob and said, "Now, let's get the hell out of here. I can have everything I need to take with me, packed and ready to go in ten minutes."

Chapter 51

Three months later

"Well, good morning. What a nice surprise. What are you doing here?"

Susan said, "I was out and about and just thought I'd drop in and say hello. I didn't know whether you would have time to see me or not, but I thought I would take a chance."

Bob stood, walked around his desk and kissed her.

"Sit, sit. Do you have a few minutes?"

"I do," she said as she sat down.

Bob smiled and said, "Last night was fun. I'm glad you mentioned going there. That was one of the few restaurants in Nashville where I haven't eaten. The food was good and the ambiance was incredible.

"I heard that from a number of people, which is why I suggested it. How is your day going? How is everything at home?"

"Everything is going well. Paul has settled in. Carrie really seems to like her new job and her apartment. Paul is supposed to be here a little later. You can ask him how he's getting along, in person."

"I haven't seen him in a couple of weeks, but he certainly seems happy He…"

Charlene knocked on his door, opened it and said, "Paul is here. You want him to wait or should I send him on in?"

"Go ahead and send him in."

Paul walked in, and said, "Is this just a party for two or is there room for one more?"

Susan stood and said, "I just stopped in for a moment between stores. This is a shopping day, and I have miles and miles left on my journey."

She gave Paul a hug, as he said, "You don't have to go. I'm only here for a couple of minutes. I need to get back to work. Sit with us."

"No, no, I really do have some things I need to finish up before the day ends. Besides, I'll see your father later anyway. We have dinner reservations. Nice seeing you, Paul."

After she walked out, Paul said, "How is everything with her? I mean, a couple of weeks ago I know you said you were enjoying her company. Does that still ring true?"

Bob smiled and said, "Yes, everything is fine. She's easy to be with and we really do enjoy each other's company. Neither of us have an agenda. It's just a day-by-day relationship and that, at least for now, is working for both of us. How's school?"

"Good between that and the landscaping jobs you lined up for me, every single day is a good one. Of course, anything would be better than my prior accommodations."

"Have you talked to Carrie today? How is everything working out for her at the station?"

"Matter of fact, that's one of the reasons I'm here. They told her this morning she is being considered for one of the reporting jobs during the evening news. She would actually be on the show reporting from somewhere most every night. She is excited, to say the least."

"Wow, that is great. I know the manager of the station was really excited about all those articles she wrote for the newspaper."

Paul looked away for a moment, clearly deep in thought.

"Is everything okay? Is something bothering you, Paul?"

"No, no not really."

He remained quiet for a few more moments, then turned toward Bob and said, "Well maybe…a little. You know, I don't know how to repay you for what you did for me. You literally saved my life. I just really don't know how to repay you."

Bob smiled. "You already have."

"I'm sorry. What do you mean?"

Bob turned away for a few seconds deep in thought…wondering where to begin. As he turned to face Paul, he said, "I've never really talked to you about what you did for me. Before you called that first time, in fact *right* before you called, I had come to the conclusion my life was over. I was in a bad place, Paul. I was convinced life wasn't worth living."

He took a deep breath, smiled and said, "Our phone call changed all that. After you called, I finally came to realize the conclusion that I had just come to was unacceptable. You saved me—much like I hope I can say I saved you. You owe me nothing."

Paul looked away, clearly deep in thought. "I need to tell you something—something you're not going to like. I've labored over what I should do…what I should do…

Bob moved forward in his chair. "Another surprise? I'm not really sure I can handle many more like that first phone call from you, so be gentle."

Paul smiled and said, "No, it's not that dramatic."

"Please go on."

"Okay. You remember that gold chain and locket you gave grandma so many years ago."

"Certainly. I looked for that chain and locket for I don't know how long. What about it."

Paul reached in his pocket and pulled out the chain with the locket still hanging from it and set it on Bob's desk.

"When I finally decided to leave, I knew I needed something I could pawn or sell for cash. I was also in a bad frame of mind toward both of you. Somehow, I wanted to hurt you. I knew how much that chain meant to her…and to you."

Bob picked it up, looked at it for a moment, smiled and said, "But, here it is."

"Yes, here it is. I tried to sell it a hundred times. I needed cash in the worst way. But I just couldn't bring myself to let it go. I couldn't…I couldn't let go…of the only family I had. I am so, so sorry, Pops. I really am."

Bob smiled, and said, "I am just glad to have it back. It meant so much to her…to your grandmother. Thank you. Now that you are here, now that you have come home, it just seems fitting that something that meant so much to her…and to me…came home too."

He laid the chain down, leaned back, cupped his hands behind his head and smiled. "Okay, Paul, what happens after you finish those courses you are enrolled in now. What's next for you? Any ideas?"

"Not really. Oh, I've thought a little about college, but that's about it. I don't really know what I'm going to do."

You know, once you do finish up, if you do move on and go to college, there's always law school. I'll be about eighty then and certainly ready to sell out, or look for a partner."

Paul smiled and said, "Tell me a little about law school, Pops. Is it really as tough as they say it is?"

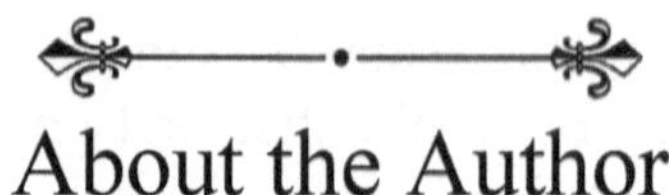

About the Author

JB Millhollin resides near Nashville, Tennessee. He has published a number of novels and continues to write, using the city and surrounding area as a backdrop for his stories. If you enjoy his style of writing, stay in touch through his Facebook author page, or on twitter (@jbmillhollin).